Heather Barnett grew up ir  English and French from from writing, her interests comedy. She is head of marketing at an agency and lives by the river Kennet in Berkshire. *Lord Seeks Wife* is her second novel.

For more information on Heather and her books, please visit her website – <u>www.heatherbarnettauthor.com</u> or join the discussion on Twitter and Instagram @WritesHeather.

Lord Seeks Wife

Heather Barnett

SERPENTINE

BOOKS

First published in Great Britain by Serpentine Books
This edition published in 2022 by
Serpentine Books Limited

www.serpentinebooks.com
info@serpentinebooks.com

A CIP catalogue record for this book is available from the British Library.

ISBN 978 1 9138 7410 0

Printed and bound in Great Britain by Clays Ltd,
Elcograf S.p.A.

For David Hart

Chapter 1

Noblet George William Chatterton de Beeble, 14th Earl of Pantling – Nobby to his friends – became aware that his mother was trying to get his attention across the breakfast table. Setting down a forkful of sausage, he raised his eyebrows at her.

'What's that, Mother?' he enquired.

Lady Caroline threw a copy of *The Telegraph* at her son, quite hard. Having smacked him in the nose, it fell into the remaining fried egg on his plate. 'I asked, you stupid boy, what you have to say about that?'

'That' was a short article on one of the inside pages:

Lord Seeks Wife: Long Hours but Excellent Benefits

Marriage is a contract, true, but how often do the clauses cover hours of employment, salary and holiday pay? It seems that in rural Mereshire, romance is dead. Noblet de Beeble, 14th Earl of Pantling, is advertising for a wife in the Situations Vacant section of his local paper, the Market Mornington Gazette. Although remuneration is not specified, the advert claims the role of wife of Lord de Beeble will appeal to those who enjoy the countryside and large houses. Curiously, a love of the novels of Wilkie Collins is also a pre-requisite. What the interview process will entail isn't clear: perhaps an essay on The Woman in White followed by a practical examination in flower arranging.

Noblet shook his head.

'Amazing how these journalists twist things.' He slapped the paper with the back of his hand. 'Quite amazing.'

'You didn't place an advertisement in the Situations Vacant section of the *Gazette*, then?'

'Oh, I did, yes. Have you not seen it? I've got it here somewhere.'

He got up and burrowed around in the sheaves of paper on the sideboard.

'Here it is. Yes, I placed the advertisement. It's entirely different to the way this fellow's made it sound, of course. See for yourself, Mother.'

Lady Caroline took the paper and read aloud:

'Thirty-something Earl seeks wife to help run ancestral home. If you love the countryside, animals and large houses, this could be the role for you! P.S. Must have a passion for the novels of Wilkie Collins. Apply in writing, stating qualifications for the role, to the Earl of Pantling, de Beeble Hall, Mereshire.'

Lady Caroline lowered the paper and ran a cold, appraising eye over her eldest son's bulky frame. Could it be that this unkempt man with his absent-minded stare was her flesh and blood and a representative of an ancient family? No matter how often she asked herself this question, the answer remained resolutely, yes. She continued to ask it regardless, in the hope that new information might come to light. If only Henry had been born first. Henry was well-mannered and capable: Nobby surfaced from the mid-nineteenth century to eat his meals before diving back into the reign of Victoria. Henry was a thoroughbred, Nobby was a carthorse. Not just a carthorse: an imbecilic carthorse.

'Nobby?'

'Yes, Mother?'

'You are an imbecilic carthorse.'

'So you keep telling me, Mother. If I could bring up the small matter of my Masters and PhD…'

'PhD? Any idiot can get a PhD. If I scribbled a few pages on an obscure author, they would no doubt be falling over themselves to call *me* Doctor de Beeble.'

Noblet's expression reminded his mother of her Labrador puppy when it received an unexpected tap on the muzzle. 'Wilkie Collins is widely acknowledged as one of the finest writers England ever produced, Mother! How you can call him obscure—'

Lady Caroline rose from the table with an air of finality, dropping her napkin beside her plate.

'You've made a pig's ear of this, Noblet. I'm going down to the village today to hand out prizes at the fête. When I come back, I shall be interested to hear your proposed solution.'

With that, she marched to the door, paused to allow her son to leap up and open it, and swept out of the room.

**

Ever since she could remember, Alice Brand had manned a stall at the Gently Rising May Day Fête. One of her earliest memories was sitting on a stool next to her mother behind the Women's Institute table, pensively drooling over the coffee cakes and treacle tarts. She had risen through the ranks over the years: from helping her mother, she'd graduated to become Colonel Markham's second in command on the tombola, and from there had made the leap to the heady heights of supervising the primary school's white elephant stall. Somehow, manning the stall always seemed to fall to Alice. The other teachers would make vague promises to relieve her during the afternoon but never remembered to – and anyway, Alice didn't mind. If she wasn't running a stall she'd be expected to 'mingle': a word that never failed to fill her with dread.

The May Day Fête was held on the playing field of St. Hilda's, the quaint Edwardian primary school, and all the teachers were expected to arrive early to help set up. At ten o'clock, Alice said goodbye to Tom the cat and hurried out of the front door of her small cottage, down the path, through the painted wooden gate and out onto the lane.

Alice loved Gently Rising. She loved the mismatched collection of cottages and grand houses that clustered round the village green. She loved the shady lanes winding their way into the surrounding countryside. She loved the circle of hills that surrounded the village like a big grassy hug. She wasn't such a huge fan of the new estate on the south side of the village, but she closed one eye as she was passing that particular spot. Gently Rising had always been her home, other than a few traumatic years studying for her PGCE at Homerton, from which she'd returned as soon as possible, sighing with relief. Alice couldn't imagine living anywhere else. Her sister, Cecily, had once got as far as 'I noticed they're building some new apartments on the riverside in Market Mornington, Alice. Have you ever thought about...' before being brought up short by the sight of Alice, aghast, grasping wildly at the nearest object (Tom the cat) as if pressing the whole of Gently Rising to her bosom. She and Tom had worn the scars of that incident, emotional and physical, for some time afterwards.

As Alice hurried up the driveway to the school, she saw Mrs Fratterbury, the headmistress, outside the entrance. Wearing a voluminous dress in stagnant-pond green, she was wedged into a wooden armchair, puffing on a cigarette. At the sight of Alice, she ground the cigarette under her large, be-sandled foot. Had *Star Wars'* Jabba the Hutt glooped his way into Gently Rising that morning and cast eyes on Mrs Fratterbury, he would no doubt have licked his lips at her Huttish beauty and suggested something outrageous involving slime – such was her similarity to his race. This wasn't something that struck Alice, who greeted Mrs Fratterbury with a cheery wave.

'Morning, Mrs Fratterbury, what a lovely day for the fête!'

'Perhaps a trifle on the fresh side, but merely a trifle. Are you well today, lovie?'

'Fine thanks, you?'

Mrs Fratterbury shook her head with the air of a weary surgeon giving bad news. Her voice became husky.

'I struggle on, Alice, and I don't complain but I'm not a well woman. It's a bit of a throaty thing, you know.' A small cough was coaxed into a dramatic spluttering fit. 'I shouldn't be here; I should be in my bed and if I was any kind of normal person I would be. But I'm soldiering on, lovie.'

Alice knew that if she gave her her head, Mrs Fratterbury would trot on through the meandering highways and byways of her many aches and pains. Normally, she would have been sympathetic, but time was ticking on and her stall needed to be set up.

'Well, you take it easy, Mrs Fratterbury, and I'll go and check on the organisation.'

'That's the spirit, Alice, lovie. See you later. I'll stay here and rest a moment,' said the headmistress, surreptitiously lighting another cigarette.

***

The 'organisation' wasn't up to much, it turned out. A weak sun was picking out the last remaining wisps of a silvery mist on the empty field. A few tables were stacked up against one of the mobile classrooms and a tangled pile of bunting lay on the single table that had been erected. A bouncy castle lay limp and forlorn over near the hedge and an old man in a waxed jacket and flat cap was prising open a plastic crate on the patio that ran along the back of the school.

'Morning, Colonel Markham!'

Caught off guard, the old man sprang to attention as if he were on the parade ground. Quickly recovering himself, he roared:

'Alice! Timed to a T! Come and lend a hand, my dear.'

As the two of them unpacked the tombola drum and set it up on a table, the Colonel grumbled, 'Same every year. All the grunt work gets left to the likes of you and me and then the dolly birds swan in and take the glory. It's the last year I'll do it, my dear. The very last year.'

Alice made a feeble attempt at dissuading him but her heart wasn't in it, as he'd been threatening to give up since 1989.

By the time Alice had brought all the white elephant donations out from the school hall, it was beginning to look more like a fête. The bouncy castle had bloomed, stalls were springing up here and there around the edge of the field and Mrs Hawsbury had arrived with her horse and haybales to set up the course for the pony rides.

The sun was hotting up in a clear blue sky. Many of the villagers were taking advantage of the sunshine to show off their new summer wardrobes; none more so than Sinead Dumper, currently setting up her bookstall next to Alice's white elephant. Wobbling a little in her blue patent stilettos, she was having some difficulty bending down to lift books out of boxes, due to the tightness of her white skirt suit.

'I'll set up here, Alice. We can help each other out.'

Ever since Sinead had moved to the village four years ago, she'd always set up next to Alice so they could 'help each other out'. Translated, this meant Alice manning Sinead's stall while she went on the prowl.

She was setting out the books with care, arranging them according to size and colour but with complete disregard of genre.

'Heard about the advert?' Sinead asked.

'What advert?'

'Not heard? Oh, Alice!' Her laugh was like a chimpanzee stepping on a drawing pin. 'Always one step behind. Got a copy here.'

She brought a newspaper clipping out of her handbag, folded in quarters.

'*Daily Telegraph*. Went back through last week's *Gazette*. Found the original.' Another pristine clipping emerged from the shiny blue bag.

Alice read the proffered cuttings.

'Mereshire in the news. How exciting. It's a shame they didn't mention Gently Rising,' she said as she passed the cuttings back to Sinead, who stowed them away again.

'Who cares about Gently Rising! Didn't you see what it said? Lord de Beeble is looking for a wife. Wonder if he's coming today,' she mused, eyes flickering around the field. 'Never met him. You?' she asked, rounding on Alice.

'Sort of. I've seen him in the village a few times. He used to live in Oxford until he came back here a few months ago. I heard he was studying for a PhD – or was it writing a book?'

'Both,' replied Sinead instantly. 'Completed a PhD on the Victorian author Wilkie Collins. Took him five years. Since then he's been working on a book.'

'Gosh! You know a lot about him.'

Sinead threw a scathing look at Alice.

'Research.'

'Oh. Right.'

'I expect he'll come to the fête. He'll want to take a look around. Get to know the villagers.'

Sinead's hands were groping in her handbag for her lipstick as she spoke, eyes darting hungrily from face to face. 'What does he look like?'

Alice thought for a moment.

'Um, I remember him being quite tall…'

'Tall – good.'

'And quite big, I think. Not *big*, big but, you know – kind of broad-shouldered.'

'Well built – good.'

7

Alice stopped.

'What else?' demanded Sinead. 'Eye colour? Hair colour? Good-looking?'

'I'm sorry, Sinead, I can't remember much about him. It must be five years since I last saw him. It was when they put on *The Moonstone* at the village hall. Lord de Beeble was the guest of honour and he made a short speech before the curtain went up.'

'Good speaker?'

'Well… He didn't stammer or anything as far as I can remember.'

Sinead did her impression of an injured chimp again.

'Useless! There's Jan Fratterbury. She'll know. Mind my stall for me.'

She stalked away towards the headmistress, heels sinking into the grass and sinewy buttocks rotating inside her tight skirt.

***

Soon the fête was in full swing. Bunting hung limply in the heat, runaway dogs raced each other between the stalls, the smell of sausages and onions wafted through the air and excited young voices rang out across the field. Alice's stall was proving popular, a swarm of people gathering round to rummage through knick-knacks and exchange gossip.

'What I want to know is what Lady Caroline will have to say about all this. I mean, it's not exactly *de rigueur*, is it?' asked a horsey-looking woman in a Hermes scarf.

'Yes, and *he's* quite the oddball, I hear,' replied her friend. 'Practically a recluse according to Tom Phipps – Tom drinks in the Lion and Lamb with the gardener from the Hall, you know. His Lordship's barely left the library since he got back from Oxford.'

'No doubt some women will degrade themselves enough to respond to his strange little advert. There are people that desperate, my dear.'

'Oh, I know, my dear.'

'Short skirt and blue heels, my dear!'

This last followed by peals of high-pitched laughter.

A little girl in a gingham dress tugged at the horsey-looking woman's sleeve.

'Mummy?'

'Yes, darling?'

'Who's got a short skirt and blue heels?'

'Be quiet, Isobel! Don't listen in to Mummy's conversations! Go and find Daddy, he's over there by the welly wanging.'

As Alice watched the little girl trotting off towards Daddy, someone else in the crowd caught her eye.

The most stunning woman Alice had ever seen was walking towards her across the field. People gawped as she passed them. At six feet tall she could have been gangly but instead, she made those around her, even the tall, willowy ones, look rather dumpy. Waves of thick chestnut hair that glinted auburn in the sunlight bounced with every step in a way that would have made a shampoo advert director's mouth water. Her simple green silk dress fell to mid-thigh and revealed slim, elegant limbs, lightly tanned as if she'd been wintering in St. Tropez. (Unlike Sinead Dumper, who looked like she'd been held hostage in a St. Tropez spray tan booth.) Cat-like green eyes, defined eyebrows, a smattering of tawny freckles across her elegant nose and a confident smile were all the details Alice had time to take in of her face before she found herself confronted by this goddess.

'Hi.'

The goddess held out a slim brown hand, silver rings gleaming.

Alice took the hand and resisted the urge to bring it to her lips. Shaking it instead, she said, 'Hi. You're new.' And then she giggled. *You're new'? What am I saying? She's not a five-year-old in my reception class!*

'My name's Mia Wild. You must be Alice. I introduced myself to your headmistress, Mrs – Fatterbury is it?'

Alice heard one of the nearby villagers snigger and hastened to correct her.

'Fratterbury – it's Mrs Fratterbury.'

'I explained that I've moved to the village and was wondering if there was someone who could show me around. She suggested you and I said you looked perfect.'

'Oh! Of course, I'd love to. So,' she fought hard to be nonchalant, 'you've just moved here?'

'Yes, I'm renting Ivy Cottage. Do you know it?'

'Ivy cottage – yes, lovely! At the end of Drove Lane. Have you got a job near here?'

The edges of Mia's lips twitched.

'No. I'm here about the advert.'

Chapter 2

Henry de Beeble shook his head at his older brother. 'What I don't get, Bob, is why the jobs section? Why not Lonely Hearts?' Henry had always felt sorry for Noblet being saddled with the – to his mind – embarrassing family name, and had switched to calling him Bob from the age of fifteen.

Noblet swirled the ice cubes around in his gin and tonic. He and Henry were sitting on the terrace which ran the full length of the back of the Hall. The vast lawn spread out before them, shaded here and there by magnificent cedars. As he gazed out past the lawn and meadows towards Eve's Wood and the village in the valley below them, Noblet seemed to be musing on the question. Henry knew that he probably wasn't musing on it at all, but grappling with some knotty problem to do with Wilkie Collins' use of the semi-colon. Turning his face up to the sunlight and closing his eyes, he prompted:

'Bob?'

'What? Oh! Sorry, Henry – miles away.'

'The ad – I was asking why the jobs section?'

Noblet drained his glass before slamming it on the table.

'Because I don't want to get married. I want a housekeeper-cum-estate-manager. But Mother is insisting children be involved, so at the last moment, I had to change the job title to "wife".'

Henry laughed.

'It isn't funny, Henry. It's alright for you. Mother isn't hounding you to get married and pull your socks up and run the damn estate. You get left alone. I'm getting it in the neck day and night; she's like a dog with a bone. You know she's moved out – well, she says she won't lift a finger to help look after the place anymore. She says I need a wife and heirs and she won't help me until they appear. I'm going crazy, Henners!' He picked up the empty glass, knocked it back, got hit in the face by a slice of lemon, and put it down again. 'I don't know anything about taxes and budgeting and God knows what else they keep on at me to make decisions on!'

'And you think your wife will? Unless you're planning on proposing to the Chancellor of the Exchequer you might be disappointed.'

'I don't intend she should know it all straight away. Of course not. But if I marry, Mother says she'll lend a hand until we're able to stand on our own two feet. Or should that be four feet? Anyway, until then the place could go to rack and ruin because I sure as hell don't know what I'm doing.'

'Mother would never let it come to that.'

'You've not seen her lately, old man! It's like an obsession.' He lowered his voice and glanced around. 'I'm not sure that she's not gone a bit... you know... loopy.'

'Yes. I can see the difficulty. With Mother, it would be so hard to tell.'

'Well I'm glad it's all so entertaining for you,' said Noblet, his tone petulant. 'You could at least take it seriously.'

'I'm here, aren't I?'

'Yes, I'm sorry. I am grateful, old man. Did you have plans?'

'I was going to take Saskia to a new exhibition of what is known as "street art" – graffiti to you and me – in a converted abattoir in Shoreditch. She's reviewing it for the magazine.'

Noblet looked askance at him and Henry laughed.

'So, yes, I was pleased to get out of it. And you sounded desperate.'

'Desperate and in need of Dutch courage.' Stepping over to the doors into the drawing room, he poked his head inside.

'More booze, Sally!'

'Get a pen and paper while you're there, Bob,' said Henry. 'We need to sketch out a plan of attack.' Noblet disappeared inside and reappeared a few moments later followed by a wiry old lady in an apron, carrying a tray.

'Here you are, boys,' she trilled. 'Not too many more, now, Noblet. You know what you're like – and sitting in the sun too, well…' She shook her head ominously.

Sally had been nanny to both boys and stayed on, taking on more and more roles until she had become butler, secretary and occasional odd-job-woman. Cooking was undertaken by a permanent fixture of the name of Martyr. She had once been called Martha, but when a three-year-old Noblet had rechristened her by mistake, the name suited her so well it stuck.

Noblet took the gin and tonic off the tray and raised it to Sally.

'Dutch courage, Sally! Can't do without it this p.m.'

Sally turned to his brother.

'Now, Henry, have you had your lunch?' she asked.

'Didn't get a chance.'

'I didn't think so. You're skin and bones – I'll step into the kitchen now and ask Martyr to rustle something up for you.'

Left alone again, Henry and Noblet settled themselves on either side of the table, Henry with pen in hand.

'The way I see it,' Henry said, 'we need to approach this as if it really were a job vacancy. It makes it a lot easier, in a way – we think about what it is that you want from a wife, and then we decide on the best way to whittle down the applicants.'

He paused and scrutinised his brother.

'That is, assuming that you're going to go through with this. I mean, this is serious, Bob. We're talking about other people's happiness aside from yours.'

'I know – Mother's.'

'No, not Mother's! I'm talking about the poor fool who marries you and becomes full-time skivvy at de Beeble Hall. You don't have to do this, just because Mother's jumping up and down. You're a forty-year-old man, for God's sake.'

'Thirty-nine, thank you very much. Still a way off my half-century yet.' He took a sip of his fresh gin and tonic. 'It's a nice idea, you know, doing what I like and all that. But we both know it's not realistic. I want to be left in peace to work and Mother's quite capable of squawking round my head like a ravening harpy until I capitulate. A quiet life, Henry, that's what I'm after.'

'Let's hope a wife is the way to get it.'

Pulling his chair into the table, he set to work again with the pad and pen.

'Come on then, Bob. What are you looking for in a wife?'

Twiddling his fingers absently in his drink, Noblet said, 'Lydia Gwilt in *Armadale*. Now there's a woman. Flaming locks of auburn hair, ivory skin—'

'And eyes of emerald green?' interrupted Henry. 'You're thinking of "Jolene" by Dolly Parton.'

'I am not! Lydia Gwilt – there's my idea of beauty.'

'I've not read that particular Collins masterpiece, but isn't she a murderess?'

'I'm not saying I want a woman with her personality,' Noblet snapped. 'I'm talking about her looks. Write that down: looks like Lydia Gwilt. Auburn hair. Ivory skin.'

'We might have to widen our criteria. I'll put "attractive".'

'Fine, fine, fine. After all, looks don't matter that much. It would be nice if she could have auburn hair, that's all.'

'Moving on…'

'It's a toughie, I've never thought about this in so much depth before. What would you put?'

'It's irrelevant what I'd put – it's your wife we're talking about.'

'I know – but it might, you know, inspire me.'

Henry thought about it.

'Well, let's take Saskia…'

'I'd rather not,' muttered Noblet under his breath.

'She's dynamic…'

'She is. Very dynamic. You can write down something like "easy-going" on my list.'

Henry raised an eyebrow and wrote it down, before continuing, 'She's also ambitious and successful.'

'She is, she absolutely is. Put down "mellow" and "homebody" on my list.'

'This isn't your cue to critique my girlfriend, you know.'

Noblet's eyes widened in shock.

'I've not said a word against Saskia, old boy! This is extremely useful, it's honing my mind, helping me focus. Carry on, old man, carry on.'

'Forget about my list. Let's focus on your ideas.'

Noblet lapsed into musing and gazing again, while Henry ate the sandwich that Sally had brought out for him.

'What do you think I should be looking for in a wife, Henry?' he asked, eventually.

'Well,' replied his brother, wiping his mouth on the napkin, 'one thing's for sure – she'll need to be happy to be bossed around by Mother. If you marry someone too strong-minded it'll be constant war between the two of them.'

Noblet shuddered.

'God, no, strong-minded's the last thing I want. Put "weak-minded". And underline it.'

'Right.' Henry took a couple of businesslike swigs from his bottle of beer. 'So, what we're looking for is a red-headed beauty with an expert knowledge of employment law who doubles up as a doormat in her spare time. Piece of cake.'

'Be reasonable, Henry. You're making things too complicated.'

Noblet hauled himself out of his chair and paced the terrace with purposeful strides.

'All I'm looking for is a nice girl, with a head on her shoulders, who doesn't mind getting her hands dirty.'

'Good, good – I'm making notes: head must be on shoulders. Dirty hands.'

Noblet paced past his chair. 'Someone who likes children, running a home and who'll get on with Mother.'

'Yes, good, carry on – I'm noting down "mythical being".'

Noblet stopped and planted one foot on the seat of a chair like an exasperated cowboy.

'This should be easy for you. This is what you do, day in, day out.'

'Wrong. I'm a headhunter. I lure greedy executives from well-paid roles into even better paid roles. Never have I had to work with a job description which includes a desire to procreate with the employer.'

'Details, details.'

'I'm glad you see it that way.'

'I do. And that's what we'll tell Mother this evening. That we have it all in hand. All it takes is for a few pleasant girls to apply for the job, we pick a couple of good ones, then present them to Mother and ask her to choose the winner. The End. Finis.'

Pretending not to hear Henry's roar of laughter, Noblet repeated, 'Finis!' before picking up his empty glass and lumbering back into the house.

Henry stayed on the terrace, enjoying the stillness: something that grew more precious to him each time he came to visit. His London flat, a minimalist warehouse conversion, was never quiet. If it wasn't noises inside – Saskia's friends, the phone, music – it was the constant traffic noise. Here, noises soothed rather than irritated. The wind rustling the leaves was like the sigh of the sea ebbing and flowing, and the owl-like sound of a faraway train horn underlined how distant he was from civilisation. Now and then, when the breeze blew from the south, some nasal-sounding megaphone announcements drifted across from the Gently Rising fête. His mother would be there now, doing her Lady Bountiful bit, handing out prizes. Henry got up and stretched. He calculated that he had at least an hour of peace before Lady Caroline returned to the Hall and set out for a wander through the grounds.

***

With no need of the megaphone, Lady Caroline's strident tones rang out across the school field, deafening Mrs Fratterbury, who was standing at her side. Lady Caroline piqued herself on her public-speaking abilities and had been known to give the Queen the odd pointer on elocution.

'Two hundred and twenteh-five! That ticket wins the set of three guest soaps!'

'That's me, your majesty!' gushed an excited voice.

Lady Caroline's eyes narrowed with suspicion until she recognised the speaker; renowned local eccentric Lorraine Watford.

Lorraine was curtseying low to Lady Caroline. Her beady eyes peered over the top of glasses perched halfway down her nose, making her look like a hen who'd accidentally stumbled into a pair of abandoned spectacles.

'Your prize, Mrs Watford.' Lady Caroline presented her with the soaps. 'I hope you're pleased with it.'

'So pink, your highness. Such a lovely fresh smell. Thank you, your ladyness.'

There was a pause as Lorraine remained curtseying; an ineffable look of feudal devotion directed at Lady Caroline's right ear. Realising she was stuck, Mrs Fratterbury stepped forward and hauled her away, safely out of touching distance of Lady Caroline.

Sinead had returned and been persuaded to keep an eye on the white elephant while Alice browsed the other stalls with Mia, who was wearing an enormous pair of sunglasses she'd picked up for a pound from the vintage clothes stall. They would have made Alice look like a worried fly but Mia carried them off with panache. Lorraine beetled past, clutching her pack of pink soaps and muttering under her breath. Mia watched her with interest.

'Who's that?'

'Oh – that's Mrs Watford.'

'Day release?'

'Sorry?'

'Is she on day release from some kind of institution?'

Alice laughed.

'No, no – she lives here in the village. She used to work for the council but she's retired.'

Alice was finding Mia something of an enigma. She was open and direct, yet had given little away about herself. She was startlingly beautiful and yet either unaware or indifferent to the effect her beauty had on others. Alice couldn't work her out. But she liked her and found herself talking a lot. From people in the village the conversation turned to Alice herself.

'Have you lived here all your life?' Mia wanted to know.

'Yes. Well, all my life bar two days – I was born in the hospital in Pantling. And of course, when I was doing my PGCE I had to move away. That was hell. The first month or so I cried every single day, I was pathetic. I missed my family so much – and being here, I suppose. I nearly came home, but Dad drove over one day and talked some sense into me.'

'What did he say?'

'He said… you'll laugh, it sounds silly, but he said I was like a tulip bulb. Everything always comes back to gardening with him. We were stuffing ourselves with scones in a tea shop and I was getting that sinking feeling in my stomach at the thought of him leaving and me having to go back to college. He started talking about gardening, for no obvious reason. He said, "Alice, you have to plant tulip bulbs in winter!" I thought he'd lost it for a minute. "You bury them deep in the cold, dark earth," he said, "and you leave them there. Eventually, the warmer weather comes and that's when the bulb blooms. One has to go through the winter months if one wants to bloom in the spring." He looked hard at me then, to make sure I got it and wasn't just picking up gardening tips.'

'And what did you say?'

'Erm, not much. To be honest, at the time it didn't make me feel much better, but over the next few weeks I'd think about what he said from time to time and it started to make sense. Anyway, sorry. I've no idea why I started banging on about that.'

'Because I asked you.' They'd reached the refreshments tent and ordered some Pimms. As they sat in the shade, sipping their drinks, Alice caught Mia looking at her.

'I want to be honest with you,' Mia said, eventually, after Alice had tried to start a conversation about the fête but stalled and sputtered to a halt. 'I've not told you the whole truth about who I am.'

'What do you mean?' asked Alice, suddenly anxious.

All the background noise seemed to fade away as Mia lowered her voice and said, 'I'd like to keep it quiet as long as I can, so please don't tell anyone…'

***

'Hallo Mother!' called Noblet.

'Watch what you're doing, Nobby! That ladder's a dangerous weapon in your hands.'

'Sorry. There's a photographer stuck up one of the trees by the lake. Going to get him down.'

Lady Caroline looked as if she'd been told there was a rat in the soup tureen.

'Tell Fletcher to deal with it.'

Noblet shook his head. 'Day off.'

'What is he doing in the tree? I didn't order a photographer. Did you?'

Shifting the ladder a little on his shoulder, Noblet set off again across the grass, saying, 'No, Mother. I don't know why he's there. Henry heard him calling for help.'

'Henry's here? Why didn't you say so!' She called after her son, 'I'll tell Martyr to hurry tea. Tell Henry to stop worrying about men in trees and come back to the house.'

Noblet raised a hand in acknowledgement, realised he needed it to support the ladder, staggered a little to the left and a little to the right then steadied himself and continued across the lawn. When he reached the lake, he found Henry, arms folded, staring up into the branches of a tree. Smoke was oozing out through the foliage.

'Filthy habit,' Henry commented.

'Yeah?' came a voice from the tree.

'Furs your arteries.'

'Couldn't give a monkey's,' responded the tree.

'Fills your lungs with black tar.'

'Whoop-di-doodle-do.'

Henry turned as his brother approached. 'I'm not getting very far with this little toerag. He doesn't want to talk.'

'About what?' asked Noblet.

'About anything, but specifically about what he's doing trespassing on private property.'

'None of your bleedin' business,' said the tree.

'It most certainly is our bleeding business,' retorted Noblet. 'It's our land you're trespassing on.'

There was a pause, then the tree said: 'Whatever,' before lapsing into moody silence.

Noblet tried a more direct approach.

'Who sent you here, chummy?' 'Chummy' was uttered in a faltering tone; that of a man aiming for the common touch but with nothing but nineteenth-century literature to draw upon. It had been a toss-up between 'chummy', and 'boy' – this last being rejected at the final moment as being too reminiscent of the language of the beadle in Oliver Twist.

'Screw you.'

'What did you want to photograph? Perhaps if you told us, we'd let you photograph it. Have you thought about that?'

Sounds of derision could be heard through the leaves.

Henry took his brother's arm. 'We're wasting our time here, Bob. Let's leave our new friend alone for a while. I think a night in the open air might improve his temper.'

The sounds of derision could be heard again, with less confidence.

'Come on, I'm looking forward to some tea.'

Noblet looked perplexed but allowed his brother to lead him away.

'Oi! You can't leave me here!'

'Sleep well. See you in the morning.'

'Arseholes! At least get me some fags, I'm out.'

'Excellent opportunity to kick the habit. Goodbye!'

Henry sauntered away across the lawn, humming a little tune and smiling at the summery scene before him: blue skies, the golden stone of the Hall glowing in the afternoon light and a table spread with silver tea things on the terrace.

'You're not going to leave him there all night, Henry?' Noblet asked, concern on his ruddy face.

'No, no. No, we'll get him down later. After tea.'

***

In London, a porcine man sitting in an expensive chair, behind an expensive desk, picked up his expensive phone. It was ringing and the name on the screen was 'Squeak'.

The man touched the screen with a sausage-like finger and raised the phone to his ear.

He grunted.

'S'me,' said the voice on the other end of the line.

'I know it's fuckin' you, that's what the fuckin' screen's for. Have you got them?'

'No.'

'Why not?'

Audible squirming. 'I'm… stuck up a tree.'

The man opened his arms wide in a gesture of exasperation, eyes rolling towards the heavens. Returning the phone to his ear, he growled:

'You fuckin' moron. I knew I should have sent Damo.'

'No! S'alright. I'll get 'em. But I need someone to come and get me out of this tree.'

The pig-man took a long breath in.

'If you wanted the fire brigade you should have rung nine-nine-fuckin'-nine. This is a picture agency. I pay people to take pictures, not rescue damsels in fuckin' distress.'

With that, he hung up, muttered 'fuckin' prick' to himself and dialled another number.

***

Two hours on a narrow branch without nicotine had done a lot to soften Squeak. At the sound of approaching footsteps, he didn't wait to be coaxed but called out, 'Alright, I give in, I'll tell you what you want to know. Get me out of this bleedin' tree. I hate the bleedin' countryside.'

'How disappointing,' drawled Henry. 'I didn't even get to say "we haf vays of making you tok", let alone threatening to attach jump leads to your nipples.'

'Eh?' gasped Squeak.

'It's alright, chummy, he's pulling your leg, old man,' Noblet hastened to explain. 'We're going to get you down now.'

Henry held out a hand. 'Hold on a second, Bob. He might not be so talkative once he's on solid ground.' Looking up into the tree he asked, 'Who sent you here?'

'Snappy Shots.'

'Snappy whats?' asked Noblet.

'Snappy Shots. 'S a picture agency.'

Noblet still looked perplexed.

'Paparazzi,' Henry explained.

'Oh. But they take pictures of famous people, don't they?' Noblet's face brightened. 'I say, is someone exciting coming here?'

'Nah,' replied Squeak. 'No one exciting. One o' you two, I reckon. Is one o' you Lord Dreeble?'

'Neither of us is Lord Dreeble. You should do your homework before you start out,' said Henry.

'I expect you mean Lord de Beeble, don't you?' asked Noblet.

'Whatever. He's the one I've got to get a picture of.'

'Him?' Noblet said, shocked. 'Why on earth would you want a picture of him?'

'Cos 'e's gonna be big news.'

'What?'

'He is,' insisted Squeak. 'My boss says so and 'e's never wrong.'

'What did he say to you about Lord de Beeble?' asked Henry.

''E said 'e's lookin' for a wife and he's a big toff wiv loads of money and the papers are gonna love it. They'll want pictures of 'im looking all posh and lonely outside 'is big 'ouse.'

'Well, I...' Noblet was lost for words. Henry led him out of Squeak's earshot.

'I was worried this might happen when I saw that piece in the *Telegraph*. The press love this kind of story, the place will be swarming with reporters soon. This is just the vanguard.'

Grasping the sides of his hair with both hands and tugging hard, Noblet moaned, 'But what am I going to do, old man? I can't work with reporters climbing in through the windows and getting stuck up trees every five minutes. Oh, this is hell!'

'Calm down, Bob. We need to think.' He pressed his palms together ruminatively for a moment and then strode back to the tree.

'If you don't get the pictures, will he send another photographer?'

'Yep. Reckon 'e's already done it. Now, are you gonna get me out of this tree before I wet meself?'

'Yes. On two conditions. One – you take some pictures of my brother and let your boss know he can cancel the other photographer. Two – you let us know whatever you hear about Lord de Beeble: when photographers are being sent here, which papers are running a story on him – anything at all that you hear. And for that, we'll put you on a retainer.'

'How much?'

'A hundred a month.'

'Pfffff! Make it a week and you're gettin' closer.'

'Two hundred a month – final offer. Unless you'd like another hour on that branch?'

Squeak grumbled something incoherent, then muttered, 'Deal. Two hundred.'

Henry brought the ladder over and leant it against the tree. There was some scuffling and then a small elf in a grey hooded top, black tracksuit bottoms and dirty trainers emerged, carrying a rucksack. He hopped behind a nearby bush, calling out, 'Back in a sec!'

The two brothers struck up a loud conversation to cover the noise of gushing water, which eventually dried up and the hooded creature scurried back out from behind the bush. Planting himself in front of Henry and Noblet, he looked them up and down.

'Which one's the Lord?'

Noblet raised a paw. 'Guilty as charged.'

Obvious disappointment spread across Squeak's face. Ignoring this, Henry asked, 'Where do you want him?'

Noblet started to splutter.

'Now, Henry, you know I hate being photographed. I…'

'Would you rather we do it now, or would you rather the other photographer comes with a telephoto lens and takes pictures of you through the library window?'

'I… Well… Oh, damn it. The first, I suppose.'

'Good, now, our friend here… What's your name?'

'Squeak.'

'No, what's your real name?'

'My real name's Gareth, but everyone calls me Squeak.'

'Our friend Gareth will show you where he wants you.'

Squeak sprang into action, beetling through the trees to recce the house and grounds while pulling a camera out of his rucksack.

'We'll 'ave a few in front of the 'ouse first. Got a swimming pool?'

Noblet shook his head. 'No.'

'Rolls Royce?'

'No.'

''Ot tub?'

'No.'

'One of them giant outdoor chess sets?'

'Not so much as an oversized bishop, I'm sorry to say.'

He seemed to be running out of ideas but then his face lit up with hope.

'Con-serv-a-tory?' He pronounced each syllable as if it were a separate word.

'Conservatory?' repeated Noblet.

'Yeah. That's what the proper rich people always have: a con-serv-a-tory. Wiv animal skin rugs on the floor.'

'Erm, no. Sorry. There's a summer house?'

He shrugged. 'That'll 'ave to do.'

He was about to beetle away again but Henry stopped him.

'As soon as you have these pictures, you'll call your boss and let him know?'

'Defo. Do it now if you like.'

'Good. And then you'll keep us informed of anything you hear about Lord de Beeble?'

'As long as you keep sending the readies, I'll keep you informed.' He headed off across the lawn, Noblet trailing behind.

'But will we know what to do with that information, that's the question,' mused Henry as he followed in their wake.

Chapter 3

A few days after the fête, a new advert appeared in the Market Mornington *Gazette* and was reproduced in the columns of many of the national papers:

Announcement Regarding Applications for the Role of Wife of Lord de Beeble

Due to the volume of applications already received for the above role, an open day will be held to interview applicants on Saturday 6th June, beginning at 9am, in the village hall, Gently Rising, Mereshire. Applicants will be registered and interviewed on a first come, first served basis. Please bring an up-to-date photograph and curriculum vitae. Successful applicants will be invited to the second interview stage.
<u>*Written applications will no longer be considered.*</u>

A story appeared in one of the tabloids under the headline 'Lonely Lord Longs for Love'. The story described how Lord de Beeble, after a series of failed relationships with unsuitable girls ('busty Bethan', 'lusty Lauren' and 'juicy Lucy' – all pictured languishing in small scraps of lingerie) had declared enough was enough. He wanted to inject some meaning into his solitary, jewel-encrusted life. The story was accompanied by a full-page picture of Noblet in his old green pullover, leaning awkwardly against the door of a summer house. Websites sprang up devoted to Lord de Beeble, offering expert advice and insider knowledge on how to become his wife (downloadable upon payment of a very reasonable fee). Local radio shows held phone-ins: women called in to say they'd applied, or that it was outrageous, or that they'd once met him at a party, or that they'd never met him at a party, or that they'd been abducted by an alien who looked like him. It was mentioned with a wry smile in the 'and finally' section of the local news. Then the national news. And still, the applications flooded in.

Stumbling over another sack of them as she popped in for a nightcap on her way home from bridge one night, Lady Caroline swore under her breath. To Sally, who was closing the front door behind her, she said, 'Would you bring Nobby here, please.'

Sally returned, trailing an apprehensive-looking Noblet.

'Hallo, Mother, how was bridge?'

'I'm not interested in talking about bridge,' she replied icily. 'I thought you said you were going to get rid of all these letters.'

'I did. I got rid of them and Henry put out the new advertisement telling people not to write, but more and more of the damn things keep arriving. I don't know what to do, Mother. People don't listen.'

Lady Caroline glared at her son for a moment longer and then seemed to relent.

'Have you opened any?'

'One or two.'

'It is just possible, you know, that if you opened some more you might find a suitable young woman. Then you could call off this whole ridiculous circus and we could all get back to normal.' She picked a letter out of the sack at random and called to Sally for a paperknife.

'Not that I'm condoning this ridiculous technique of yours for finding a wife. You know my views on it…'

'I do, Mother, yes,' said Noblet, firmly, hoping this would avoid the need for her to set them out again. It didn't.

'I offered to take you with me to stay with the Purvos in Norfolk, I offered to invite the Cholmondeley-Lumleys for a weekend with their three sweet daughters, I suggested you come with my little party of pals to Glyndebourne. In short, I offered to introduce you to some of the best girls in the county – what am I saying? The best girls in the *country*. But you'd rather put a grubby little advertisement in a grubby little newspaper and invite the world in to gawp at our private lives. Strange way of going about things, Nobby, but then you were never quite normal, were you?'

'I wonder where I get that from,' he muttered.

'Pardon?'

'I wonder where that came from, Mother? That letter.'

'The answer to that can be ascertained quite simply by reading the address.' She looked down at the piece of paper which she was holding by the very tips of the corners.

'It has come from 15 Downton Close, Birkenhead. It says "Dear Mr Lord, Even though I'm fifteen". Oh dear, no. I don't think so.'

She dropped the letter on the floor beside the overflowing sack.

'Bring a handful, Nobby, and we'll go through them somewhere more comfortable.'

There was only one lamp lit in the drawing room – the evenings were getting darker later and later, and even tonight, at nearly nine o'clock, the terrace still gleamed silver in the dusk. Lady Caroline went to the drinks table and poured herself a generous measure of whisky from the decanter before sitting down in a severe-looking armchair. Noblet came in with a stack of envelopes.

'Turn that lamp on so I can read. It's too dark in here.'

Lady Caroline was supposed to wear reading glasses but preferred to blame her poor eyesight on not enough light, other people's handwriting, bad paper – anything other than her own eyes. She picked up a pink envelope from the pile Noblet had dumped on the small mahogany table beside her. It smelt of roses and for a second, she was propelled back in time, to her youth, when she had been courted by Noblet's father, Nibs. Nibs had arrived at each meeting (they could hardly be called dates, with most of the extended family also in attendance) with an armful of pink roses. That was, until she had told him they made her feel about eighty-five and he had moved on to other, less elderly, blooms. The eldest son of each generation of the de Beeble family was always christened Noblet and then given a different nickname to distinguish them from each other. Noblet was Nobby, his father had been Nibs, and Nibs' father, inexplicably, had been Tutu. Nibs had been picked out for Caroline, and she for him, by their parents. There had been nothing melodramatic or tragic about this to Caroline's nineteen-year-old mind. Marriage was a way of getting what you wanted in life. If you were married you would have your own servants, your own garden, your own house, your own friends. Yes, there would also be a husband that these things must be shared with, but he would have his own interests. Caroline didn't expect love from marriage. Marriage was the base from which you went on to do all the things you wanted to do in life. She knew Henry, for one, didn't agree with her on this. Things had changed, or so he liked to tell her. Henry was a romantic. He thought one's spouse should embody in one person many different roles that, Caroline believed, could as easily be played by several separate people. Caroline had had a husband for security and, sometimes, companionship. She had children for love, friends for friendship and lovers for sex. To expect to find all of these things in one person appeared to her infantile in most people; but in Henry it was charming. Noblet, on the other hand, was more malleable. He was the kind of man who, in her day, would have been married off very young, bumped into his wife from time to time at breakfast, then disappeared for the rest of the day to shoot or fish. He would have been very supportive of his wife's desire to travel abroad or to spend weeks without him at their London house; and if he had found out about the lovers, he would have shrugged his shoulders and said 'good for you, dear.' He was so like his father, she reflected as she read through the rose-scented job application.

Noblet had hurled himself onto the opposite sofa and was watching her glumly. 'Any good?'

'Not the kind of person we're looking for, I'm afraid. Too many references to her physical attributes and too few to her mental ones. If there are any mental ones.'

That one got crumpled up and thrown at the empty fireplace. Lady Caroline picked up another, slashed at it with the paperknife and glanced at the contents. Another one for the fire. The slashing, reading and throwing continued in silence for some minutes until Noblet reached down and smoothed out one of the crumpled letters.

'What's wrong with this one, Mother?'

'Which one?'

'From a lady called Terri in Hull. She says…'

'Noblet,' Lady Caroline interrupted, 'she is called Terri and she is from Hull. Beyond that, we need know no more. Put her in the fire.'

Noblet rolled the letter up into a ball again and dropped it onto the hearth.

'If you were organising this wife-business on your own,' she continued, 'I'd have serious concerns. Thank God Henry's helping you.'

'I don't know why you say that. Henry's not a snob. He wouldn't dismiss a girl because she was called Terri and came from Hull.'

'Henry's got an instinct where women are concerned. Take Saskia, for instance.' Her face softened. 'She is the right kind of girl, Noblet. I approve of Saskia. Find yourself a Saskia and we will all be happy.'

'All except me,' groaned Noblet into the sofa cushions.

Lady Caroline reached the end of the stack of envelopes, finished her whisky and stood up.

'Well, look at the time. I must be making my way to my humble home.' Her humble home being the eighteenth-century Dower House, a seven-bedroom pile with six acres of grounds and separate chauffeur's quarters complete with chauffeur.

'These letters have been rather a disappointment, but there's still hope. Perhaps Henry will find you someone wonderful at this cattle market he's organising in the village. And if not,' she smiled archly at him, 'there's always Glyndebourne.'

***

In the secret recesses of Alice's brain lurked a secret fear. Her secret fear was that she was boring.

On a day-to-day basis, this wasn't something that tormented her. She didn't lie awake for hours debating whether or not to make a grand statement in order to stand out from the crowd. Such as painting each fingernail a different colour. On the whole, she was content with her life and too busy enjoying it to fret over its probable dullness. However, once in a while something would happen to make her feel that she had fallen into a rut, and that something would niggle at the edges of her consciousness. This time it was Mia. When she'd said goodbye to Alice after the fête, she'd flown to Argentina to 'tie up some loose ends'. Alice, on the other hand, had gone home to eat leftover pizza before watching an old episode of *Poirot* with the cat on her lap. Life carried on as usual but since saying goodbye to Mia, it was as if someone had taken a paintbrush and painted a grey wash over everything.

On the Sunday morning after the fête, Alice cycled over to her parents for lunch, as she did every Sunday. When Alice's father had retired from the church some years previously, he and Alice's mother had moved from Gently Rising's vicarage to a neat Georgian house in the hamlet of Pipper, some half a mile away.

As she cycled down the sun-dappled lane which led from Gently Rising to Pipper, something was lurking near the gates to de Beeble Hall. It gleamed, shiny and pink, in the morning sun, and to Alice's short-sighted eyes it looked like a skeleton which had been dipped in molten pink plastic and left to set. A small grey bundle of something like tumble-dryer lint broke away from the feet of the figure and hurled itself, yapping, at the front wheel of her bicycle.

'Coco! Get back here! Coco!'

The staccato voice revealed the owner of the lint creature to be Sinead Dumper, wearing a shocking pink PVC catsuit and matching platform heels.

'Can you stop cycling,' she snapped. 'It's irritating him. I've only just got him under control.'

Alice pulled up and reached down to stroke the dog, then changed her mind after catching sight of the manic eyes and bared teeth.

'New dog, Sinead?' she enquired.

Sinead nodded. 'Picked him up from the breeder this morning. He's a Bichipoo. Cost two grand.'

'He's a what?'

'Bichipoo. It's designer. Cross between a bichon frise and a poodle.'

'And you've called him Cocoa? That's… unusual.'

'Classy,' she corrected her. 'Named after Coco Chanel.'

'Well, I don't think Tom's going to like the new addition to the village,' said Alice, with a smile.

'I didn't buy him to please your flea-ridden old cat. He's for walking. Good way to get out and meet people.'

'And is this what you'd consider a suitable dog-walking outfit?' she shot back, smarting at the slight on Tom's personal hygiene.

'This is what I'd consider fashion. Upping my game. Striking while the iron's hot.' She jerked her head in the direction of de Beeble Hall, which lay hidden behind trees at the end of the mile-long drive. As she spoke, they heard the low hum of an engine and a large black car came into view around a bend in the drive.

'Quick! Get out of the way! You're blocking me.'

Alice wheeled her bike over to the other side of the gates while Sinead gathered up Coco and draped herself stiffly against the wall. The car continued its slow progress down the drive. Sinead remained frozen in position, Coco struggling a little in her arms, while Alice looked on, unable to tear herself away. As the car paused at the gates, anyone in the back seat would have had a clear view of Sinead, clad in pink PVC and grappling with a struggling ball of grey fluff. The car remained at the gate, the engine ticking over. One of the back windows rolled down with an expensive-sounding whirr. Alice, on the other side of the car, couldn't see anything through the tinted windows. There was silence for a long moment, then a carolling peal of female, upper-class laughter which continued, albeit muffled, as the window rolled back up and the car pulled away.

Sinead dumped Coco on the floor. 'Wasn't him. It was Lady Caroline.'

'Never mind,' said Alice, kindly. 'She's quite old-fashioned, isn't she, Lady Caroline. I doubt she knows what's fashionable and what's not.'

'Couldn't care less what she thinks,' said Sinead, clipping a pink lead on to Coco's diamanté collar. 'Not her I want to impress.'

'Don't be too sure of that. From what I heard at the fête, Lord de Beeble won't marry anyone his mother doesn't approve of.'

Sinead stopped what she was doing and stared at her.

'Anyway, enjoy the rest of your walk.'

Alice hopped back on her bike and cycled off, Coco half-strangling himself against the lead in his attempts to chase after her, yapping his little designer heart out.

***

Arriving at her parents' house she found her older sister Cecily laying the table in the garden and talking to a tall man who stood nearby, legs akimbo and arms folded across his broad chest. Cecily had had few boyfriends and Piers was the first to be brought home to meet the family. Introductions were made and everyone sat down in deckchairs under the trees to enjoy their aperitifs.

Alice's mother smiled at Piers.

'It's such a pleasure to meet you, Piers. We've heard a lot about you from Cecily of course…'

'Oh dear! All bad I expect!' He guffawed and beamed round the circle.

'Not at all. But tell us about yourself. How did you and Cecily meet?'

'Well, Felicity, that's a funny story as it happens. Isn't it Cess?'

Cecily looked as if she wasn't one hundred per cent convinced of it being amusing, or indeed something she wanted to share with the group. She started to intervene but he playfully slapped a meaty hand over her mouth and continued.

'She doesn't like me telling this story because she thinks it's embarrassing. But I say that's life, Cess! If people don't like the truth, they can lump it.' He beamed round at everyone again. Alice's mother started to look uncomfortable.

'I rolled into the surgery one day in absolute agony and she was my ministering angel. When I knocked on the door marked "Dr Brand" I was expecting some old duffer with a beard but instead, this rather attractive young saucepot welcomed me in.'

Alice shifted position in her chair.

'Still, couldn't be helped – I was in pain and there it was. I dropped my trousers, bent over and said "Do what you've got to do, doc!" And God bless her, she did. I'd got a boil the size of your fist and I'd not sat down for a week. She set straight to work, rammed the needle in up to the hilt, patched me up and packed me on my way. But not before I'd made her promise to come to dinner with me that night. So, there you have it ladies and gentleman – how a boil on the backside was the beginning of true love!'

More guffawing, feebly echoed by Alice and the Reverend Brand. Alice's mother looked stony-faced as she said:

'Well, what an unusual way to meet. To table everyone!'

***

Lunch was a stilted affair. Piers appeared not to notice that his jokes weren't to everyone's taste but on the whole, Cecily seemed rather proud of him. He was certainly very gregarious and entertaining, reflected Alice, as she tucked into pink slices of roast beef and crisp Yorkshire pudding, but not at all what she would have expected Cecily's boyfriend to be like. In her professional life, Cecily had the reputation of being a little cold, but this was because she was misunderstood, Alice felt. She was, in fact, scrupulously fair, giving the same amount of thought and attention to everyone, from the overwrought parents with a feverish baby to a doolally old lady convinced she had prostate cancer. Piers was the kind of man Alice had thought Cecily would shy away from, but perhaps they just proved the cliché that opposites attract. She had a sudden vision of herself in Cecily's shoes, bringing a new boyfriend home to meet the family for the first time. Despite the fact she was knocking on the door of thirty, it had never happened. There had been the odd short-lived relationship – one at Homerton, a few online dates in the years since – but nothing serious enough to get the family involved. In fact, Alice realised, the last time she'd been with someone for more than a couple of weeks was at least four years ago. She was more likely to be found at home of an evening baking cupcakes for a colleague's birthday than downing cocktails on a hot date.

'Not hungry, darling?' She realised that her mother was talking to her. 'You've not touched your roast potatoes.'

'I think it's the heat. It's delicious, as usual, Mum, thanks.'

Piers had launched into a story about a recent scuba diving trip and Felicity turned politely towards him to listen, leaving Alice to her own devices again. Almost thirty and still single – was there something wrong with her? All her friends were settling down, why couldn't she? And – perhaps more importantly – why wasn't she more bothered about it? Boyfriends, in her experience, were overrated. Dating made her feel anxious and inadequate; more often than not she spent the evening feigning interest in a tedious conversation while wishing she was at home on the sofa with the cat. She couldn't relate to those internal fireworks that always seemed to be triggered in romcoms when the heroine was kissed by the hero. Whenever she'd kissed a man she'd experienced a couple of damp squibs at most. In fact, the last time she'd felt anything approaching fireworks was when Mia had smiled at her. Did she have a crush on Mia? She jabbed at some peas. That would make things complicated. No, no, she told herself. She was blown away by Mia, in the same way you would be by any exotic creature. She was sure she was attracted to men. Perhaps not in the same way as other women seemed to be, though – or not to the same extent. It was all very confusing and she was glad to turn her attention to the much simpler question of whether she'd like second helpings of roast beef.

Her distraction over lunch hadn't gone unnoticed. While they were carrying dirty pots into the kitchen, Cecily said, 'You alright, Al? Not overdoing it are you? You didn't laugh at Piers' rabbit joke and that one is hilarious.'

'Oh! No, I'm fine, thanks. Sorry, I must have missed it. He seems nice, though, Sissy. How's it all going?'

'Good, thanks,' said Cecily. 'But are you sure you're OK?'

'Honestly, I'm fine. Sunday blues, that's all.'

'You with the blues? Something must be wrong.'

Alice gave her sister a quick hug. 'It isn't. I'd tell you if there was something serious.'

Felicity came into the kitchen, carrying some empty glasses. 'What's serious?'

'Cecily and Piers,' Alice replied quickly.

'Ooh!' Cecily mock slapped her sister on the arm. 'You little minx, I never said that.'

Felicity tensed up a little as she said, 'He's very confident, Cecily.'

'I know he might seem a bit full-on when you first meet him, but he's just trying to make a good impression.'

'Yes, well, you can leave these dishes – Alice will help me, won't you, poppet? Your father's taken Piers to look at the greenhouse. Why don't you go and rescue him? You know he'll keep him there for hours otherwise, inspecting the tomato plants.'

***

That night, Alice had a nightmare. She dreamt she was being chased up a mountain of cold roast beef by an enormous grey woolly monster. The monster was snapping at her heels but as she clawed at the slices of beef, they kept slipping away beneath her. A strange man was at the top of the mountain, reaching out a hand to pull her up. When she got nearer, she realised it wasn't a man at all, but Mia who was waiting for her. The surprise made her stagger and then she was falling down a sheer cliff face, evil-looking roast potato rocks rushing up to meet her. When she woke, she was sitting bolt upright in bed, drenched in sweat, heart pounding.

Chapter 4

When the alarm went off on Monday morning Alice was still tired and irritable. The usually uplifting sight of the village green sparkling with dew did little to improve her mood as she made her way to work. At nine o'clock, the Senior Teacher was forced to take assembly as Mrs Fratterbury hadn't turned up, and Alice found herself thinking disrespectful thoughts about her headmistress. Mrs Fratterbury often rolled into work late with no explanation of why she'd been held up. All the teachers knew what had held her up anyway: sheer laziness and, more often than not, a hangover. This morning she shambled in at 9.20, in time to catch the end of assembly and to congratulate Mrs Denton on a job well done.

'I couldn't have done it better myself, Margaret. I like you to have these opportunities. I'm not one of those headteachers who keep all the glory for themselves. I believe that you reap what you sow.'

Making her way into her office, she turned on the kettle and settled down to give serious attention to a jam doughnut. There was a knock at the door and she hastily pulled out some papers and pretended to be studying them.

'Come!'

Alice opened the door. Mrs Fratterbury smiled toothily at her, unaware that most of her lower face was dusted in sugar.

'Good morning, Alice. Shouldn't you be in class?' She tapped her watch.

'Yes, I'm about to go in. I wanted to find out if you'd had a chance to write a letter about the outing. It needs to go to the parents today.'

'The letter about the outing... Yes, I was working on that yesterday, I believe. Now what did I do with it. I take on too much, you know, Alice. That's my problem. And then I don't know where I am with things.'

She shuffled papers on her desk, going through the motions of searching for the letter, which they both knew didn't exist.

'Do you know what's probably the easiest thing, lovie? Go and ask Mrs Fairlie to knock one up for you. She'll know what to put. I can't lay my hands on my draft at the moment.'

Mrs Fairlie's job description was school secretary, but when it came to the organisation and administration of the school, she was headmistress in all but name. Mrs Fratterbury delegated so well that she had delegated ninety per cent of her job to her secretary.

'OK,' Alice said, not attempting to smile. She turned to leave the room but Mrs Fratterbury called her back.

'Are you poorly, Alice? You don't seem your usual sunny self.'

'I'm fine, thanks. I'd better get back to my class.'

'Yes, off you go. Mustn't keep the little people waiting. My door's always open though, dear, if you need a chat. A problem shared is a problem solved, you know.'

The door closed and Mrs Fratterbury dismissed Alice's odd demeanour from her mind by concentrating instead on making a nice cup of coffee to go with the remainder of her doughnut.

**

A day with the reception class had lightened Alice's mood somewhat, and she felt close to her old self again by home time. They could be so endearing sometimes, when they weren't squabbling or having tantrums, which happened quite a lot. One of them had told her she was nearly as beautiful as Barbie (only her hair wasn't as nice) and a little boy called Jacob had given her his second favourite digger. She'd had to give it back, of course, but it was the thought that counted. On the way home from school she popped into the community shop to pick up something for dinner. The term 'community shop' always made her think of 'care in the community' – and never more so than when Lorraine Watford was on duty, as she was today. A committee ran the shop and approved people's requests to volunteer. Nobody had thought Lorraine would be a suitable shop assistant but nobody was brave enough to tell her so, and her request had been granted. Today she'd been making a new display on the counter.

'Ooh.' She giggled as Alice entered. 'You'll like this. Like what you do with your kiddies.'

'Mmmm,' said Alice. She had no idea what the display was supposed to represent, but she knew better than to ask. Most volunteers would make pyramids of attractive jars or fill a wicker basket with a selection of seasonal fruit and vegetables to brighten up the counter. Lorraine had cleared all nonsense of this sort off the surface and instead scattered random objects across it, including a couple of packs of Marigolds, some sugar cubes, lemons and a pack of Bird's custard.

'It's all summery and lovely, isn't it?' she chirped.

'Lovely,' agreed Alice.

The little bell jangled on the door and Alice turned with relief to see Colonel Markham. She divined his hesitation when he realised who was serving; and also his realisation that it was too late to retreat. He lifted his chin and marched up to the counter.

'Good afternoon, Mrs Watford. Good afternoon, Alice.'

Lorraine simpered a little and pushed a pair of Marigolds at the Colonel.

'For your washing-up. No wifey, to do it, have you, Colonel? You need a good little wifey to look after you.'

Colonel Markham glared at her.

'May I remind you I served three years in the catering corps, Mrs Watford. I am perfectly capable of looking after myself.'

'Lovely and bright,' she urged, continuing to push the gloves at him.

Ignoring her, he turned to Alice.

'Enjoy the festivities on Saturday, Alice? Rushed off your feet, I expect? I noticed Ms Dumper deserted her post as usual.'

'I had a great time, thanks.'

'And,' his voice seemed to have a slight catch in it; his eyes taking on a dreamy look, 'I noticed you made a new friend. Charming-looking woman. Is she… ahem!' He cleared his throat. 'Is she going to be visiting the village again, do you know?'

Alice tried to hide her amazement. Colonel Markham seemed to have shed twenty years and looked almost dashing as he twirled his grey moustache.

'Yes, she is. She's renting Ivy Cottage.'

'Is she? Well. That is interesting.' He reverted hurriedly to his normal tone of voice. 'Interesting for you I mean – having a new friend in the village.'

To Lorraine, who was humming at him while rearranging the lumps of sugar, he said:

'One of those steak and kidney pies, please, Mrs Watford. I'm in a hurry.'

Lorraine picked a chicken and mushroom pie out of the fridge behind her and presented it to him. He opened his mouth to protest, thought better of it and handed over the money before beating a retreat. Alice made haste to pay for her items and followed hot on his heels.

***

The week rolled on, following its usual pattern. Work during the day, watching TV, baking or chatting to a friend in the evening. There was no return of the irritability of Monday, but Alice was still conscious of a lingering dissatisfaction. She felt as if she was waiting for something to happen – but a voice at the back of her mind kept whispering that it never would. This was it, for life. She tried to cheer herself up with the thought that soon Mia would be back but even that made her gloomy. Mia was passing through: she would leave Alice behind.

She was turning these dreary thoughts over in her mind as she walked home from school on Friday afternoon. Passing the village hall, she spotted something new on the noticeboard.

NOTICE OF MEETING

Public meeting to be held on Saturday 16th May at Gently Rising village hall.

Topic: Lord de Beeble's proposed use of village facilities for an interview process.

All welcome. 7pm start. Refreshments will be served at the close of the meeting.

The meeting will be chaired by Mrs Elaine Jowlett.

Initially, the reaction in the village to Lord de Beeble's advert and the surrounding media interest had been one of curiosity and excitement but over the last couple of days, Alice had noticed a turn in the tide. There had been rumblings of discontent from certain members of the community – dark prophecies of what all this attention would mean for the village: traffic, noise and perhaps even litter. It seemed that these discontented elements had come together under the leadership of Elaine Jowlett, local scout leader and a lifelong Gently Risinger. If she had set her mind against Lord de Beeble using the village hall for his interviews the meeting promised to be a lively one. Alice reached for her phone; Mia had asked her to keep her up to date with any developments and this was, if she knew Gently Rising, a development.

***

The famine-ridden cheeks of the model were barely visible above the stretchy tube of white trellis packaging, more normally found around wine bottles, that formed the tall neck of her dress. Her body, to just below her pelvis, was clad in a blue mesh made out of twisted and stapled salt and vinegar crisp packets. Her feet were in sandals created from polystyrene trays.

Something was wrong. Saskia called the stylist over.

'It's not working. She looks too… alert, you know? And something's missing.' Rummaging through the pile of garments on the table, she picked out a blue cone-shaped hat; chains of figure-of-eight packing chips cascading from the point of the cone down to the floor. She watched as the stylist arranged the hat on the model's head and gave her some instructions on her pose and facial expression.

'That's it, man. That's the vacuum.'

When Saskia had launched her magazine, there had been some speculation over the meaning of its name: *The Vacuum*. Certain commentators had assumed it was an ironic reference to society's perception of woman as a domestic animal. It wasn't. It was Saskia's way of referring to something that was so painfully, achingly cool, it was off the scale. 'Cool' was no longer cool enough for Saskia Stonor. Things were categorised into 'icy' (quite cool), 'forty below' (really cool), and 'the vacuum' (off the scale). Young, rich and pretty, Saskia had done what everyone had expected her to do by heading straight from St. Andrews University to an indecently well-paid job in the City. The CEO was an old friend of Daddy's and he'd ushered her into a plum role from where she could expect to progress year on year with a fat bonus every Christmas and a guaranteed directorship by the time she was thirty-five. Life was easy for Saskia. A couple of years passed, years in which she had hung out with other rich City friends: skiing in Courchevel, holidaying on friends' yachts in the Seychelles, long weekends in Miami and Monaco. Cabs, bags, heels, jewels, tans, booze, coke and late, late nights – these were precarious props of her day-to-day life. And then, a breakdown.

Totally unexpected, embarrassing for friends and family, and not at all part of the grand plan. Gone were the late nights, priceless morsels of food and ten-thousand-pound drinks bills; instead life contracted to the hushed, airbrushed interiors of an exclusive rehab clinic and private convalescent home. The empty space that appeared in her circle of friends was referred to with thinly-veiled contempt, before closing up completely. Breakdowns happened to the weak. Saskia was consigned to that other, lesser part of the world that was beneath notice.

'OK, that's a wrap, guys. Meditation time. Gather in, everyone.'

Models, stylists and photographer alike shuffled into a circle and held hands. Saskia closed her eyes and hummed. The others joined in, modulating their pitch to hers. Yoga and meditation were two of the things she'd picked up at the ayurvedic retreat in India. Crabs was another, but Saskia didn't drop that into the conversation quite as often. After leaving the private convalescent home, Saskia had moped around at her parents' house in the country for a while, directionless. The chance mention of ayurvedic healing in a newspaper article had set her off on a quest to find out more, throwing herself in at the deep end with a month-long stay at a retreat in Goa. She had been an instant convert. The calm of the retreat had suited her post-rehab introspection and the ideologies discussed there seemed to fit with many of the big questions she'd been asking herself. Pre-breakdown, her life had been hectic and superficial. At the retreat, she learnt a New Way. This New Way involved respecting and contemplating nature, taking time each day to meditate alone, and regularly disappearing off to an out-of-the-way hut to have sex. Hence the crabs.

Her salvation could have been Christianity, homoeopathy, scrapbooking, power-walking or Toby-jug-collecting. Saskia was a lost soul looking for succour, and she would have grasped at the first plausible-looking system of beliefs to come her way.

In Goa, she found herself.

In New York, she temporarily misplaced herself again.

A new friend she'd met in the retreat had invited her to come and stay for a while. This friend, Zelia, was the fashion editor of a major women's magazine. For something to do, Saskia had gone into the office with her a few times, and in the end, they found her a job helping out one of the stylists. Yoga and meditation were still a major part of her daily routine, but she found herself being lured back into her previous lifestyle of long hours and hard partying. Zelia warned her to slow down, but she'd got the taste for it and soon was tumbling down the slippery, champagne-soaked slopes of debauchery towards the precipice. Fortunately, at the vital moment, her grandfather died. Summoned back to England for the funeral, Saskia had time to step back, reflect, and breathe a sigh of relief. New York had nearly succeeded in dirtying her newly-cleansed soul, but she had been plucked to safety just in time. Standing at the edge of the grave in a black Miu Miu dress, she sent up a silent prayer of thanks to her grandfather for sacrificing his physical body in order to save her soul. And for the inheritance of around twelve-point-five million, of course.

'OK guys, thank you for sharing that with me. Let's get this all cleared up now and Bo, I want to see some copy by midday tomorrow, no excuses. Chop chop, guys, let's move it.'

The magazine had been a flash of inspiration. Back in Britain with cash piling up in the bank, she needed a new focus. She thought about setting up a yoga centre, but it seemed too small-scale. She wanted to educate... not the masses, exactly: more the chosen few. Saskia had learnt a hell of a lot and it would be bordering on immoral not to share her insights with others. With her mixture of life experience in the superficial City, spiritual Goa and stylish New York, she knew now what was authentic, what was beautiful and above all, what was cool. Or rather, what was the vacuum. And so, the magazine was born – its objective to raise humanity out of the gutter and on to solar-powered, ethical-diamond-encrusted scooters; to lift their eyes from their suburban shagpile to the eco-luxe headpieces worn by the cognoscenti. *The Vacuum* repudiated everything vulgar, mundane and crass – such as making lots of money in the City – and instead promoted the avant-garde, the ecologically innovative and the dazzlingly odd. It didn't make money, but then that had never been the intention. Making money was greedy and base. The magazine was a work of art and like many artists, its editor did not always receive the acclaim she deserved. If she had, the whole point of the magazine would have been missed – it was opposed to what was popular and was, itself, often misunderstood. Saskia preferred to run *The Vacuum* at a loss, pouring in a few hundred thousand from her own pocket now and then, rather than succumb to the tastes of the general public.

'Ciao, guys. Good work today. Ciao-ciao.'

Outside, the traffic roared past and Saskia picked out the welcome yellow light of an available black cab. She abhorred climate-destroying cars and didn't own one herself. Instead, she used public transport whenever she wasn't running late, and a cab when she was. Ninety-nine times out of a hundred, she was running late. Inside the cab, she had time to post an enlightening TikTok and tap out a couple of motivational tweets, before they pulled up outside La Vache Qui Pleure, an upmarket steakhouse. Not a big eater of meat as a rule, she'd suggested a new experiential plant-based restaurant, where diners were encouraged to chant over their food for good energy but Henry had demurred. 'Bob hates London as it is,' he'd said, 'the least we can do is help him face it on a full stomach.'

***

Noblet spotted Saskia approaching through the candlelit restaurant and stood up to give her an awkward peck on the cheek. She hugged him to her for a few moments, despite the stiff resistance.

'Noblet,' she breathed. 'Great to see you, man.'

Noblet muttered something that sounded like 'very pleasant' but she'd already turned away to kiss Henry full on the mouth and give him an even longer hug.

'Are you OK, babe? You look pale.'

'How can you tell in this light?'

'Call it a sense then. Your aura's faint.'

'My aura and everything else is fine, darling. Sit down. Let's order some wine.'

'Yes!' agreed Noblet. 'Wine! Wine, wine, wine. Lovely, lovely wine.'

Then he picked up his menu and studied it with close attention.

'Everything go OK at the shoot?' asked Henry.

As Saskia related the events of the day at the magazine, Noblet continued ostensibly to inspect the menu whilst drifting into reverie. For once, the topic of his thoughts was not Victorian literature. It was something far weightier. It was socks. It had all started that morning when his mother had eyed him over her cup of tea, glanced at the open doorway and then beckoned to him. He'd leaned towards her, eyebrows raised. She had beckoned again.

'I can't get much closer without dipping my shirt in my kippers, Mother,' he said, without attempting to lower his voice. 'Do you want me to come over there?'

'Sshhhh!' she hissed. 'Try to be discreet for once in your life, Noblet. I want to talk to you,' her voice sank to as close to a whisper as she could manage, 'about socks.'

'What?'

The teacup was replaced on its saucer with an irritated rattle.

'Socks,' she rasped.

When Noblet had told his brother that he suspected their mother might be losing her marbles, he hadn't exaggerated. Here was yet another symptom of her decline into senility. He humoured her.

'Go on,' he nodded, brightly.

'It's a subject I doubt you have given much thought to. When you marry, you will need to be prepared for it,' she continued, in the same voluble attempt at a whisper. 'Your wife will expect it.'

'She'll expect socks?'

'I beg your pardon?'

'I'm sorry, I don't quite follow. Are you saying my wife will expect me to give her socks?'

Lady Caroline looked like she might explode – and then did.

'Sex, you imbecile! I quite clearly said sex!'

Sally, walking into the room with a fresh pot of tea, swivelled on her heel and exited without spilling a drop.

'For goodness' sake, Mother! Do you think I want to discuss that with you over the breakfast table? Or over any kind of table if it comes to that?'

'What you want and what you need are entirely different. You need to know what you're doing, Noblet.'

'Goddamn it!' Noblet banged one fist on the table, causing a kipper to bellyflop out of his plate and land on the tablecloth where it lay, beached in a pool of its own grease, looking like it wished it were somewhere else. 'I'm thirty-nine years old. We live in the twenty-first century – or some of us do, anyway. I have enough experience of…' he glanced behind him and dropped his voice, '"socks" to be able to acquit myself in the marital bed, thank *you*!'

His mother looked surprised but for once allowed the subject to drop.

Ever since then, however, socks kept popping unbidden into Noblet's mind. Despite his show of confidence, his experience was limited. He'd never met, let alone stripped down to his socks with any of the 'busty Bethans' selling stories on him in the tabloids. A few forgettable flings in his twenties and a more recent relationship with a professor of Jacobean literature formed the sum total of his vaunted experience. What would be expected of him by the successful candidate? Having come through gruelling rounds of interviews, would she expect her prize to swing from chandelier to chandelier, Tarzan-style, naked but for a pair of pants embroidered with the de Beeble coat of arms, before ravishing her on a copy of *Who's Who*? Personally, when it came to socks, he could take it or leave it. He knew it wasn't very manly to admit it, but he preferred a bit of snuggling in bed to wild nights of passion: all that thrashing and grunting and sweaty flesh and—

'Rump?'

'I'm sorry?' Noblet pinged back to the present.

'Or fillet? I hardly ever eat meat these days – evil methane – but when I do it's got to be a rump steak. Call me bourgeois' –

Noblet thought 'boring' was more likely to spring to mind – 'but I love it. The steak here is unreal, isn't it, babe?'

'It's good,' agreed Henry.

'And you've got to have it bloody, of course,' said Saskia, lasciviously. As she tipped up her glass, the red wine leaving purple, feathery trails over the inside of the bowl, Noblet thought of raw garlic and crucifixes. The waiter was hovering by the table and Noblet chose and ordered.

'Fillet steak, well done, please.'

'So suburban to be scared of a little blood, man. Get out of your comfort zone.' Looking up at the waiter she changed the order to rare. Noblet reiterated his request that it be well done. Saskia wagged her finger and overruled him; Noblet all but yelled his order at the man and their table began to attract attention from fellow diners. Henry intervened.

'Let it go, Saskia. You've got to let the man order his own supper, sweetheart. He can try some of yours if he wants to.'

The waiter, having allowed the corner of his mouth to twitch once, withdrew with a flourish reminiscent of a triumphant matador.

'So, Bob…' said Henry, with the air of a man who hasn't quite decided what he's going to say, but who knows it won't be anything to do with steak, 'looking forward to tomorrow?'

'Absolutely not.' Sulkily balling a piece of bread in his fingers, he flicked it across the room, not noticing as it hit a neighbouring diner in the eye. She shrieked and he glowered at her. 'Bloody Londoners. Attention-seekers, every man jack of 'em.'

A waiter came over and topped up their glasses. Noblet picked his up and tossed it back.

'You're gonna look the dog's after Henry's taken you shopping, man. If I had it my way, he'd be more experimental but you can't deny the man's got taste.' Saskia smiled as she ran a finger down Henry's well-cut lapel.

'If you ask me, the whole idea is verging on the ridiculous. You can't make a silk purse out of a sow's ear and dressing me up in Savile Row suits isn't going to make me James Bond.'

Aged ten, Noblet had been forced, kicking and screaming, into a pageboy outfit which included velvet knickerbockers and a frilly collar. Looking at his face now, Henry was vividly reminded of that moment.

'Don't worry, Bob – there'll be no velvet. Or frills.'

'What?'

'Nothing. Listen, we need to smarten you up a bit. Your potential wives will be making an effort, it's only fair that you do too.'

From somewhere within the gloom of the restaurant, a three-piece band oozed into the first bars of 'Summertime'. A husky female voice seeped like syrup into Noblet's veins, mingling with the wine and softening the edges of the evening. Maybe this wasn't such a bad little restaurant after all. Maybe London wasn't such a bad little town. Maybe the shopping trip wasn't such a bad little idea.

'You know what, Henners? Maybe you're right. Maybe this shopping trip won't be hotal tell after all.'

'You should have stayed with us, Noblet, man. There's plenty of room. We've had the spare room redone and the energy in there now is unreal.'

At the sound of Saskia's voice, the syrupy, winey sensation seemed to hold its breath for a moment, but after another gulp and a particularly breathy note in the song it continued on, slithering right down to his toes. Noblet had made the mistake of staying with Saskia and Henry once before. He wouldn't fall for that again. Fermented drinks, activated charcoal, jackfruit with everything and chanting before breakfast. Somehow Henry had avoided most of it, but like all honoured guests, Noblet was forced to partake of his hosts' most outlandish delicacies.

Noblet said something that included 'very kind' and 'Savoy' and 'convenient' but not necessarily in any kind of coherent order. The food arrived and they all fell to, Saskia offering a piece of her gory steak to Noblet five or six times.

'Anyway, babe. I was saying to Henry, I can't make it tomorrow because I've got meetings, but I'm gonna be there on the big day, so you needn't worry about that.'

The steak hadn't quite soaked up the wine yet and things were still blurry.

'Shorry, don't follow. Big day?'

'Saskia's offered to come and help out on the sixth, Bob. She thought we might need a female point of view on things. I think it's a great idea.'

'The sixth?'

'Yes, the open day at the village hall.'

'Village hall?'

'Yes, Bob. Keep up – the interviews.'

'Oh! The interviews. At the village hall. Yes. On the sixth. What about them?'

'Saskia's coming to help.'

'What!'

'I offered as a favour,' snapped Saskia. 'If you don't want me there, believe me, I've got plenty of other things to be doing.'

She whipped her phone out of her handbag and jabbed at the screen.

'No, no, I didn't mean… I'd be very apprehensive… I mean appreciative…' He turned to Henry, a plea for help stamped in crimson across his face. 'Don't I?'

'Bob would be very grateful, darling, you know he would. He's a bit nervy about the whole thing, that's all.'

'Exshtremely nervy,' agreed Noblet.

'Oh yeah, he sounds really grateful,' sneered Saskia.

'Come on, sweetheart, you know he didn't mean it like that.'

'Silly, silly old Bob,' said Noblet, with a pitying shake of the head.

'Well...' putting down the phone she seemed to relent. 'I don't see how you can do without me, to be honest. You need a woman's eye. Caroline's fabulous, of course, but I can't imagine she'd want to get involved?'

'Mother refers to it as the cattle market,' confirmed Noblet.

'And I can see her point of view. But on the other hand, it's everything that *The Vacuum* stands for. It's a platform to allow an ancient family to embrace the twenty-first century in an ultra-modern way.'

'Is it?'

'God, yeah! It's sweeping away the old-fashioned traditions of courtship and reducing the marital process down to its essential elements of barter and exchange.'

'Is it really? Well.' Noblet was taken aback.

'Absolutely. And Henry's a goddamn genius for thinking it up.' She beamed at him, then pulled him towards her for a kiss.

Smiling back, Henry said, 'I'm not going to disagree with anyone who calls me a genius, but I think you'll find yourself in the minority. It's not a new idea – most TV talent shows started with an open auditions round.'

'Yes, babe, but the genius comes in taking an existing idea and applying it to an entirely new sphere. You've got one of those minds that refuses to be bound by tradition – you're an innovator, like me.'

Noblet had one of those minds that thought some kind of chocolate pudding was in order after a main course of steak and chips. He tried to attract the waiter's attention with one eye, while keeping the other trained on Saskia's face in an effort to appear keen and alert. The restaurant was at its busiest and the band were struggling to be heard over the buzz of voices and clatter of cutlery on crockery. When Henry's phone rang, he was alerted by the discreet blue light of the screen next to his wine glass.

'Henry de Beeble. Who? I'm sorry, who? Oh – Gareth! Yes.'

'Who's Gareth?' asked Noblet.

'No idea, babe. Maybe someone from Henry's work.'

'Yes, go on. When? How many? Right. Thanks, that's useful. Keep in touch.'

Henry hung up.

'That was Gareth, Bob. He's heard something.'

'Who the devilled kidneys is Gareth?'

'The chap up the tree – the paparazzo. He's been told to cover a meeting in Gently Rising on the sixteenth. Some of the villagers are agitating.'

'Agitating?'

'Yes. Not too happy about us swanning in and playing Lord of the Manor apparently.'

'But I am the Lord of the Manor. Aren't I?'

'According to him, certain villagers are accusing us of riding roughshod over them. Using their facilities without proper permission.'

Saskia rolled her eyes.

'We should have expected this, babe. Villagers are worse than small-town people in some ways. Narrow-minded, you know?'

'But all we're doing is borrowing the village hall, Henry! Where's the harm in that?'

The waiter arrived to take their dessert orders and conversation ceased for a moment. When the waiter had withdrawn, Henry said, stroking a thoughtful eyebrow, 'Perhaps we should have been more diplomatic. If we'd involved the villagers in the process, we could have got them on side. Stupid of me.'

'Oh, come on, babe. Like Noblet says, you're only using the village hall.'

'It's the principle. People like to be consulted.' The eyebrow seemed in danger of being rubbed off entirely. 'Maybe there's a way to smooth things over, though,' he mused.

'Does it involve me?' asked Noblet.

'No.'

'Excellent! Do whatever you need to do, young Henry, you have my complete support.'

Chapter 5

Canter canter canter. Turn. Canter canter canter. Turn. More cantering.

What was the point, wondered Chip? Either they want to be in one place, or another. Why the turning? Why the cantering in the other direction? Why the turning again? Chip knew where she wanted to be. She wanted to be back in the stable flirting with Don Juan and nibbling seductively on a little fresh hay. Once she got back there, she sure as hell wasn't going to be turning and cantering away again. She had a little bit more nous, she liked to think, than these bossy pink barnacles. Not that she minded this one so much. This one was light and agile and didn't hurt her mouth like some of them. She smelt like hay and trees and other nice things. She gave Chip lots of pats and stroked her nose with soft fingers. Off they went again, cantering. Then turning. This one might be nice, but she had no more sense of direction than the rest of them. Pick a place, get there and stop, that was Chip's motto. Much more restful and less strain on the joints.

Something small and hard hit Chip's back and she reared up, imagining monsters throwing rocks. Her rider slipped off and a couple of people darted across from behind the railings.

'Are you OK?'

'Naughty Chip! Bad girl!'

'No, no,' laughed Mia. 'It wasn't her fault – my mobile fell out of my pocket. It must have scared her.'

She got up and stroked Chip's nose. The pony refused to make eye contact.

'Sorry, sweetheart. It won't happen again.'

Chip was unimpressed. Fine words buttered no parsnips in her book. Someone had picked up Mia's phone and handed it back to her. Noticing a text message, Mia touched the screen and read: 'Local bigwig Elaine Jowlett holding meeting on the 16th about Lord de Beeble's interviews. Could be interesting. Hope you're well, nice and sunny here, love Alice.'

Interesting, certainly. Particularly if Lord de Beeble put in an appearance. But she had plenty of time to organise a flight; no point missing the rest of the polo match. Handing her phone to the groom she remounted Chip and, after a couple of pats on the neck they set off again, cantering and turning and cantering. Chip let out a whinny of exasperation. Where would it all end?

***

Tap tappity tap tap tap went Sinead Dumper's acrylic nails on her computer keyboard. The curtains of Lake House (known from 1870–2016 as Pond House but promoted to lake status by its current owner) were drawn and the only light was the glare of the screen as it picked out the sharp angles of Sinead's face. Her jaws were clamped shut, her shoulders hunched and her body motionless other than the fingers flying across the keys. She was concentrating hard. A former legal secretary, her typing speed was a hundred words a minute and her brain struggled at times to keep up. Coco lay at her feet, fluffy head slumped on his front paws. He was silent other than an occasional sigh of disgust.

Strategy for 'Becoming Lady de Beeble' (BLDB)
"If you fail to plan, you plan to fail"

Phase 1
Appearance
- *Increase St. Tropez sessions from fortnightly to weekly*

- *Trip to West End for hair restyling consultation (Duchess of Cambridge? Victoria Beckham? Claudia Winkleman?)*
- *Facial expressions. Practice aristocratic looks in front of mirror daily (pull chin in, frown, loosen mouth, avoid eye contact)*

Research and preparation
- *Daily revision of Wilkie Collins facts*
- *Learn five entries of Who's Who (Mereshire residents) per day*
- *One chapter of etiquette manual per day*
- *Flower-arranging lessons*

Action
- *Daily walks with Coco past gates of d B Hall*
- *Increase volunteer sessions at community shop to ensure hearing all local news*
- *Execute strategy for attaining first place in queue 6th June (Operation Bouncer)*
- *Exploit all opportunities of bumping into Lady Caroline (church?)*
- *Remember to smile!*

Next steps
- *Keep daily log of all new information and progress*
- *Note main competition*
- *Go for gold!!*

Sinead pressed save and reviewed her work. It looked good. It looked businesslike. It would give her the edge. She liked plans. Plans were the framework around which a successful life was built. Her ex-husband had been the fruit of a lever arch file full of research, notes and Gantt charts. He'd been quite startled when he came across it one day, but by that time they were safely married and there was no turning back.

He'd been last on her list of targets when she started work at Rowe, Rowe, Rowe and Yibbut; but having discovered that the three Rowe brothers were married, she had moved on to the acquisition of, and merger with, Simon Yibbut. He seemed timid and so rather than scare him off with an immediate revelation of her sexual attractions, she took tips from a book by an American author she'd found in the library called *The Husband Trap – Softly, Softly, Catchee Money*. She lowered her lashes in what she understood to be a 'coy' manner when he entered the room. She tried making her chest heave a little when he spoke to her, although soon gave up on this; concerned that it might look like she was doing buttock clenches at her desk. She allowed herself the luxury of time and built up her attack over several weeks.

Her hard work, research and continual reapplication of make-up paid off. Simon Yibbut surprised himself one day, when he and Sinead chanced to be alone in a meeting room, by inviting her to go to *La Traviata* with him that Friday evening. He had been somewhat bewildered at Sinead's instant declaration that she loved Italian food, but on the whole, she appeared keen to accept the invitation and he hurried away to his own office, to marvel at his audacity. The date went brilliantly. Sinead had learnt sections of the latest issue of *The Lawyer* by heart and spent the moments before curtain up probing Simon on his opinion of the latest amendments to section 34 of the Property Act. He was thrilled to discover that someone so attractive could also be such a sparkling conversationalist, and at the interval relaxed enough to regale her with his thoughts on the likely ramifications of the proposed white paper on the standard due diligence process. One thing led to another and before the year was out Simon had persuaded Sinead to dump the Dumper and say yes to

Yibbut: a proposal she accepted with the same businesslike attitude she had brought to the entire transaction. Barely were the words out of his mouth than she was slipping engagement ring catalogues out of her handbag and firming up provisional reception venue bookings. The wedding was elegant in the extreme: nothing was omitted, from the salmon-pink-plumed horses pulling her glass carriage, to the 'sunset and rainbows' theme and the seven flower girls in shades of red, orange, yellow, green, blue, indigo and violet. She had done it. She had set out to marry well, she had planned it down to the last flutter of eyelashes and she had achieved her goal. From now on she knew whatever she set out to achieve was within her grasp, as long as she applied herself.

Compared to the effort she put into snaring him, divorcing Simon Yibbut was a cinch. Almost before he knew what had hit him he was on his own again, one or two million pounds the poorer and with considerably more grey hairs. And Sinead, unpacking in her new house in the country, had filled a shelf with pristine and – as yet – empty lever arch files.

***

'Jack Sprat could eat no fat, his wife could eat no lean.' No matter how hard she tried not to, Alice would find herself reciting these words in her head at the sight of Elaine and Ted Jowlett. Elaine was a mountain of flesh and beside her Ted looked like a sliver had been sheared off and then remoulded into something resembling a man. He was narrow everywhere: narrow hips; narrow, sloping shoulders; long, narrow head and narrow lips. Even his hair was narrow: an oval island of brown marooned in the middle of his white, waxy forehead.

Alice was looking through the serving hatch doing a rough headcount. There had to be at least a hundred people crammed into the hall. Thank goodness she'd made extra of her home-made brownies and millionaire's shortbread. Elaine and her husband were standing by the stage, surrounded by a gaggle of villagers. Behind them, the rows of wooden chairs were filling up with familiar faces. Sinead Dumper was prominent in the front row, glammed up to the nines in a little black dress and diamonds. Colonel Markham was a few rows back, sitting bolt upright, one hand on his walking stick. Alice had spotted one or two other village stalwarts arriving: Mrs Fratterbury looking windswept, Lorraine Watford with her jumper on inside out and Jerry Brewer, the aptly-named landlord of the Lion and Lamb, potbelly straining against the buttons of his short-sleeved shirt. Elaine glanced up at the clock, which was showing three minutes to seven. Raising one rather mottled hand, she hushed the group of villagers that surrounded her and strode to the stage. Ted, lost in admiration, was brought to heel with a sudden look shot from under his wife's caterpillar brows as she ascended the rickety wooden steps. Everyone hurried to find seats and settled themselves with some muttering and rustling before an expectant silence leached across the room. Elaine approached the edge of the stage and paused, feet shoulder-width apart and arms folded as if she were drawing breath before throwing herself into a demonstration of traditional Cossack dancing.

'Gently Risingers!' The way her voice swelled and rolled around the room called to mind a great warrior, rallying her clan before battle. There was a certain air of the Highland chieftain about her with her tartan kilt, squat black shoes and white tights; and had any ancient chieftains been endowed with magnificent bosoms, no doubt they too would have displayed their fearsome arsenal in a tight black polo neck, thus striking terror into their flatter-chested opponents. She raised her right forefinger and lowered her voice to a penetrating stage whisper.

'I ask you one question. What does Gently Rising mean to you?'

Taking one step backwards and clasping her hands behind her back she seemed to be inviting her audience to take a quiet moment to ponder her question. And, obediently, they pondered.

Colonel Markham thought of an Englishman's home, castles, manicured lawns and a cosy billet.

Sinead Dumper thought of a small smattering of houses viewed from the height of a grand Hall on a hill.

Jan Fratterbury thought of glasses of wine in the garden, pleasantly fuzzy summer afternoons and endless columns of neat schoolchildren parading away into the distance.

Lorraine Watford thought of something impossible to put into words but which resembled globules of bright paint being splattered onto a large, ragged canvas. But then, she wasn't thinking about Gently Rising.

Alice thought of a happy child in a safe place and unknown dangers beyond the perimeter.

Stepping forward again, Elaine smiled around the room, before nodding vigorously several times.

'Gently Rising means different things, no doubt, to all of us. But whatever those different things may be, they are ours and they are sacrosanct,' bringing one fist swinging down from shoulder height to emphasise her final word, 'Gently Rising is ours – nay, it is us, and we,' again swinging the fist, 'decide its fate and its future.'

Catching her breath, she leant forward onto the lectern and continued, switching to a more businesslike tone, 'And so, the second question I ask you all is, do we allow the sacred body of this most gentle village to be violated by the many-headed monster?' No immediate response being forthcoming, she paraphrased. 'I put it to you: are we to allow crowds of rampaging strangers to overrun these hallowed streets, lanes and green places?'

Ted, overcome by the emotion of the moment, shot out from the wings, bellowing, 'Never!' and waving one narrow fist in the air. Finding himself alone centre stage, a look of horror spread across his face and he continued at full pelt straight on into the wings on the other side.

Some villagers were stirring and a few approving noises had followed Elaine's words, but Jerry Brewer now rose to his feet.

'What about businesses in the village? Don't we get a say? If His Lordship wants to invite coachloads of young ladies to Gently Rising, I say let 'em come! I'll be stocking up on white wine and Babycham!' Laughing heartily at his own wit, his belly wobbled over his low-slung belt as he winked at a couple of regulars. Some appreciative chuckles and 'hear hear's followed this from certain factions in the room, along with some tutting and dark mutterings from others.

Elaine attempted to quell the revolt.

'What I say to you, dear Jerry, is don't be short-termist. We mustn't put profits above people. Yes, an influx of strangers into the village would herald a mini economic boom for our greatly appreciated local businesspeople. But what devastation would be left in its wake? We must learn from the mistakes of others. We mustn't let the name Gently Rising become synonymous with that of Glastonbury!'

'Oh, come on!' expostulated Jerry, who was still on his feet. 'You can't seriously be comparing a few birds in the village hall to one of the biggest festivals in the world? Keep some perspective, woman!'

Amongst the ensuing hubbub a shrill voice rang out:

'What about the double standards? That's what I want to know!' The speaker – Miss Tipperton, a firm friend of Elaine Jowlett – flushed as people craned to see who was speaking, but pushed on regardless. Voice quavering and hitting notes a dog-whistle would have been proud of, she piped, 'The Brownies had the hall booked a year in advance for that date! The Brownies always have the first Saturday in June for their summer jumble sale, everyone knows that.' She nodded at her near neighbours. 'Why should Lady Caroline be allowed to push the Brownies out?' She managed one final exclamation of headache-inducing shrillness, 'Let's hear from the village hall committee!' before dropping back into her chair and trembling all over.

An awkward smile on her face – Miss Tipperton had forgotten that she, Elaine, was on the committee – Elaine said, 'I'll address that point, if I may, Valerie. When the committee granted the request, the full extent of His Lordship's plan wasn't clear. Now that the potential ramifications have become known, I feel it my duty as a Gently Risinger to spearhead a protest group. We should demand a hearing with Lord de Beeble to lay our concerns before him.'

Alice, taking a quick look through the hatch at that moment, noticed that Mia had come in and was looking glamorous in black jeans, a grey silk top and huge silver hoop earrings. She was leaning against the back wall and waved when she caught sight of Alice. And then Mia wasn't there anymore. No one was there, the room was blurred - one panel of clarity remained at the entrance to the hall where a man was standing. As if she'd been trying for some time, and with some frustration, to turn a key in a rusty lock, Alice experienced a release as the door swung wide, and fresh air flooded through her senses. Time had stopped and she was glad of it because it meant she could let her gaze linger on strong, straight features and eyes that held a mixture of humour, intelligence and determination. The eyes looked into hers, briefly; her heart stopped, briefly; and then pounded so hard and fast she suspected those hadn't been cocoa nibs in the brownie she'd just eaten but shotgun pellets. Of course. These were the elusive internal fireworks she'd heard so much about.

The man stepped forward and, looking towards the stage, called out, 'Excuse me. Could I address the meeting?'

Interpreting surprised silence as acquiescence, the stranger passed down the central aisle and took the wooden steps at one agile bound. Holding out a hand to Elaine who, clearly discomfited, wasn't sure whether to curtsey or spurn it, he said, 'Mrs Jowlett. A pleasure to see you again.'

Pink with pleasure that he'd remembered her name, Elaine took the proffered hand and introduced him to the hall with a flourish and a sonorous, 'The Honourable Henry de Beeble.'

The crowd perked up. This was more like it. The handful of dejected journalists and photographers sprang to life, turning on recording equipment and snapping away.

'I'm sorry to arrive unannounced, but my brother asked me to come and speak to you on his behalf.' Henry looked straight out at the crowd, catching people's eyes, drawing them in.

'He would have come himself but urgent business called him away at the last minute. We realised we've gone about this very stupidly – or rather I have, my brother's not to blame at all. I should have organised a meeting with you all before anything was decided. I apologise that it didn't happen.' He looked so earnest and sincere that the audience found themselves unbending – the women perhaps a trifle quicker than the men.

'I wanted to come here today to reassure you that we are ready to listen to any concerns you may have and to take appropriate action. Starting now. If there are any questions or comments…'

A shiny blonde bob of hair popped up above the crowd and a terracotta-coloured hand, laden with gold and diamonds, shot into the air.

'Sinead Dumper,' growled Sinead, in her best impression of a seductive purr. 'Personally delighted about your brother's idea. Wonderful thing for the village. Keen to help in any way I can. Also. What's the criteria? Do local women get preference?'

A few titters flickered round the room.

'Great question. My brother is proud of his Mereshire roots and is keen that his marriage should benefit the local community. With that in mind, he will be giving precedence to any applicant who has been resident in the county for more than three years.'

Sinead looked smug and sat down, keeping her eyes glued on Henry. Around the room various women were totting up how long they'd lived in the area.

Henry allowed the general chatter to die down before continuing. 'I understand that due to our booking the village hall, a long-standing engagement has had to be cancelled.'

Elaine nodded, motioned to Miss Tipperton and murmured 'Brownies' in Henry's ear.

'My brother would be mortified to hear that the Brownies had been affected and so on his behalf I invite them to hold their…'

'Summer jumble sale,' hissed Elaine.

'…their summer jumble sale at de Beeble Hall this year.'

Valerie Tipperton, still pink with embarrassment from her public-speaking, now turned puce with pleasure. The tears sprang into her eyes and she fanned herself with a copy of *The Puzzler* while nodding her thanks to Henry. From then on, the villagers' backing was assured. No objection was raised but Henry had a solution, no suggestion that he didn't agree to or promise to take back to his brother. There was one awkward moment when Lorraine Watford stood up and waved her arms at the stage.

'I don't wish to be dyspeptic, but it would have been the correct thing to do of course. We would have appreciated it, not just I, but all of us.'

'What's that, Lorraine?' questioned Elaine.

Lorraine motioned towards Henry.

'I'm telling His Worship how upset we all were that he didn't ask our permission to get married in the village hall.'

Henry opened his mouth but before he could speak Elaine whispered something in his ear and then called out to Lorraine, 'Quite, quite. We'll minute that, Lorraine, thank you. Now, we must move on if we're to fit everyone in, yes, Mrs Hawsbury, what point did you want to make…'

***

Meeting over and promises of further consultations minuted, the hatch disappeared under a barrage of hungry and thirsty villagers. Alice, rushing to keep up with the orders, had no time to think about anything other than teas, coffees and cakes. Jerry led a large contingent off to the Lion and Lamb 'for some proper drinks', and in time the rush died down enough for Alice to escape from the kitchen. She made a beeline for Mia, who had been cornered by Lorraine Watford and Colonel Markham. An amused smile played about her lips, while Colonel Markham was alternately frowning at Lorraine and dimpling at Mia. Lorraine was holding forth.

'...nothing against you in particular, Mina. Such lovely teeth. But others, you know... They come here and do things.' She motioned darkly, although what she was intending to communicate was beyond the ken of either of her listeners. 'One of them moved into Oak Lane for a few months. They put something in the garden, some kind of symbol. It made me nervous. Voodoo, you know...'

'Oh, Mrs Watford, what will Mia be thinking of us?' The Colonel patted Mia on the arm and explained, 'It was a reproduction of the *Venus de Milo*. Nothing sinister.'

Lorraine nodded and glared over her glasses at Mia's right ear. 'Sinister, that's the word. Armless. It's some kind of black magic thingamajiggy. It's not what we do here, not in Gently Rising.'

'Hi, Mia.'

'Alice!' Mia leant over to kiss her on the cheek and then took her arm. 'Excuse us, will you?' They went and perched on the edge of the stage, Colonel Markham casting a wistful look after them and Lorraine darting off on some unknown mission of her own.

'What did you make of Henry de Beeble?' asked Mia. 'Have you met him before?'

'Not since he was a child – and that was once or twice at a distance. He's not been around much,' said Alice, managing to avoid the first question.

Mia scrutinised her face. 'You look great, by the way.'

She did look well that evening. Her eyes were bright, her skin luminous and there was a rosy colour in her cheeks.

'Well... thanks. So do you. How was Argentina?'

'Oh, fine. What's been going on here, though, that's what I want to know? Tell me everything...'

Chapter 6

Strangers arrived in the village. A trickle at first, not long after the village meeting. Villagers noticed unfamiliar, heavily-made-up faces in the Lion and Lamb and the community shop. B&Bs in the area reported an unusual lack of vacancies.

Sinead, popping into the library in Market Mornington to swap her copy of *The Woman in White* for *The Moonstone*, was told that the library's entire catalogue of Wilkie Collins was loaned out; a discovery which made her bare her small, pointy teeth at the librarian like a terrier catching sight of a juicy-looking postman. Proceeding to the bookshop, she discovered three or four Collins remaining on the shelves and promptly bought the lot to save them falling into the wrong hands. The trickle became a stream, and soon both hotels in Market Mornington were full to bursting and every holiday cottage in a twenty-mile radius had been hired out. Gangs of glamorous, and not so glamorous women were seen roaming around the village and surrounding lanes in clothes surely not meant for country rambles, hoping to bump into Lord de Beeble. Henry was forced to hire a security company to patrol the estate after Noblet complained of trespassers. He'd been very shaken one morning by the discovery of a strange woman in the house. Shambling into the breakfast room half-asleep, he was confronted by a naked intruder lying flat on her back on the table, modesty preserved by a couple of fried eggs and a portobello mushroom. He had turned faint, swayed from side to side and then bawled for Sally. Galloping in, Sally had taken in the scene at a glance and shooed the, now rather greasy, naked woman into the garden with a broom. Noblet had porridge for breakfast that morning.

When tents started appearing on the village green, Henry found himself in receipt of several heated emails and phone calls. His initial proposition of inviting the campers to move onto de Beeble land was dismissed out of hand by Lady Caroline. Instead, he called a meeting with the de Beeble Interview Village Liaison Committee (headed, naturally, by Elaine Jowlett) to thrash out an agreement. It was decided that the tents would be tolerated but any campers remaining on the Monday after the interviews would be 'encouraged' to leave by Henry's security company; and any damage to the green would be made good at the de Beebles' expense.

Gently Rising was surprised to find a number of men amongst those invading the village, but a story in one of the tabloids soon shed some light on this development. One afternoon, as Noblet was ensconced in the library, working on his theory that Wilkie Collins had foreseen, and very possibly invented, the electric trouser press, Henry received a phone call from Squeak. Henry was staying at the Hall for the week running up to the interviews to give Noblet moral support.

'Morning, Guvnor.'

'Gareth. What news?'

'I fort you might not get *The Sun*, so…'

'Well deduced.'

'Yeah – so, I fort I'd let you know about the story. About the men.'

'Men?'

'S'right. You know what it's like these days, don't yer – all political correctness and women's lib an' that?'

'Women's lib, yes – where do the men come in?'

'They got their rights too, innit? They reckon it ain't legal to only let women apply for the job so there's men comin' to the interviews.'

Henry's bark of laughter penetrated as far as the library, where Noblet looked up and frowned, before resuming his two-fingered assault on the computer keyboard.

'They're right,' Henry said. 'It didn't cross my mind but of course, we can't discriminate on grounds of gender.'

''F'you say so. Anyway, they're gonna mount a protest an' that if you don't let 'em into the interviews, so I thought I'd better warn you.'

'Don't worry, they'll be welcomed with open arms.'

Henry felt a pang of pity as he made his way to the library, but it couldn't be helped.

'Sorry to interrupt, Bob, but this won't take long.'

'As long as it doesn't, old man. I've hit rather a rich vein, you see.'

'Yes. Small change of plan about the interviews.'

'Change of plan?'

'Yes. Or rather an addition to the plan. There'll be… a masculine element.'

'Masculine? What do you mean, masculine?'

'The thing is, Bob, legally we can't discriminate against job applicants on the grounds of race, age – or gender. So if any men apply we'll have to consider their applications.'

'Are you saying…'

'Theoretically, your future life partner could be a man or a woman so…'

'It bloody couldn't!'

'…so we have to consider both. In order to be legal.'

'Oh, of all the ridiculous… Oh, I mean… Henry, you're pulling my leg, old man?'

'Afraid not. Look, Bob,' he said, pulling up an uncomfortable-looking chair and sitting down next to his brother. 'You and I both know you won't be marrying a man at the end of this.'

'Damn right we do! I've never so much as kissed a man on the cheek, despite what that French pal of yours had in mind.'

'Right. So you'll be choosing a woman to be your wife. But in order to remain above the law, and to avoid protest marches and newspaper campaigns and all that kind of extra fuss, you must appear to be seriously considering all male applicants too.'

Noblet shook his head from side to side like a bulldog trying to rid itself of a demeaning bow.

'What is the world coming to? I ask you? This wouldn't have happened in Collins' day you know. Far from it. Ha! I would have liked to have seen the outcome of their newspaper campaigns and their protest marches if Victoria had got word of them! Ha!'

'No doubt. Elizabeth takes a more open-minded view, so we need to keep everything non-gender-specific.'

'Non-gender-specific? Trying to find a wife? You couldn't find something more gender-specific if you tried, man!'

Henry held up his hands in mock defence and got up, backing towards the door. 'Not my fault, Bob. You'll have to bite the bullet I'm afraid. Just make sure that's all you bite,' he added with an impish grin before darting out of the door in time to dodge an airborne stapler.

***

The front door of the picturesque Tudor cottage known as Bluebells opened and Lorraine Watford appeared on the threshold. She leaned out, peering both ways to check that none of her neighbours were in the vicinity. What she was about to do was perfectly justifiable, but experience had taught her that some of her fellow villagers – in fact, all of her fellow villagers – tended to disagree with her on certain matters. The matter of outsiders, for instance. Gently Rising, Lorraine believed, was for the Gently Risingers. Non-Gently Risingers did not belong in the village and should be discouraged. They could come to visit, if they wished, to admire the village – but then they must leave.

Reaching into the hallway behind her, she picked up something heavy and staggered out into the road with it. She locked the door behind her. Not something she would normally do, but with outsiders around, well... It was dawn and the village was quiet. Lorraine tiptoed with her burden across the empty street onto the green. Gently Rising's village green was famous in Mereshire. It was either the biggest, or the oldest, or something else that Lorraine couldn't quite remember. She knew it was special though, and it was sacrosanct. And what had happened to it, practically overnight, was an outrage. Tears of indignation welled up in Lorraine's eyes as she surveyed the desecration before her. A city of tents, sheltering outsiders, had sprung up. Big tents, little tents, pointy tents, round tents, khaki tents, flowery tents – even a caravan with a tent bulging tautly out of the side of it like a blister. Lorraine worked at speed, propelled from tent to tent by righteous indignation. She was nearing the other side of the grass, her task almost complete, when an unseen guy rope sent her flying into the side of a fluorescent pink tent. She scrabbled for purchase against the canvas, sliding downwards in slow motion until she came to rest, still scrabbling, on the ground.

Muffled sounds were heard from within.

'What the...?'

A dishevelled blonde head popped out through the zip at the front. It took in Lorraine, prostrate on the ground, and screamed.

'Amy! There's an old woman out here bleeding all over the grass!'

Lorraine managed to extract her foot from the paint tin and her head from the guy rope and heaved herself to her feet, dripping red paint. Other heads were poking out of tents now.

'What's going on? Who's painted an effing great red cross on that tent?'

'And that one! Bloody hell, it's on ours too!'

'Get her – it's that woman, look! She's covered in paint!'

A bare-chested boy made a lunge at Lorraine but she picked up her empty paint can and bounced it off his head before galloping, surprisingly quickly, off the green and up the hill towards the church. One or two people set off in pursuit, but in bare feet and still half-asleep they soon gave up. The last they saw of her was a large bottom wobbling up the lane, enormous polka dot knickers visible through the paint-splashed white linen trousers.

**

Later that Saturday morning, Alice was sitting on a stool behind the counter of the community shop daydreaming about Henry de Beeble when a strange man sauntered in. Removing his midnight-blue fedora, he dropped it on the counter and, resting his elbows beside the hat, leant towards Alice and asked, 'Where are you hiding Geriatric Van Gogh? Red Hand Gran. Where is she?'

Alice shook her head, bewildered.

'Geriatric what? I'm sorry, I've no—'

'I know what these little close-knit communities are like, I grew up in one. So don't try and pretend you're not covering for her.' Picking up an apple and biting into it with an amiable grin, the stranger waited for Alice's response.

'That'll be forty pence, please,' said Alice primly, holding out her hand, 'and I don't know what you're talking about.'

The stranger looked her up and down while crunching away at his apple. Finishing it and dropping the core into Alice's outstretched hand, he conceded, 'Fair enough. Maybe you don't know anything. Let's start over. I'm Jay.'

Looking from Jay's proffered palm to the core nestling in her own, Alice dropped the fruit in the bin and wiped her sticky hand as best she could on her jeans.

'Alice. And what are you talking about?'

'Unlikely as it may seem, not everyone in this village is in favour of our impromptu campsite on the village green. We awoke this morning to find our tents being defaced by an old dear in white slacks.'

'Defaced?'

'Large red crosses painted on the sides. Now, I'm not denying that some of them have benefited from a splash of colour, but mine was a pink and violet Cath Kidston and the red clashes horribly. I'm quite depressed if you must know. That tent was my pride and joy.' He picked up a chocolate bar and unwrapped it. 'It was a birthday present – first time out of its little flowery canvas bag.'

As he seemed genuinely dejected, Alice decided not to mention that the bill had now risen to £1.20 and instead murmured something consolatory.

'So who is this menace, do you know?' asked Jay, when he had finished the chocolate and handed the wrapper to Alice.

'What did you say she looked like?'

'Blonde hair, sticking up in all directions. Didn't get much of a look at her face but she was a spectacles aficionado. Resembles a butternut squash from behind. White slacks. Polka dot underpants. Runs like a pregnant rhino.'

'Oh.' Even before the description there'd been little doubt in Alice's mind about the identity of the culprit, but now it was indisputable.

'I think I know who you mean. It sounds like Mrs Watford.'

'Bingo. And where does Mistress Watford live?'

'Why, what are you going to do?'

'It's alright, I'm not planning on going round there with my heavies and doing the old dear over. I want to have a chat, see if I can't bring her round to our way of thinking. Employ a little diplomacy to improve relations between natives and pioneers.'

'I wouldn't bother. You won't get anywhere. She's a bit, well….' As Alice tried to think of a tactful phrase her eye fell on a bag of mixed nuts. She jerked her head towards them.

'How disheartening. I did so want to practice my diplomatic skills. Maybe I'll try them on you instead, dear Alice.'

'Me?'

'That's right. We can strike a blow for homelander/foreigner relations. Show them all that we won't let boundaries get the better of us.'

'Well…'

'I'll meet you in that quaint-looking pub on the green, eight o'clock. Bring your tam-o'-shanter.'

'My what?'

But Jay had gone, warbling 'Cheerio' over his shoulder and swiping a packet of salt and vinegar crisps on the way out.

Chapter 7

Jerry Brewer and his belly stood at the back door of the Lion and Lamb, surveying the busy beer garden with an air of complacency. The air was scented with woodsmoke and blossom; a violet haze on the horizon supported a darkening sky of indigo blue and, in the lush countryside all around, tiny noises signalled the night creatures coming to life. Jerry wasn't pondering the beauty of the evening, however, he was totting up the night's takings, and his belly was proudly watching him work. The past couple of weeks had broken all records. He'd had to order in extra deliveries from the brewery and many of the kitchen staff were working double shifts to keep up with the orders of steak and ale pie and sausage and mash that flooded in regardless of the heat. Jerry nodded at one or two disconsolate regulars, squeezed onto tables that they would usually have spurned, their regular spots having been nabbed earlier in the afternoon by prospective interviewees and their hangers-on. A few of the villagers were hobnobbing with the outsiders: something which to Lorraine Watford's mind would have been marginally more reprehensible than collaborating with the Nazis in 1940s Paris. There was that little mouse, Alice Brand, sitting with the tall, tasty piece Jerry had spotted around the place a few times and a camp-looking bloke in a silly hat. He wondered what they were talking about, but upon his belly growling at him, he resumed his mental book-keeping.

***

Jay complimented Mia on her surname and asked if it was made up.

'No,' she replied. 'If I'd made it up, I would have gone for something interesting, like De'Ath.'

'Wild's pretty interesting,' said Alice Brand, wistfully.

'I grew up in a commune. We were all called Wild. It was about being free spirits instead of someone else's property.'

'You grew up in a commune?' asked Jay and Alice in excited unison.

'Much less outrageous than people imagine. No naked dancing in the fields, as far as I can remember. Apart from when I was about two, but I didn't know any better then...'

Alice was fascinated. 'But didn't your parents mind that you didn't have their surname?'

'Well... That's a complicated question. I have several parents – four mothers and three fathers. But all of them believed in what the commune stood for: they were happy for me to be called Wild.'

'But your biological parents?' insisted Jay. 'They must have had more say than the others.'

'I don't know, I never knew which were my biological parents,' said Mia with a smile. Raising her glass, she continued, 'but Wild I am and wild I'll stay, so here's to free spirits and free love.'

'Free spirits and free love,' they chorused – Jay and Mia at the tops of their voices, Alice rather less so. They all clinked glasses and downed a good portion of their drinks.

'So where was this commune?' asked Jay.

'In the countryside outside Nice.'

'And how about you, Jay? You must have grown up somewhere rural?' hazarded Alice. 'I remember you said you knew a bit about living in a close-knit community.'

'Do I.' Jay pushed his fedora back on his head and crossed his forearms on the table, flicking cigarette ash into an empty glass. 'The things I could tell you would make your blood curl.'

'Curdle, don't you mean?'

'Curl,' insisted Jay, prodding the air with his cigarette for emphasis. 'Curdling's nothing, curling's far worse.'

'What kind of things?' coughed Alice as she breathed in a cloud of second-hand smoke.

'Wife swapping. Affairs. Sadomasochism. Incest.' He took a long drag on his cigarette. 'But enough about me...'

The evening wore on and Mia and Jay were getting on like a house on fire. So much so that Alice felt like a spare part. *Am I so boring?* she wondered. The drinks kept coming, the conversation kept flowing, and the electricity kept buzzing between Mia and Jay. At one point Jay was at the bar, and Alice heard herself saying to Mia, somewhat in the tone of a jealous lover:

'Well. You and Jay seem to be hitting it off.'

Mia looked at her, a sleek, dark eyebrow raised. 'He's funny. I like him. Don't you?'

'Oh,' retaliated Alice with a hollow laugh. 'I like him, yes. Not as much as you do, clearly.' Somewhere deep inside her, a sober Alice was cringing.

Mia gave her a funny look and then turned her attention to Sinead Dumper, tottering across the road in a cotton tea dress and court shoes.

'Look, here comes Princess Diana.'

'Mmmm,' agreed Alice, absently. 'She's wearing a lot of that kind of stuff at the moment. I think she's trying to make a favourable impression on Lady Caroline.'

'And I'm absolutely sure she is. Subtle as a brick but I love her for it.' Standing up and waving, she called out, 'Sinead! Over here!'

Sinead's eyes darted around, picked out Mia, and a mixture of surprise, resentment and fury spread over her face. She hesitated for a moment and then headed towards their table.

'I didn't know you knew her,' Alice said.

'I don't, yet.'

As Sinead approached, Mia beckoned her over and charmed a neighbouring group into lending them a chair.

'Hi there! You don't know me, my name's Mia.'

'Nice to meet you,' snapped Sinead.

'Sit down, won't you? Jay's gone to the bar but we'll send him back – what are you drinking?'

'Can't stay, sorry,' said Sinead in her best supercilious manner. 'Meeting someone. Thought you wanted to say something to me.'

'I did. How much I admire your style and hope to get to know you better,' replied Mia with a winning smile.

'Oh. Thanks.' Sinead's expression suggested she harboured strong suspicions that she was being made fun of, until Mia's gaze, clear and frank, thawed her an infinitesimal amount. 'I might be able to come back later. After I've met... my friend.'

Mia clapped her hands. 'Oh, I do hope so. It would make my evening – please try.'

Sinead's suspicions seemed to spring back to life – but again she was confronted by that open countenance and candid smile.

'Well. No promises. Have a nice evening.' She stomped off again, having spat an ungracious greeting at Alice without looking at her.

The two sat in silence for a moment until Alice spoke.

'She despises me,' Alice observed, into her wine glass.

'What do you think of her?'

Alice hesitated and then dug down into her soul to tap previously unmined depths of negativity.

'If you want the truth, I don't like her very much.' She experienced a little thrill of surprise as she heard those cutting words hanging in the air. Her sober self looked pointedly at the empty wine bottle and shook its head.

'If you don't like her, why care that she doesn't like you? You wouldn't want the good opinion of someone you loathed, surely? What would be the point?'

'Loathed is a strong—'

'The trick with people like that is to see them as entertainment,' explained Mia, waving away her qualms. 'Think how dull the world would be without them. Don't take her personally, just sit back and marvel.'

Alice wondered with a jolt if that was how Mia saw her. Reassurance came instantly, however, with the thought that she wasn't interesting enough to be classed as entertainment.

The evening progressed, time passing unnoticed by Alice, who was wrapped in a cosy blanket of alcohol-induced fuzziness. A general air of debauchery had settled over the beer garden of the Lion and Lamb. Staff were struggling to keep up with clearing away empties and some had given up, leaving towers of pint glasses curving into the sky, fairy lights twinkling off the dregs of lager inside. Tables were overflowing and people spilt onto rugs on the floor, eating illicit picnic food smuggled across from their tents.

'So is this a serious ambition, Jay?' asked Mia. 'Marrying Lord de Beeble?'

'God no, the man's a boor, have you seen him? No, this is just a jolly old trip to the country to kill some time.'

'Before what?'

'Before… I don't know, the next thing.'

'Do you have a job?' asked Alice, conscious that she was enunciating her words very carefully and yet they still sounded like they were pushing their way out through a mouthful of pebbles.

'No need, unfortunately. Grandpapa made a fortune in light bulbs and left me and my brother a trust fund each. Not enough to live in luxury but too much to force me to get a job and stop floating around the country looking for a purpose to my life.'

'Ooh, very deep,' chuckled Alice before glancing at the sombre faces around her and realising she'd hit the wrong note.

'What kind of purpose are you hoping to find?' asked Mia.

'A vocation? A passion? Love? Any of the above,' he murmured, fiddling with a cigarette stub in the ashtray, then throwing it aside.

'Love?' repeated Alice. 'So you're hoping to meet someone here, even if it's not Lord be Deeble?'

Something was wrong with that sentence, but she'd work out what it was later. Jay was forcing a smile, sensing he was dampening the mood.

'Jesus H, whatever gives you that idea? I'm not ready to plight my troth, I prefer to play the field. I'm only twenty-seven, after all.'

'Are you? I'm going to be thirty on Wednesday,' said Alice, slurping the last drops of wine in her glass.

'This Wednesday? Are you having a party?' asked Mia.

'No. I expect we'll have a family dinner.'

'Come on, it's your thirtieth. Why don't you have a party?'

Alice fiddled with the stem of her glass.

'I don't enjoy parties – you have to do all the organisation and then you don't know if anyone will come, and if they do everyone looks at you and…'

Mia waved these objections away.

'You don't need to worry about anything. Jay and I will organise it, won't we Jay?'

Jay had been staring at the ashtray but at the sound of his name raised his head.

'Erm. Pardon?'

'See, Alice? You won't need to do a thing,' said Mia, smiling her dazzling smile.

***

Ever since Henry had described the village hall meeting to her, Saskia had been aware of the germ of a genius idea beginning to sprout in the layers of fertile compost in her brain. Something about the way Henry had described the different characters at the meeting had fired her imagination. How about, mused her genius, an article on English eccentricity? Setting the great wilderness of the human mind against the tidy cultivation of country gardens, tea rooms, duck ponds and chocolate box cottages? She could combine it with a fashion piece while she was down there. It was all coming alive in her imagination now – models clad only in St. George's cross knickers, whimsical headpieces made to look like roast dinners, models dressed as punks sitting atop red phone boxes, English designers, English photographers, English models – it would be the English Eccentric Issue. Something, some uncharacteristic modicum of tact, whispered to Saskia that it might be best not to mention to the villagers themselves that she was doing a piece on eccentricity, though. No, traditional village life, that would be her cover.

She phoned Henry to tell him the good news.

'Babe, I've had the most outrageously brilliant idea. It's the vacuum.'

Henry was lounging in the garden at de Beeble Hall, scanning the papers, pleasantly drowsy from the heat of the sun.

'What's that, darling?'

'I'm going to come and stay with you at the Hall and—'

'I know, darling, we're seeing you on Friday night. Looking forward to it.'

'No, I'm going to drive over on Wednesday afternoon with Joel and Annabel. I've had an idea for an article. I'm excited about it, babe.'

'Great. I'll let Martyr know you'll all be here for supper on Wednesday.'

'Oh yeah – can you remind her about my gluten and dairy intolerances? She seems to have a problem remembering stuff like that. Last time she made lasagne – that's like death to me, you know? Maybe she could do a salad - alfalfa sprouts, pea shoots?'

'Mmm,' said Henry, non-committally. 'Drive carefully and I'll see you on Wednesday, OK?'

'Ciao-ciao, babe, ciao.'

***

After dinner on Wednesday night (lobster bisque, beef wellington with dauphinoise potatoes and tarte tatin, much to Saskia's voluble chagrin), Henry, Noblet, Saskia, photographer Joel, and Annabel, Saskia's assistant, spread out around the terrace, letting their food go down and sipping post-prandial tipples. Noblet was sitting apart from the rest and sulking behind a newspaper. Annabel sat on the steps, drinking vodka and messing around on her iPhone. Joel picked up his drink and set off to investigate the garden in the gathering dusk. Saskia stood behind Henry as he lounged in a chair, stroking his hair and watching Joel.

'Did you miss me, babe?'

'Mmm.'

'I missed you. It was weird not having you there when I got home. I mean, I was out most nights – but when I wasn't, you know. I'd had a shitty day on Monday and didn't have anyone to tell about it. That was when I tried calling you and your phone was off, remember?'

'Sorry about that, darling. Flat battery.'

'Yeah, so I had some houmous and carrots and called Katie instead.'

'I see. So you missed me for a bit, until you got hold of Katie.'

Saskia bent down and kissed the top of his head.

'Silly. Katie can't take your place. I missed lots of other things. I missed you massaging my feet. I missed your cooking…'

Before Henry could respond, they heard Joel calling up to the house from somewhere down near the lake.

'Can you hear that?'

Then he appeared, jogging back across the lawn.

'Sounds like something's going on in the village. If I didn't know better, I'd say it sounds like The Proxy playing live.'

Saskia looked scornful, but they all stopped to listen. There was a pounding heartbeat echoing dully around the valley, and from time to time they heard a higher-pitched melody.

'It's probably a school disco. You're not in London now, Joel babe, you don't stumble across The Proxy playing live in your neighbourhood.'

'All the same,' said Annabel, 'maybe we should go down and see what's going on? For the article?' Annabel was twenty-four and lived in the bars, pubs and clubs of Hoxton, Brixton and Shoreditch. Most of her friends had no idea where she lived because she would always be found out somewhere, usually having taken too many pills, always awake and looking for the next party. The prospect of a quiet evening surveying the hushed, moonlit lawns of a country house, with a glass of vodka and Coke as her only stimulant, struck terror into her.

Support came from an unexpected corner.

'Damn good idea. Make the most of it, that's what I say. Could be some great material for your article.' Noblet nodded at them, newspaper discarded.

Saskia stroked Henry's head again.

'Would you mind, babe? I'd need to borrow your car. We'll rock up, take a few shots of their little disco or whatever it is and come straight back.'

'Knock yourself out, darling. We'll be here.'

'Oh yes,' agreed Noblet. 'We're not going anywhere. Take your time.'

***

Saskia, Joel and Annabel jumped into Henry's Aston Martin and roared down to the village.

'This'll be a waste of time,' Saskia was saying as they parked up by the green, 'but I felt sorry for you guys having to hang around up there. Boring as fuck, I know. That place is crying out for a festival – you know, drape the whole place in white silk, yurts on the lawns, book some new wave folk acts, chill-out zone in the library, pseudo-vintage tea parties on the lawn. That'd be the vacuum, man, remind me to speak to Henry about it.'

She continued setting out her vision for de Beeble Fest as they followed the sound of pounding music to the village hall, but when they opened the double doors and looked in, the words died in her throat. There, on the poxy, cramped stage of a poxy, cramped village hall, were The Proxy; the hottest band to come out of London in the past six months. Saskia had been trying, unsuccessfully, to get an interview with them ever since she'd first seen them play under some railway arches in

Waterloo, but they kept turning her down. And yet here they were, entertaining a pack of country bumpkins who would have been just as happy listening to Disco Dave's Hits of the Seventies, Eighties, and Nineties.

'What the f…' she hissed. Someone had done this, someone had got them here. Scanning the room her eyes locked onto a familiar face. She couldn't be sure if the face was familiar because she knew this woman or if she recognised her as being from her world, rather than from this little village in the sticks. She was taller, glossier, and more beautiful than anyone who lived in this village could be. She was the culprit.

'Do you know her?' she asked the others. No need to ask who she was talking about; Joel and Annabel were both gawping at her already.

'She looks familiar…' Joel couldn't quite place her either. 'Supermodel?'

'Too fat,' spat Saskia.

Joel and Annabel exchanged a meaningful look. Saskia was usually far too secure in her own importance to be jealous of other women, no matter how attractive.

'Let's get a drink and go and speak to the band when they break. Joel, get some shots of these inbreds, man. Too, too shabby.'

'I think it's a private party,' whispered Annabel as they walked in.

'So what? They're hardly going to chuck us out, come on.'

91

Chapter 8

Arriving earlier that evening, Alice had been gobsmacked and a little scared. This party had been organised for her. This band was playing, these tables had been loaded with food, this bar and these waiters had been arranged, these people had turned up at the drop of a hat, all for her birthday party. She'd never heard of The Proxy, but the look on Jay's face had given her a good idea of how famous they were. The guests were a mixture of old friends, villagers and sophisticated strangers, no doubt invited by Mia. She could protest all she wanted that Jay had had a hand in the organisation; Alice had no doubts who was the mastermind behind this evening. Walking in with Mia and taking all this in, she shook her head, bewildered.

'Who are you?'

Mia laughed and tucked her arm under Alice's. 'I'm your fairy godmother. Now we need to find Prince Charming. Come and have a drink. I invited a few friends; I hope you don't mind. This is José, Ben, Tia – that's Corey...'

Ordinarily, this would have been Alice's cue to slip off and hide, but somehow with Mia by her side, nothing seemed to faze her. She took a deep breath and plunged into the mass of friendly faces, knocking back a drink that had been thrust into her hand. She appeared to be mingling, and for once she was – almost – enjoying it.

***

After a tumultuous first half, the band took a break. Luc, lead singer of The Proxy, prowled over to Mia and kissed her hand. He was hopelessly in love with her. Four of The Proxy's last five singles had been inspired by her (the fifth, 'Life on the Line' had been inspired by waking up with an epoch-making hangover inches away from a railway track). His love was unacknowledged and unreciprocated. Luc preferred it that way; nothing would have stamped on the delicate bud of his inspiration like the unromantic foot of requited love.

Mia's eyes smiled at him over the rim of her whisky glass.

'I've never heard you sing better.'

'I always sing well when you're listening.'

'Do you need anything? Have you got a drink?' She hailed a passing waiter. Luc took a glass of champagne and a vodka shot off the tray, then pointed a tobacco-stained finger over the waiter's shoulder.

'Who invited the journalists?'

Saskia had backed Stein Avery, The Proxy's drummer, into a corner while Joel took pictures of him. Annabel was in the background, exchanging sultry looks with Rollo Carr, the floppy-haired bass player.

'I wonder,' said Mia, with a frown. Turning round she caught the eye of a burly man in black and gestured him over. Luc kissed her hand again before oozing away.

***

Saskia felt a tap on her shoulder and froze. Someone was touching her vintage Narciso Rodriguez violet distressed leather jacket. Someone with a large and no doubt greasy finger. She turned, fixing a grade A look of hauteur to her face. It encountered a barrel-like chest. She adjusted the look upwards.

'Can. I. Help. You?' Her words shot like peas from a particularly vicious pea-shooter.

The man growled at her.

'Sorry? Can't understand you.'

The man growled at her again. The words weren't clear but the West Country accent was.

'No. Sorry, still didn't get it. Do you speak English?'

'Maybe you'll understand this,' rasped the man, grabbing her and propelling her across the room and out of the door with a firm shove between the shoulder-blades. Joel and Annabel appeared more fluent in West Country than Saskia as they shot out behind her with no need of translation. With the sound of the slammed door ringing in their ears they looked in horror at the indignant figure in violet leather who was doing an Oscar-winning depiction of a fish out of water. Inside the hall: laughing, chattering and the band tuning up for the second half. Outside the hall: silence, punctuated with violent gasps. When Saskia found her voice again, it was shaking.

'That is NOT fucking cool, man.'

They knew how moved she was by the fact that she'd forgotten to use one of her trademark phrases rather than the mundane 'cool'.

'Who the fuck is she to treat me like that?'

'Erm… that wasn't a woman, Sask.'

'Not the monkey, I'm talking about the piper. She's the one behind this.'

Annabel deciphered the metaphors. 'You think that glamorous woman told him to chuck us out?'

'Glamorous is not a word I'd use to describe that bitch – and not one you'll be using to describe her again if you want to keep working for *The Vacuum*. Shocking lapse of discernment, babe.'

Annabel looked flustered and started to stammer a retraction. Saskia paid her no attention. Stalking off, the others trailing behind her, she headed for the car. Halfway there she stopped, turning to stare at the village hall.

'No, man. No way. I'm not going to let her scare me off like a little kid. She doesn't know who she's dealing with.' Looking round at the others and smiling a vicious little smile, she took off her towering heels. Motioning to Annabel to do the same with her stilettos, she put both pairs of shoes in the back of the car.

'Got plenty of film in that thing?' she asked Joel, pointing to the camera round his neck.

'Er, no, it's digital…'

'OK then. Come on you guys, we're journalists, let's chase down this goddamn story.' She jogged off in the direction of the small copse which pressed up against the boundary of the village hall grounds.

'I'm a fashion photographer, not bloody Kate Adie,' grumbled Joel, traipsing along behind her.

'What story is she talking about?' hissed Annabel.

Joel shrugged and then flinched as Annabel let out a piercing shriek; her bare foot encountering a thistle in the grass. Saskia emerged from the wood to motion furiously at them for silence, then retreated again into the shadows.

They pressed on towards her.

***

The bouncer emitted a short, sharp grunt of satisfaction after the door had slammed behind the interlopers. He enjoyed bouncing – or door supervision to give it its correct title. Door supervision was an art, and an underappreciated one at that. A door supervisor had to be all things to all men. When an event was going well, he faded into the background like a piece of wallpaper. When there was trouble, he materialised like… like a strip of wallpaper peeling away from the wall and collapsing on people. Or something even more dramatic than that. The worst parties were those at which no actual ejections were required. He hated a boring party. Tonight, he'd only needed to eject those three pathetic specimens so far, but he was hopeful that it was the start of better things to come. Scanning the room to ensure no jiggery-pokery had ensued in his few moments of distraction, he lumbered back to his preferred vantage point against the wall near the fire exit and resumed his impersonation of a piece of wallpaper.

'Saw you in action. Very impressive,' purred a voice somewhere near his right nipple.

He looked down and recognised the shiny blonde bob and whip-thin body of Sinead Dumper.

'Urr.'

She continued flashing seductive looks at him while he scanned the room. He growled apologetically, 'On duty.'

'I know. No need to talk. Like to watch you work.' Sinead stared into his face. 'Fascinating.'

'Urr.'

The bouncer found Sinead disconcerting. She had first accosted him when he was doing his day job, patrolling the borders of the de Beeble estate. She'd been wearing a very short leather mini-skirt and a black vest top, and if he hadn't known better, he'd have said she was lying in wait for him. The door supervisor – Derek to his mother and one or two other close confederates – wasn't used to overt female attention. His mother believed that he would be quite a catch for some lucky lady but there, it must be said, she was in the minority. Derek had discovered early in life that although the ladies love a bit of brawn, they are less partial to small, deep-set eyes, a piggy nose, trumpet-like ears and a propensity to sweat buckets even in arctic conditions. Whence, then, came this sudden interest from what Derek termed to himself a 'fam fatal'?

Sinead squeezed his arm and allowed her fingers to linger on his boulder-like bicep.

'Like a drink? Something soft? Won't affect your reflexes?'

Undeniably she had a certain sense of the complexities of door supervision. When they'd met in the lane, and again when she'd arranged to meet him at the Lion and Lamb, she'd shown a flattering interest in his work and a thirst to know more. How often did he patrol the estate, for instance? Was he a specialist, focussing on estate patrols, or would he be involved in, for example, crowd control at the village hall interviews? Questions such as these had drawn him out and he'd introduced her to the secrets of his profession. The Stance (legs apart, arms crossed high on the chest, chin up). The Stare (unflinching, unblinking and best carried out by small, deep-set eyes looking down a piggy nose). The Customer Address System, to be applied when accosted by customers requesting access to a venue without the correct ticket (engage Stance and Stare, grunt monosyllabic responses whilst maintaining Stance and Stare and permitting mouth and head to move as little as possible). Sinead had drunk all this in and even attempted the Stance, Stare and Address herself, which Derek had found endearing.

'Orange juice,' he grunted, and Sinead darted away to the bar, returning with his drink and one for herself. He glugged the juice, draining the glass, never letting his attention wander from the crowd in front of him. Sinead took his empty glass and shook her head in admiration.

'Amazing concentration.'

He shrugged modestly and said, 'S'my job.'

Nevertheless, she continued to shake her head and remained glued to his side, watching and admiring.

***

Luc bent over the microphone, dark hair flopping down, but through the mane his eyes were trained on the tall figure of Mia near the front of the crowd. '*Oh you,*' he sang, '*you're that first day when winter's through. The world's not good enough for you.*'

Gosh, thought Alice, champagne bubbles bouncing and popping in her brain, *it almost looks like he wrote that song about her.*

This is a nice song, was her next thought, and she hummed along. One of the other teachers from work was standing next to her and they swayed together from side to side.

'You, you're all my winters too,' Alice warbled. 'Yeah, yeah, yeah, yeah, yeah, yeah, blue…' Possibly not the right words, but so what. No one was listening.

(In fact, everyone was listening as Alice was yelling at the top of her voice.)

'Here you go, Alice, have a mojito.'

'Thanks!' Who was that? Someone with a big smile and a tray of cocktails, it didn't really matter what his name was. It didn't matter what anyone's name was. They were all smiling and swaying and singing and having a lovely, lovely time at her thirtieth birthday party.

Only… now she appeared to be surveying that birthday party from the floor… and then from the arms of a burly man in black who was carrying her out into the fresh air.

Recalling it later, everyone agreed that things had happened fast. One minute, Alice was being doused in water and fanned by a circle of people on the grass, the next someone was snapping away with a camera.

'That's it, man! Get it on film! Bouncer brutality, he's knocked that poor little frump out.' And then – 'Come on, Joel! Let's get out of here, man!'

At the sight of Derek barrelling towards him, Joel hadn't waited for Saskia's exhortations and the two of them scrambled desperately to get back over the wall. Joel, six-foot tall and athletic, was over and on the other side with Annabel while Saskia was still getting a foothold.

'Help! Pull me over! Help me, man!' came Saskia's increasingly frantic voice.

With a final heroic leap, she hurled herself at the wall and was halfway over when Derek reached her and grabbed an ankle. As he dragged her back down, Joel gripped her scrabbling hand and tried to heave her over onto his side of the wall. The two men were pulling in opposite directions, Saskia was screaming and trying to kick Derek in the face, Annabel was shrieking hysterically – and then all of a sudden something happened that no one was expecting. Derek's absence from the village hall had allowed a couple of gatecrashers to sneak in. One of these darted over and slapped a large cross on Saskia's bottom in bright red paint. Instantly a camera started flashing, lighting up Derek's bewildered look; Saskia's white leggings now adorned with a big red cross; her anguished face as she twisted back to try to see what was happening; and the satisfied glint of a job well done in Lorraine Watford's unfocused eyes.

The stress of the situation was too great for Derek to bear in silence. He lifted his great head and roared like a wounded guinea pig, sending people scattering. Mad hair, spectacles and paint pot bowled back into the village hall, paused to daub one or two outsiders in red paint, then continued on into the night. Flashing camera, grey hooded top and mischievous grin fled for the far wall, scrabbled over and disappeared into the wood on the other side. Bare feet, white leggings and red, sticky bottom fell heavily onto something soft, which squealed, before being heard to rustle away through the leaves.

***

Alice sat up.

'Ooh. I think I must have nodded off. Is everyone having a nice time?'

Mia sat down on the grass beside her. 'I, for one, have not had so much fun in a long time.'

'Oh good.'

Closing her eyes Alice curled up again to resume her refreshing sleep.

***

Inside the hall, pandemonium. Someone had assaulted Stein Avery and several partygoers with red paint and an enraged-looking bouncer had pounded through the hall in hot pursuit of the perpetrator, scattering people in all directions. Rumours were flying around that the tabloids had airlifted journalists and paparazzi in to secretly film the party. Scores of people were said to have collapsed in the grounds and been rushed to hospital.

In short, Alice's 30th birthday party was a huge success.

Despite splashes of red paint leading to the door of a picturesque-looking cottage by the green, Derek was unable to rouse anyone with repeated hammerings on the door. In the end he was led away, head hanging in shame, by a whippet-thin woman with a shiny blonde bob.

Chapter 9

In the lamp-lit drawing room, a companionable silence was broken by the sound of a powerful engine roaring up the drive. Noblet felt his heart sink a little as he put aside his book.

'Are they back already? Barely been gone five minutes.'

Henry looked at his watch.

'It's been over an hour and a half.'

'Has it? Goodness. Time flies when you're having fun.'

The door opened and Joel and Annabel appeared, looking sheepish.

'Hi, guys.'

'Hi. Where's Saskia?'

'She's in the car.'

'What's she doing there?'

'She's waiting for your housekeeper to bring her a pair of trousers.'

A pause. Henry looked at them.

'She had to take hers off – there was a bit of an… incident.'

Henry's look at Joel had turned menacing and he now hastened to explain about the undignified ejection from the party, the investigative journalism and the red bottom.

Noblet spluttered, chuckled and then laughed out loud. Henry forced the corners of his mouth down with an effort and Joel allowed himself to smirk, but Annabel was too scared and still dazed from having Saskia fall on her head to do anything but stand, silently, in the doorway.

Henry got up. 'I expect you could do with a drink.' He waved them towards the decanters on the sideboard as he headed out of the room. 'I'll go and check on those trousers.'

Sitting alone in the Aston Martin outside the quiet house, naked from the waist down other than a flesh-coloured thong, a tear rolled down Saskia's face. The sensation of that tear on her skin intensified the shame and the hurt, and all at once she was sobbing, cheeks drenched. She wasn't an evil person. She didn't deserve this. However much she tried to block it out, the image kept elbowing itself back in front of her eyes: the vicious old woman with her dripping paintbrush; the sweaty bouncer with his grubby hands all over her legs; the smirking faces of bystanders; and her Chloe leggings, stiff with red paint and nestling at the bottom of a public rubbish bin.

When the door opened and she saw Henry looking in at her, holding a pair of trousers, she grabbed his hand and pulled him into the car, throwing herself into his arms.

He looked at her with concern. 'Darling! Are you alright?'

She shook her head and cried even harder.

'Ssh.' He squeezed her to him and kissed her wet cheeks. 'Are you hurt?'

She managed to calm down enough to say, between juddering sobs, 'Not hurt, but it was so horrible, babe.'

He tried to comfort her but she pulled away, sobs dying down now and indignation starting to take over.

'That's the worst thing, babe, someone was taking pictures. I don't know if it was someone at the party or if I'm…' the sobs started up again, 'if I'm going to end up in the papers!'

It crossed Henry's mind that she wasn't important enough to end up in the papers but he kept the thought to himself.

'Don't worry, darling, I'll speak to Gareth and see if he knows anything.' At her look of incomprehension, he explained, 'The paparazzo we found on the estate that time. He might know if any professional photographers were in the village tonight.'

***

Thursday morning dawned brightly, with a hint of haze on the fields; but in Alice's bedroom, the outlook was less sunny. The beeping of her alarm ripped open the cosy cocoon of sleep and she reached over towards the bedside table, hammering at anything her hand came across in an attempt to end the noise-induced pain. It yelped into silence and she lay back on the pillows, spent. After a minute or so of mental preparation, some deep breathing exercises and a short internal pep talk, she got up. Moving with care around the room to avoid banging her fragile-feeling brain against the inside of her skull, she managed to scrape together an outfit and headed towards the bathroom. Sitting on the floor of the shower, head resting against the tiled wall, it crossed her mind to call in sick. But everyone knew about the party, she would have to drag herself in somehow.

Compared with Alice's journey to school that morning, Scott's polar expedition was a Sunday afternoon ramble. Stopping regularly to allow the waves of nausea to subside she would lean against the nearest wall or hedge before struggling onward. Once or twice she passed an acquaintance, looming out of the mists of stale alcohol fumes that surrounded her. Colonel Markham was coming out of his garden gate as she passed. He seemed to hesitate, and then instead of returning her husky 'good morning' he reached out and patted her on the arm with a look of ineffable pity, before turning away. Strange, but maybe he'd had a similar hangover himself in his heyday. As she passed the newsagents, two teenage girls were lounging on the bench outside – former pupils of hers who'd since moved on to secondary school in Market Mornington. It was probably coincidence, but they both started giggling when they saw her. They were teenage girls after all: giggling was their equivalent of breathing. Still, a little strange.

Turning into the lane that led to the school, she saw a familiar form in the distance. Sinead Dumper. Oh God. She cranked up a gear, from snail pace to hyper-tortoise drive. The school entrance was at the nearer end of the lane, she should reach it before Sinead got to her. Sinead had other ideas, however. She seemed to want particularly to speak to Alice and held up a hand, motioning her to stop. At the risk of instant vomiting and/or death Alice revved from hyper-tortoise drive to arthritic pony trot, calling out to Sinead – 'Sorry, late!' – before whisking in the school gates and through the front door in the nick of time. Inside she paused, panting, sweating and praying for a quick release from this vale of tears. The extremity of feeling passed, however, and she set off for assembly. She didn't get there. Mrs Fratterbury was lying in wait and as Alice passed her open door she called out.

'Cooee! Alice lovie, in here. Step into the pantry, said the spider to the fly and close the door behind you, there's a love.'

Alice sighed and complied.

Mrs Fratterbury had the look of a spider which had swaddled a fly and now couldn't decide whether to pop it straight in her mouth or rock it to sleep with a lullaby first. Admittedly, thought Alice, it was rare to find overweight spiders with frizzy hair and mustard stains down their jumpers – but that was what made the resemblance all the more surprising. Mrs Fratterbury wasn't in a hurry to speak. She reached out a hand and took Alice's resisting one across the desk. Then she looked at her and sighed. Alice wondered if this would be a good time to throw up.

Finally, the headmistress spoke.

'Alice, lovie, we're all behind you.'

Instinctively, Alice looked around. There was no one behind her, just a hat stand with several of Mrs Fratterbury's sagging, bobbly cardigans on it and some yellowing paintings by long-departed children, depicting the Battle of Hastings. The sight of so many arrows gouging out bloody eyeballs made Alice's stomach heave and she closed her eyes. When she turned back around and opened them again, a tabloid newspaper was lying on the desk. It hadn't been there before and Alice hadn't heard it arrive. Perhaps Mrs Fratterbury was trying to distract her from the arrows and gore with a demonstration of magic.

'We've all seen it, lovie, so we all know. At least – Annie C hasn't seen it yet because she'd already popped over to St. Joseph's for her IT training when I got here, but everyone else has. So you mustn't worry about trying to keep it to yourself, putting on a brave face like Patience on a monument.'

Vague, troubling ideas started to creep into Alice's weary brain. What had she done last night? Anything so embarrassing it was newsworthy? There was the drinking, the singing, the dancing. Some kind of al fresco nap, she remembered the smell of earth and the feel of damp grass against her cheek. None of this was illegal though, surely, or even that interesting to people who didn't know her?

Mrs Fratterbury watched her. Did Alice know? Did she suspect? No – there was no embarrassment, no shame, just bewilderment. All of Mrs Fratterbury's fondest hopes were realised: she would be the one to break the news. Picking up the newspaper very deliberately while keeping her eyes glued to Alice's face, she unfolded it and placed it flat on the table. Alice looked down.

'Booze-fuelled orgies in wife-hunt village!' gasped the outraged headline, above a set of three pictures. The first showed what looked like an outlandish sexual act against a wall. A woman daubed in red paint was poking her bottom in the air and twisting round to leer at a burly man as he fondled her legs.

Beside them, a buxom woman brandished a paintbrush. (Was that Lorraine Watford? Hard to tell with the brush obscuring half her face, but it looked like her mad hair.) The second picture was of a tousled-looking girl in a green dress, lying on the grass with a group of men and women kneeling around her – a girl who turned out on closer inspection to be Alice herself. Her gaze lingered on that photograph for a moment or two before dragging itself to the third picture. This was a close-up of Alice's bottom half, revealing the unfortunate fact that her skirt had ridden up on one side to her waist, revealing the full glory of her Spanx control pants. A hand could be seen grasping the skirt's hem – most likely to pull it down, thought Alice, but in the context of the picture, looking as if it was undressing her. A ball of ice dropped from a great height into Alice's stomach.

Mrs Fratterbury let the image sink in for a moment and then murmured, 'Read the article, lovie.'

Alice obeyed.

"'Last night, in Gently Rising, our spies witnessed disgusting scenes of depravity and debauchery never before seen in the sleepy Mereshire village. Readers will be familiar with the name of Gently Rising as the home of Lord Noblet de Beeble. Naughty Noblet is on the hunt for a mate and doesn't care who knows it, posting saucy adverts in the local press to lure luscious lovelies to his posh Mereshire mansion.

"'*The Daily Hack* wonders if the judging committee of the Mereshire Best Kept Village Competition has visited Gently Rising recently. This quaint backwater has won first prize three times in the past ten years, but it won't pick up any honours in its current state. The village green has been trashed by an encampment of scantily-clad women, all hoping to become Lady of the Manor. The Beeble Babes, as these women have become known locally, can be found in the village pub, the Lion and Lamb, at all hours, boozing and wearing little more than their underwear. According to local reports, it's not safe for men to walk the streets at night with these sex-mad hussies on the loose.

"'Last night, according to our spies, the debauchery reached epic proportions with an orgy in the village hall to celebrate the birthday of local woman Alice Band – teacher by day and sex addict by night. Revellers were stripping off and daubing each other with strange pagan markings. The nearby fields and woods were a hotbed of wild sex, with good-time girl Alice's party guests romping among the ancient English oaks.'"

The article went on to savour each outrageous act of depravity in minute detail but Alice's attention had wandered. She couldn't stop looking at the photographs.

Mrs Fratterbury was making comforting noises and now enquired, 'Alright, lovie? At least they got your name wrong, eh?'

Alice looked up. The headmistress's hand was hovering over a box of tissues, ready to stem the tide of tears which was surely moments away. That gesture seemed to call up something primaeval in Alice's soul. The block of ice that had landed in her stomach became molten iron and shot through her veins. She sat up straight and looked Mrs Fratterbury in the eye.

'Of course I'm alright, Mrs Fratterbury. I mean, I can see why you'd be worried – it's a bit embarrassing having your picture in the paper like that, drunk, but it'll blow over. And we all had such a wonderful time. It'll be something to tell the grandchildren.' She smiled at the headmistress.

Mrs Fratterbury's look of patronising concern faltered. She pushed the paper nearer to Alice and placed a chubby finger on the article.

'Are you quite sure you read it properly, dear? They called you a sex addict and a good-time girl,' she added at last, to avoid any chance of a misunderstanding.

Alice continued to smile. 'Oh yes! Ridiculous isn't it? Anyone who knows me knows that's all rubbish – and who cares about people I don't know?' The smile had become almost challenging now, and Mrs Fratterbury dropped her eyes.

'Well. I must say. That's very brave of you, my dear, and I'm so glad you're not upset about it,' she said. 'Of course I was hoping you'd feel that way,' she continued, fighting to regain some of her usual complacency, 'I was hoping there wouldn't be waterworks and the boy standing on the burning deck and all that kind of hysterics but you never know.'

'No,' agreed Alice. 'Well, I'd better be getting to class.'

'Oh, no need, dearie. I called a supply teacher as soon as I saw the paper. I felt sure you wouldn't be up to taking class today.'

'No problem,' countered Alice brightly, 'I'll pop along and let her know she can go home now I'm here. Ta-ta, Mrs F.'

The supply teacher was duly dismissed and Alice threw herself into lessons: gluing straws, sharpening pencils and reading stories as if there were no tomorrow. Somehow, she made it through that grimmest of all grim days, fuelled by adrenaline, diet Coke and crisps. Healthy eating was for days when you hadn't been libelled as a sex addict in a tabloid newspaper alongside an enormous picture of your control pants. At long last, it was the end of the day and the children were gone. Normally she would have stuck around in the staffroom doing some prep for the next day, but even her newly-found iron resolve couldn't stomach the thought of that so she headed for home.

Dropping her bag in the hall she turned her phone back on and listened to a series of anxious messages from her sister, her mum and various friends. Slumped down at the kitchen table, she tried and failed to gather the energy to call them back. Having texted everyone the same message – that it was all a silly mistake, she was fine, was having an early night and would call them tomorrow – she scooped up the cat, a cup of tea and the biscuit tin, and retreated to her bedroom. Shutting the curtains, ignoring the knocking at the door and Mia's voice calling through the letterbox, she turned off her phone again and got into bed.

Chapter 10

The day of the interviews wasn't exactly greeted with a pealing of church bells and villagers with doffed caps lining the streets to the Hall, but expectation shimmered in the air along with the heat. Even Lady Caroline herself unbent so far as to observe to Noblet, when she popped in for an early breakfast, that today 'was the day of his little social experiment.' Saskia, who was sitting beside her, picking at a bowl of organic spelt muesli and hemp milk, opened her eyes wide.

'You're so right, Caroline, it's a social experiment.' She turned to Henry. 'We should have invited the Royal Institution down to monitor it, babe.'

'I can't imagine they'd have been that interested,' said Henry, half listening to the conversation and half scanning the papers. Since the fiasco on Wednesday night he'd relieved Gareth of his duties, reasoning that a payment of £200 a month to a paparazzo ought to be enough to receive due warning that one's girlfriend's paint-daubed bottom is about to appear in the tabloids. Particularly when he suspected not only had Gareth failed to alert him to the photographs taken in Gently Rising that evening, but had taken them himself. Henry's calls on Wednesday night had gone straight to voicemail and by the next morning it was too late, the damage had been done. Gareth had sworn blind that he'd known nothing about the pictures, but a little hesitation in his voice told a different story. So now Henry's link to the press, however ineffectual it may have been, had disappeared and he was forced to keep tabs himself on any de Beeble-related tittle-tattle. He was relieved that Saskia's name had been kept out of the article and he'd managed to persuade her that no one would recognise her from the photo with her hair obscuring much of her face.

Noblet's plate was piled as high as usual with bacon, eggs, mushrooms, sausages and tomatoes but the pile didn't seem to be diminishing.

'Feeling nervous, Noblet?' asked Saskia, eyeing his plate. 'It's natural, man – all those women lining up to meet you, expectations are going to be high,' she continued blithely, setting aside her cereal bowl and turning her attention to a cup of green tea.

Noblet sprang up. 'Something I need to check – er – in the library,' he growled, before shooting out the door.

'Typical Nobby,' drawled Lady Caroline. 'He's always been like that. No stomach for public engagements. Not like dear Henry. See how calm he is.'

Saskia squeezed his shoulder. 'Nerves of steel, haven't you, babe?'

'Seeing as I'm not the one interviewing my prospective wife, it's rather easier for me to remain calm than it is for Bob, wouldn't you say?'

'Nothing to do with it,' retorted Lady Caroline. 'Nobby would be nervous if he were manning the door.'

***

Those manning the door did in fact have good reason to be nervous. All the applicants seemed to have had the same idea of arriving hours early in order to be at the front of the queue. Derek and his confederate, a dour-faced man called Keith, glowered from the steps of the village hall at the snaking queue of deckchairs, rugs and small tents. These belonged to incongruous-looking creatures whose sparkling finery was gruesomely at odds with the summer morning. Perhaps at midnight in the finals of the Delectable & Divine Drag Queen Dance-Offs these individuals would have passed without comment, but they looked out of place between the fresh green hedgerows. Barricades had been set up the previous evening to force people to queue single file, rather than surrounding the hall in a mass, but these were already bulging under the pressure of numbers. On a grubby beanbag under a Cliff Richard golf umbrella, right at the very front of the queue, was Lorraine Watford. At the sight of Derek emerging from the hall and surveying the crowd, she poked him hard in the stomach.

'Ugh!'

'Yes. I was here first. Lorraine Penelope Eric Watford, local resident. *From* the village, you see. Not like those.'

Derek rubbed his stomach and unleashed The Stare. Lorraine took this to be a most promising sign, and continued.

'Age thirty-six, excellent teeth,' she bared them at this point to demonstrate, 'childbearing hips' – she looked as if she were about to bare those also but Derek put out a restraining hand – 'excellent family, related to George the Third, sunny disposition, GSOH, piano to grade eight and above.' She wound up on a triumphal note and fell back a step, evidently expecting to be waved straight through to the matrimonial suite.

Derek maintained The Stare.

'Nothin' to do with me,' he observed. 'Save it for in there.'

Lorraine frowned at him for a moment and then comprehension seemed to spread across her face along with a knowing smile. 'Enough said. Mum's the word.' She tapped her nose.

Derek cranked The Stare up a notch before pointedly looking over her head towards something important in the distance. It was hard to ignore her, given that at regular intervals she would yell comments at him such as 'Nod nod, wink wink!' and 'Charlie's your uncle, Bob's your maiden aunt!' but Derek was a professional. Other door supervisors would have crumbled under the strain, but he stood back and thought of England.

By a quarter to nine, the village was at a standstill. The lane leading up to the hall, the streets surrounding the green, and several lanes leading out of the village were all crammed with prospective interviewees. Henry, driving himself, Noblet and Saskia down to the village, was glad of the accompanying security escort ploughing a path through the crowds. Noblet, who had planned to walk down through the fields to get a bit of air before his ordeal, was relieved he'd allowed Henry to talk him into coming in the car.

'Great...' he paused, open-mouthed, 'God.' He shook his head, staring out the window at the press of people all around the car. 'Where have all these people come from? What on earth do they want?'

'They want to marry you, Noblet, man!' laughed Saskia. 'You're in trouble if you've not worked that out by now, shit!'

'No, no, I mean, I know what they want... but what do they *want*? What do they think will happen if they marry me? Has someone been telling them we're billionaires?'

'They saw your picture in the paper, Bob.'

'Oh ha-ha, Henry. Ha bloody ha. This has all been a big joke to you from the beginning, hasn't it?'

They were pulling up to the village hall and Saskia caught sight of Derek at the door.

'Fucking hell! That's him! That's the asshole who threw me out of the party and attacked me! You've got to get rid of him, babe! I don't want him here!'

'You don't have to speak to him, darling, we're going round the back. I can't get rid of him, we won't have enough crowd control.'

Saskia continued protesting until she clocked the photographers making a beeline for the car as they parked up. Assuming a look of utter boredom, she slid out of her seat and prowled into the hall, giving the photographers plenty of time to snap her electric blue tea dress and bondage-style boots. Conversely, Noblet cannoned from the car into the building as if propelled by a misfiring ejector seat, deaf to the shouted invitations to give the assembled photographers a smile, a wave or a flex of his muscles.

And so the interviews began in earnest. Weeks of speculation, hours of agonising, gallons of ink and acres of online comment came down to this one moment: the front door of the village hall opening with a sound like an angry duck and the apparition of a dishevelled, portly woman, peering over her glasses and proffering a battered photograph album.

'Name?'

'Lorraine P. E. Watford, NVQ.'

'Age?'

'Thirty-three, Your Honour.'

Pregnant pause. 'I'm sorry, I think you misheard me. I asked your age?'

'Thirty-three, Your Honour. Although they say I look a lot younger. More like thirty-two.'

'Thirty-three,' Henry repeated, noting something down on the paper in front of him. 'And can you tell us, in a few words, what makes you think you'd make a good wife to Lord de Beeble?'

The photograph album was slapped down onto the table and Lorraine riffled through.

'My father – there, you see. And my mother. Aunt Bea. Aunt Cissy. Uncle Deirdre. Auntie Ed.'

'What…'

'Connections. Excellent connections. Trace our family back to George the Third via a wet nurse and the groom.'

Noblet was blenching and Saskia seemed to have been struck dumb for once, but Henry remembered Lorraine from the village meeting. Taking the album off her and closing it firmly he handed it back, saying, 'Wonderful. We'll make a note of your excellent qualifications and we'll be in touch if you're successful in making it to the next round. NEXT!'

Once Derek had succeeded in unclasping Lorraine's fingers from Noblet's ankles, the second applicant was ushered in.

'Name?'

'Sinead Desiree Dumper.'

Sinead had rolled up a couple of minutes after nine and been ushered to the front by Derek, to the accompaniment of furious catcalls from the rest of the queue.

'Age?'

'Thirty-three.'

'Really? Remarkable coincidence.'

'Pardon?'

'Nothing. Could you tell us why you think you'd make a good wife to my brother?'

This was what she'd been preparing for for weeks. The phrases flowed off her tongue; carefully crafted and planned, planned and planned again. She covered the main points – her age, neither young and flighty nor old and desiccated but perfectly experienced and mature. Her background as a legal secretary, demonstrating her excellent organisational skills. Her interests – never was a woman as eloquent on the themes of flower arranging, gardening, charity work and smallholdings as Sinead Desiree Dumper. Even these, however, were eclipsed when it came to her main passion in life: Wilkie Collins. Had she been teleported there and then to the *Mastermind* chair, she would have received full marks on the specialist subject of that particular author. Noblet himself was taken aback at the depth of feeling she displayed for his works and her knowledge of even his most obscure scribblings.

As Sinead concluded her pitch and sat back, there was a moment of stunned silence before Henry said, taking her proffered CV and application form, 'Thank you. I think that about covers it, unless?' He looked around at the others.

Noblet cleared his throat, loosening his collar with one finger.

'Ahem. There was one thing. I – er – I wondered…'

Sinead leant forward, lips parted, gimlet eyes trained on his.

'Yes?'

'I wondered – in *The Woman in White*, would you say the relationship between the Count and his wife stands up to scrutiny? You know, in your opinion, as it were?'

Whatever she'd been expecting, it wasn't that. Recollecting herself, however, she (remembering to smile first) answered brightly, 'Amazing writer, Collins. Could make you believe anything. And some men do have a magnetic attraction for women.' Her gaze dropped from Noblet's eyes to caress his mouth, throat and chest before dropping to about the point his crotch would have been, were it not chastely concealed by pants, trousers and the table. Noblet blushed and even Saskia spluttered a little, staring agog at Sinead. The interview was concluded, Sinead withdrew and the next candidate was ushered in. It took several more interviews before Noblet was able to regain his composure. As he did so, a tall, languid man slid into the seat before them.

'Name?'

'Whatever you want it to be.'

Henry put down his pen.

'Thank you for coming. We'll be in touch.'

'Oh dear. Not even afforded the courtesy of a proper interview? Some might say His Lordship is paying lip service to the anti-discrimination laws. Some newspapers, for instance.'

'If you'll do me the courtesy of telling me your name, I'll do you the courtesy of interviewing you.'

'Delighted, old sport. The post office, police, passport office and my mother know me as Jason. Everyone else knows me as Jay.'

'Do you have a surname, Jay?'

'Not yet. I'm hoping to acquire one shortly. JdB. Quite a ring, no?' he asked, treating Noblet to an intimate glance from under his eyelashes.

Some of the panel seemed to be finding the room a little hot. The sun shone relentlessly through tall, narrow windows, lighting up Noblet's pink face. Saskia had slipped on a huge pair of sunglasses and manoeuvred herself into a patch of shadow.

'Tell us why you think you'd make a good partner for my brother.'

'Don't get me started! Firstly' – counting off the points on his fingers – 'we've got so much in common. We're both stylish, intelligent gentlemen of leisure with a predilection for queens. Victoria, in your case,' inclining his head towards Noblet, 'several, lesser-known monarchs in mine. Next, His Lordship needs someone to help him run his estate. I was raised on a smallholding, and have a natural affinity for the beasts of the field, mulching, husbandry, composting and all those sorts of words. Thirdly, we're both crazy about literature. His Lordship is an aficionado of the English Victorian era, while I myself favour American writers of a later period: F Scott Fitzgerald, Kerouac, Steinbeck, Schulz. I flatter myself that we can educate each other – filling in each other's gaps, if you like.'

Henry was leaning back in his chair, arms folded, listening.

'Shouldn't you be making notes?' enquired Jay.

'Oh, I won't forget anything.'

'Which segues into my next point. Number four, if my top-class arithmetic skills don't deceive me. I stand out from the crowd. His Lordship needs – I hesitate to say a trophy wife, but the learned panel get my drift. Whereas Earls up and down the country are hauling dowdy frumpsters in pearls to the altar, imagine the publicity if Lord de Beeble announced he was taking *me* up the aisle.'

'Yes. I can imagine it. But what makes you think Lord de Beeble wants any publicity?'

Jay gazed above their heads.

'Tres interessant. Yes, what makes me think that? Why would I imagine that a man who poses for pictures in national newspapers and conducts his courtship via the local news bulletins would want publicity? Why, why, why? No,' he shook his head apologetically, 'the answer eludes me, I'm afraid. We'll chalk that one down to interview nerves.'

'Now look here—' began Noblet, but Henry carried on.

'I take your point. If the interview nerves aren't too overwhelming, I wonder if you could answer another question. My brother is keen to start a family.' Noblet twitched and looked at the ceiling. 'Can you tell us how you would fulfil this particular element of the job specification?'

'The same way all the best people do. I would fly out to, say, Angola – or Kazakhstan, or wherever, I'm not picky – with a large entourage in tow, sprinkling silver and gold as I went, and I would gather up the nearest photogenic cherub from the local orphanage, before sweeping back to my husband's arms via a double-page spread in *Hello!* magazine.' He cocked his head on one side. 'What else?'

Henry held out a hand.

'Thank you. It's been entertaining. We'll be in touch if you make it to the next round.'

Jay pouted.

'Over so soon? I haven't even touched on my firm, smooth body.'

'That is a shame, but perhaps you can touch on that outside – we've still got hundreds of people to see.'

With a nod to Derek, Jay was dispatched. As he flounced out of the door, Noblet expelled a lungful of air so enormous he seemed to have been holding it in through the whole interview. He stood up.

'I need a break. And some air.'

He lurched over to the tea table, sloshed some tea into a cup and headed out the back door; reappearing almost instantly, slamming the door shut on the noise of overexcited photographers, journalists and interviewees.

'Can't get away from it! Can't even pop outside for a bit of p and q without grown men demanding I strip down to my undies!'

Stumping over to the stage, he heaved himself up onto the edge and slurped his tea.

Saskia murmured to Henry, 'Shall I have a word with him, babe? A woman's voice is scientifically proven to be soothing, you know.'

'To be honest I think he just needs to be left on his own for a bit.' Henry got up and stretched. 'Tea?'

'I'll have a herbal if there is some. Camomile.'

They sipped their tea together, occasionally glancing at the stage where Noblet was eating ginger nuts with an air of hurt dignity.

'We're going to have to speed up or we'll never get through them all,' remarked Henry, loud enough for Noblet to hear. 'Perhaps we should have some sort of code. If Bob can tell it's going to be a no, he could…'

'Sing a verse of "What shall we do with a drunken sailor"?' proposed Noblet, interested in spite of himself.

'I was thinking something more discreet. Like blowing your nose.'

'Yes. Yes, I could do that.'

'OK If she's a definite no you blow your nose and we move on to the next one.'

'Good-o.'

'And if she's a definite yes? So, we all know to pay particular attention?'

They all considered what could be the sign for a definite yes.

'I could clear my throat?' suggested Noblet.

'But mightn't you clear your throat from time to time anyway?'

'Well, I would do it in a very definite manner. Like this.' He drew himself up to his full height and placed a large fist before his mouth. 'Ahem!'

Pleased with himself, he repeated the process, louder this time. 'You see. Ahem!'

Derek came shooting through the door.

'Yes, sir?'

'Er – we're ready for the next candidate,' blustered Noblet and Derek hurried to usher her in.

By lunchtime, Noblet's handkerchief was beginning to look worn, and the panel had found their rhythm. Perhaps one in ten candidates would not be greeted with a sound like the trumpeting of a baby elephant, and these fortunates were accorded more than thirty seconds. The pile of 'yeses' was about an inch thick compared to a foot of 'noes'. Riffling through the yes pile as he stuffed a prawn mayonnaise sandwich in his mouth, Noblet asked, 'Where's the first lady?'

'The first lady?' repeated Henry incredulously. 'You'd like to invite the lunatic offspring of George the Third and a groom back to the second interview?'

'Not her! I don't count her. No, the Irish lady. Who knew so much about Collins.'

Henry was taken aback.

'I assumed she was a no?'

'Did you hear her speak about Collins?' demanded Noblet, eyes sparkling. 'For that alone she should be invited back. I forgot to ask her opinion on an interesting minor character in *Armadale*.'

Noblet found himself receiving support from an unexpected quarter.

'Babe, I thought she was quite promising. Vulgar and pushy – but that could be toned down, and otherwise she was strong. Good organisational skills, eager to please…'

'If I was looking for a new PA, she would be my number one candidate. But as Noblet's wife?'

'It's my decision, old chap, and I say she's through to the next round.'

***

Sinead, unaware of how precariously her fate had been hanging in the balance moments earlier, was tapping an impatient court-shoe-clad foot on Alice's doorstep. She needed something to fill her afternoon, and happily, the thought of Alice had sprung to mind. Interrogating her on all the gory details about the tabloid article and boasting about how well her interview had gone would take her to, say, 4pm; which was perfect as her elocution teacher was due at half-past. And now bloody Alice was threatening to ruin her plans by not answering the door. Sinead was sure she was in. She'd heard something that sounded like a body falling to the floor as she'd clip-clopped up the garden path. She peered through the window but the living room appeared to be empty. She considered calling out 'Yoo-hoo, Alice! It's Sinead!' but doubt as to whether that would hasten the opening of the door or ensure it remained closed, sealed her lips. She held a finger on the doorbell for a minute and snapped the letterbox for good measure. Coco helped her out with a couple of sharp barks.

'Hello there,' said a silky voice behind her. Mia stood in the lane, looking, in her gauzy blue dress, like an off-duty water nymph.

Sinead flicked a strained smile at her.

'Trying to get hold of Alice.'

'She's not in, I'm afraid.'

'But I heard something…'

'Must have been the cat,' said Mia. On cue, Tom hurled himself through the hedge like a stuntman through a paper hoop and butted her legs, purring at top volume. 'Or something else,' she continued, undaunted. 'She popped in at my house earlier on the way to her parents. I'll let her know you called.'

Sinead looked like she might protest, but in the end shrugged and marched back down the path. Passing through the gate, she said, 'So what are you doing here? If you don't mind me asking,' she added, with a sneer.

'Not in the slightest. I'm getting a breath of fresh air.'

Sinead stared at her. Mia smiled back and, very deliberately, inhaled. 'Lovely,' she confirmed.

As soon as Sinead was out of sight Mia walked up to the house and tapped on the living-room window.

'The coast's clear.'

There was a moment of silence and then a pale face rose from beneath the windowsill and hung there like the moon over a desert. The window opened.

'Are you sure she's gone?'

'Yes.'

'How did you know I was here?'

'Just a guess. Why don't you get up and open the door?'

Alice looked down at her grubby dressing gown and let out an involuntary sigh. 'I'm not very good company at the moment.'

'Never mind, I am. Come on, I feel like I'm at a very low-tech drive-in. Run by a vampire.'

Inside Alice shuffled into the kitchen and put the kettle on. Flopping into a chair she asked, 'Have you been for your interview?'

'Not yet.'

Alice glanced up at the clock. Half-past one. 'Shouldn't you be in the queue?'

'I don't like queuing.'

'Oh. Right.'

She lapsed into silence. A cup of tea appeared in front of her.

'Thanks. Sorry, didn't hear the kettle boil.'

'How are you?'

'Fine.'

Mia sipped her tea and waited.

'I mean,' Alice clarified, 'obviously I'm not fine. All the village saw the pictures in the paper, I can't face seeing anyone. I'm a laughing stock and the worst of it is I'm so far from being a sex addict; I've not had sex in years. I'm thirty years old, living on my own and likely to stay that way forever. My life's in a rut and I don't know what to do about it. I want to curl into a ball and die.'

A tear rolled down her face and splashed in the cup of tea. She pushed the cup of tea to one side and let the tears fall onto the table, leaving little dark splodges on the wood.

'It's probably going to get worse,' remarked Mia.

The tears redoubled in intensity.

'Unless you do something about it.'

'I don't want to do anything about it,' sobbed Alice, grabbing a tissue and rubbing at her tears and runny nose.

'No, that's the problem in these situations, one never does,' agreed Mia.

'Oh, and I suppose you've been in this situation, have you?' snapped Alice through the sobs. 'Front page news in your elasticated pants?'

'But the thing is,' she continued, as if Alice hadn't spoken, 'if you make an effort now, everything will be easier in the long run. You need to show the village that you're not embarrassed to be the centre of gossip for a while. You need to stop crying and have a shower. I'll be back in an hour and we'll get to work.'

With that, she was gone and Alice's sobs dried up with a sound like a hiccup.

'Well of all the…'

An hour later Mia was back and somehow Alice had got herself into the shower, changed into a clean pair of jeans and splashed enough cold water on her face to stop it looking quite so much like a pink marshmallow.

Mia wasn't alone.

'Alice, you remember José from your party.'

Alice remembered one or two things from the party but sadly José wasn't one of them. She wondered if he'd had that large vanity case with him at the time.

'Luckily he was still in the area. He's going to effect a transformation. Aren't you, José?'

He grinned, revealing perfectly white, even teeth.

'I am a man who loves a challenge. I accept!'

Chapter 11

Midnight. The last, bedraggled stragglers had filed in and out of the village hall, stifling yawns and stashing half-drunk bottles of wine behind bushes. Derek had brought the glad tidings that the final interviewee had been seen, and he was now helping his associates to put the room to rights. Noblet shoved his chair back from the table with a harsh scraping sound.

'At very long last! That was, without doubt, the longest day of my entire existence.'

Henry picked up the pile of 'yeses'. 'Productive, though. I didn't expect there to be so many good interviews.'

'Me neither, old chap, me neither.'

The three of them made their way wearily to the car, Henry and Saskia in the front and Noblet in the back. Henry flicked on the headlights and did a double take. Two female figures had emerged from the darkness and stood in front of them, blocking the way.

Saskia tsked. 'Beep the horn, babe.'

Before he could, one of them came round to the driver's side and tapped on the window.

'Ignore her!' squawked Saskia as Henry pressed the button to lower the window. 'For God's sake, babe, we'll never get home.'

A husky voice said, 'I'm sorry to disturb you,' and Noblet and Saskia both gasped, for very different reasons, at the sight of Mia's beautiful face.

'Are we too late for the interviews?' she asked.

'Yes!' yelped Saskia, hissing aside to Henry, 'That's the bitch that got me thrown out of the party!'

Simultaneously, however, Noblet was saying in a strangled voice, 'No! Not too late at all, the night is young!'

As Henry switched off the engine and undid his seat belt, Noblet leaned forward and whispered into Henry's ear – 'Lydia Gwilt!'

***

José, it had turned out, was a magician. He was a conjurer with concealer, a shaman with shadow: a sorcerer of slap. Out of his case came tubes, pots, bottles, brushes, cloths, tonics, ointments, powders and creams. Alice had found herself seated beside the kitchen table in a towel, her head being massaged as she inhaled fragrances so exquisite she began crying once more. Rather than try to stop her, José urged her on, crooning in her ear, 'Yes, yes, releaze it all. Cry yooer 'art away and we start again.'

After the massage came the application of cleansers and lotions. This was the first stage, José explained, in the pre-pre-cleansing phase. Three more cleansing phases were yet to come. Alice awoke halfway through the second phase to find Mia sitting cross-legged on the table drinking coffee and reading Alice's A-Level copy of *Cyrano de Bergerac*.

She noticed Alice was awake and said, 'I love this guy. Panache. That's my idea of a man.'

Alice nodded and drifted off again, waking when José nudged her.

'You must wake oop now, Lady Alice. It's time for ze pre-base base, and for thees every 'ole in ze skin, every leetle cell must be awake.'

Mia had disappeared but José made some strong coffee and waved it under Alice's nose.

'Normally, I say no to ze caffeine, ze skin e don' like eet, but just thees once I allow eet.'

Later Mia reappeared, in a different dress and looking, if possible, more beautiful than ever.

Her cat's eyes widened when she saw Alice. 'You look amazing.'

José pshawed.

'I 'aven't even begun yet! Thees is ze pre-make-up!'

The light was fading outside but José and Mia gathered an arsenal of lamps which blazed in a circle around the chair where Alice's transformation was taking place. Mia had found some chilled rosé and as José worked, they drank wine and ate a strange combination of olives, cherries and chunks of parmesan from the fridge.

At ten o'clock he stood back, put down his brush and declared, 'I am finished! My greatest work yet!'

Whipping his phone out of his back pocket he snapped a startled-looking Alice, explaining, 'As a record. You must give me another photo so I 'ave somefin' to compare.'

He pulled a mirror out of his case but Mia put out a hand.

'Not yet.'

From a bag at her feet, she produced a billowing strip of material, some jewellery and a pair of expensive-looking wedges.

'Put these on.'

The strip of material turned out to be a long, flowing strapless dress of silk; palest turquoise with small silver stars and flowers. There was a silver bangle to go with it and chandelier earrings that sparkled like raindrops in the lamplight.

'But…' So many questions tumbled into Alice's brain. 'Where did these come from? They won't fit me. I don't wear clothes like this…' Her last words were muffled by the T-shirt that Mia was pulling up over her head.

José slipped discreetly into the next room.

Mia dropped the light-as-air dress over her head and zipped it up. Alice found herself pulling off her jeans and socks in a daze and slipping on the sandals as Mia fastened the jewellery.

She stepped back and considered Alice from head to foot.

'José!'

He bounced back into the room.

'Eez ready?'

'One more thing.'

'Ah! Of course. Ze scent.'

Turning back to his case he tried bottle after bottle before inhaling deeply and nodding his head.

'Thees one.'

Alice found herself enveloped in mimosa, jasmine, rippling cornfields and breezes rolling down from Tuscan hills.

'Now! She is ready.'

He lifted the mirror, reflecting first her face and then tilting it so she could see her dress.

What she saw was Airbrushed Alice. Not your everyday, bog-standard Alice with limp hair, a tendency to chubbiness and the odd spot or two, but the Alice from her daydreams. This Alice was made to turn heads when she walked into a room. Her eyes were bigger, her lips plumper, her flesh firmer and her skin was bouncing golden rays off the walls. Her neat bob had been tousled, giving her a bohemian, spontaneous kind of look. And she felt rather spontaneous. After all, hadn't she wanted something unusual to happen to her, to flip her out of her comfortable little rut? The events of the last few days weren't what she had had in mind, but you couldn't always choose your rut-flippers.

Looking at the kitchen counter, she clocked two empty bottles of wine and wondered how much of it she'd drunk. She hoped her newfound confidence wasn't purely alcohol-fuelled.

Before the first furrow of concern had wrinkled her radiant brow, however, Mia had taken her by the arm. Kissing José on the cheek, she said, 'You are a god among men and we thank you from the bottom of our hearts.'

'Oh! Yes, thank you, José, so much! I've never looked like this before, you're amazing.'

Outside the cottage, Mia began humming one of the songs The Proxy had played at Alice's party. Alice joined in, humming happily until she realised they were approaching the Lion and Lamb.

'Where are we going?'

'Phase One of Operation Anti-Rut. Give the neighbours something to talk about.'

Alice hung back. 'Wasn't being plastered across the tabloids enough?'

'Give them something else to talk about. Something they're not expecting. Sinead and Co. are no doubt envisaging you crumpled in a heap on the sofa watching *Sleepless in Seattle* and overdosing on Dairy Milk.'

'I like *Sleepless in Seattle*,' said Alice irrelevantly. 'And Dairy Milk.'

'However, instead, here you are, like Cinderella with her fairy godmother, stopping off at the pumpkin for a quick tipple of magic potion before dancing away into the sunset with your prince.'

Alice looked at her.

'That doesn't make sense.'

'Not yet.' She set off again towards the pub, calling over her shoulder, 'Come on Alice Brand – it's time for the tulip to bloom.'

Alice looked down and caught sight of her silk dress rippling gently in the breeze. It would be ungrateful in the extreme to waste all of José's work and Mia's thoughtfulness by creeping off home again. Lifting her head, she followed Mia into the crowded bar of the Lion and Lamb.

The record didn't exactly stop with a screech of the needle, and not quite everyone turned round to gawp at them, but other than that they could have been re-enacting a barroom scene in a Western. Mia paused for a moment before slinking across to the bar; allowing everyone plenty of time to drink in the sight of Alice, transformed. Alice followed, attempting a slink of her own. It needed some work – she had a suspicion it made her look like a toddler waltzing in quicksand.

Someone tapped her on the shoulder. She turned to find Colonel Markham, pink and beaming.

'Alice, my dear. You look splendid! May I buy you and your enchanting friend a drink?'

Mia smiled her lazy smile at him and asked for a whisky. Alice ordered a gin and tonic. As Jerry served the drinks, other people started to gravitate towards them. Mrs Fratterbury was so pleased to see that Alice was getting over her little 'contre-tete'. Sinead nodded towards them from a distance and remarked that Alice was looking surprisingly well, considering. Lorraine Watford wandered past to congratulate Alice – or Angela, as she insisted on calling her – on looking so fresh and clean, and was prevented from spilling red wine all down the turquoise silk dress by the quick reflexes of Jerry Brewer; honed over years of working behind a bar. By the time they were the hub of the crowd at the bar all thoughts of embarrassment were forgotten – or at least much subdued.

When, at around eleven thirty, Jerry Brewer managed to shoo everyone out, Alice was almost disappointed that the night was over, and said so to Mia.

'The night isn't over. You haven't forgotten about my interview, have you?'

'At this time of night? I thought you must have gone earlier while I was asleep.'

'No, I was waiting for you.'

'For me?'

'Absolutely. Phase two of operation Anti-Rut. We're both going to have an interview.'

'Oh, no.' Alice shook her head, inadvertently adding to its tousled look. 'No, I couldn't do that.'

'Why not?'

'I don't want to marry Henry de Beeble for a start.'

'You're in luck. It's his brother who's looking for a wife.'

Oops. Freudian slip.

'Anyway,' Mia continued, 'I don't want to marry Noblet either, remember.'

'Yes, but that's different. You're—'

'Shh!' Mia glanced at the little groups of people still lingering nearby. Alice lowered her voice.

'Well – anyway, it's different for you.'

'Fine, so you don't want to marry Noblet de Beeble. But it'll be fun. And what else are you going to do? Go to bed with a cup of hot chocolate? What have you got to lose?'

What did she have to lose? It could be embarrassing, but hell, she'd plumbed the depths of embarrassment in the last few days. Plus, she might get a glimpse of Henry de Beeble.

'I suppose I could… keep you company,' she conceded.

And so, she found herself at midnight in the village hall, Mia beside her and three tired-looking faces before her.

Chapter 12

They interviewed Mia first. Despite Saskia interjecting with snide remarks, Mia shone – as Alice had known she would. Articulate and utterly at ease, she out-interviewed every previous interviewee a hundredfold. Noblet was transfixed. Barely able to string a sensible question together, he drank her in from head to foot. Even the admission that she'd never read any Collins raised not a flicker of disappointment. Mia was through. So far, so predictable. Now for Alice.

'Name, please.'

Alice appreciated how it would feel to be in the *Mastermind* chair. What would she choose as her specialist subject? Tabloid humiliation? The history of Gently Rising, 1988–2018? The beauty of Henry de Beeble? The beauty of Henry de Beeble seemed most apt, being, as it was, before her and flooding her thoughts. How could the others sit there so calmly, seemingly unaware of those eyes, deep brown and shaded by blackest of black lashes. Not to mention the perfect lines of his cheekbones, two diagonals pointing down to his mouth. To his mouth…

'Your name? Please?'

Had she not answered already?

'Alice Louise Brand.'

'Age?'

'Thirty. And three days.'

Saskia sneered. 'Very precise.'

'Sorry, yes, it was my birthday a few days ago so I…' she trailed off.

Henry lowered his eyes as if he felt Saskia had been a little unkind.

'Could you tell us why you think you'd make my brother a good wife?'

Alice considered the question. After all, she was here, at an interview, and these people were taking the time to interview her. It was only polite to put some thought into the matter.

'I'm not sure if I would make him a good wife.' They all stared. She hastened to explain. 'What I mean is, I wouldn't make anyone a good wife if I didn't love him, and as I don't know His Lordship yet, I couldn't say if I could fall in love with him.'

Saskia rolled her eyes and yawned, loudly.

'I suppose that's not a very helpful answer. Sorry.'

Henry smiled at her. 'It makes a lot more sense than most of what we've heard in this hall today.'

Noblet nodded. 'I agree. Quite right.'

'But,' continued Henry, 'setting aside the question of love, for a moment, do you think you have any qualities that would make you a good companion to my brother?'

'Um… I love Gently Rising and this area, so we'd have that in common, I believe. I couldn't live anywhere but the countryside. I like children – I'm a primary school teacher here in the village. I love cooking and baking – although I expect you've got cooks for that, haven't you,' she went on hurriedly. 'I – I like animals, and gardening, and seeing family.' She looked down at her lap, wishing Mia and José had given her some interview coaching along with the makeover.

'That's fine.' Henry gave her a reassuring smile. 'If you could let us have your application form.'

'I don't have one, I'm afraid.'

He pushed a piece of paper across the table. 'Put your contact details down here.'

Alice neatly printed her name, address and telephone number on the paper and pushed it back across the table. Her hand brushed Henry's and she flinched. Leaping up from the chair she blurted, 'Well, thanks so much for seeing us at the last minute, I'll see myself out. Good luck, I hope you find someone nice. Thanks, bye.'

Outside, Mia was leaning against a tree, smoking something that looked suspiciously like a joint.

'How did it go?'

'Terrible. I babbled.'

'The upper classes are all babblers. You'll fit in like a dream.'

Alice pulled a face. 'So, what now?'

The night was mild and there was something magical about the village huddled in the moonlight. Alice didn't want to go home to her lonely cottage.

'The world's our oyster. London? Paris? Or margaritas and a smoke in my garden?'

'Erm – the last one, I think. Although maybe not the smoke. Or the margaritas. A cup of tea would be nice though.'

In the end, margaritas seemed more appropriate. The air was thick with perfume in Mia's garden. Beyond the hedge, a wildflower meadow sloped towards the star-speckled sky. Sprawled on cushions with the chirruping of night insects all around they gazed up at the starkness of the moon in the deep black above. When Mia lit another joint and passed it across, Alice found herself, in her new guise of spontaneity, accepting it. She'd not smoked anything since university, and then not much, but tonight it seemed to suit the mood. Everything started to become a little indistinct, and then very defined and then very, very funny. They couldn't say a word without the other laughing, and the more they said the more they laughed until their stomachs ached and their cheeks hurt. Louise

Crawley next door threw up the sash of her bedroom window and asked if they could please keep the noise down. And that was the funniest of all.

***

The following day, Lady Caroline stood on the terrace watching the dismantling of the marquee on the lawn.

'Hello, darling, you're up late,' she said as Henry appeared with a cup of tea and the papers. 'Late to bed?'

'Very.'

'Have you found a wife for Noblet?'

'Not yet, but I'm hopeful.'

One of the main upright supports was lowered and the empty canvas billowed and sank to the ground. Half-naked men hauled poles away towards the waiting truck.

'Those Brownies are worse than hooligans, you know.'

'What happened?'

'You might well ask, what didn't happen. Rioting, looting, savagery of all descriptions.'

'You're exaggerating, Mother.'

'Indeed! Would you call girls vomiting in the rose garden rioting or would you not? Would you call Martyr having to expel thieving girls from the pantry looting, or would you not? Would you call girls running half-naked into the lake savagery, or would you not?'

Henry smiled. 'Sounds no worse than anything Noblet and I got up to in our time.'

'Well. Perhaps not. But multiplied by several hundred it is extremely tiring, I assure you.'

Saskia shuffled out of the house looking wan.

'I'll never understand why it's so hard to get a good cup of lemongrass tea outside of London. Hi, Caroline.' She pecked the older lady on the cheek.

'Good morning, Saskia. I'm sure Martyr will do her best if you let her know what you want.'

'It's fine, she's getting me some hot spring water and lemon juice. I haven't done my stretches yet, that's why I'm not myself.'

Descending the steps to the lawn, oblivious to the comings and goings of the workmen, she assumed the yoga pose known as 'downward-facing dog': a position which presented the others with the sight of her small, pert bottom. Henry had a flashback to red crosses.

Lady Caroline raised an eyebrow. 'And what do you have planned for the day, Saskia dear?'

'I've got work to do,' Saskia called through the gap between her legs. 'I still haven't got the shots for my English eccentricity piece so I'm gonna take Joel down to the village and see what we can find. What about you, babe? Want to come with us?'

'Can't, I'm afraid. I need to work on the format for the second interview stage. Then Noblet's got some media interviews this afternoon.'

'Does he know?'

'Does who know what?' Noblet stood framed in the doorway, eyeing Saskia – now balancing on one leg, holding her other ankle behind her head – with annoyance.

'Saskia was asking if you knew about the media interviews this afternoon, Bob.'

'Media interviews? No, I do not. What media interviews?'

'I told you, Bob – a couple of papers and local TV news. They want to hear how yesterday went.'

'What! You did not tell me, Henry. I am sick and tired of everyone in this house treating me like a forgetful halfwit. I refuse to do them.'

Turning on his heel he stomped back into the house.

Saskia and Lady Caroline looked expectantly at Henry.

'He'll do it. Once I explain it's all for his own good.'

'His own good?' Lady Caroline enquired.

'Yes. Positive PR. I'd rather the media told the story we want to tell. Bob'll listen to reason.'

'It'll be the first time,' drawled Lady Caroline as the final piece of the marquee was rolled up and borne away.

***

Down in the village, the green looked almost normal again. Most of the tents had been dismantled; only a handful remaining half erect or spread out on the grass ready to be packed away. The main route out of the village towards the A4 was clogged with cars and camper vans edging their way, nose to tail, into the countryside. Beside the 'Welcome to Gently Rising – Please Drive Carefully' sign, Lorraine Watford was waiting to salute each exiting car with a loud raspberry followed by an exhibition of her tongue.

Elaine and Valerie were supervising the exodus from a bench outside the Lion and Lamb.

'They may all be gone by this afternoon, Elaine,' ventured Valerie.

Ted appeared at Elaine's side, awaiting permission to speak.

'Report?' barked Elaine.

'All clear, my love. I made a complete circuit of the village and apprehended no obvious theft or criminal damage. I checked,' flipping open a small notebook, 'the church, the telephone box, all eight benches, the bridge, the postbox, the bus stop, and the war memorial.' The notebook snapped shut and he stood to attention.

'And the village hall?'

He looked stricken.

'The village hall!' He flipped the notepad open again. 'I omitted to include it in my itinerary. God forgive me for my forgetfulness.' And he was gone, a thin brown flash across the grass.

***

Saskia, tottering across the green on her Vivienne Westwood platforms, nudged Joel. 'Look at those two, man. They'd be perfect for the piece.' Waving a hand as she approached, she called out 'Hi there! We're doing a feature on village life for a magazine in London. You two look so – quintessential. Can we take a couple of shots?'

Elaine seemed to double in size.

'Of course, my dear! We'd be proud to represent Gently Rising, wouldn't we, Valerie? That's Valerie – V-A-L...'

'Great, now don't move – we've got to capture you just as you are.'

Click.

Captured in the frame are two ladies in the autumn of their days, seated side by side on a wooden bench. The larger lady is clad in brown tweed and sensible shoes; meaty arms crossed, supporting a prize-winning bosom. The smaller lady cringes, pale face strained beneath colourless hair; pale hands grip a shapeless beige handbag on her shapeless beige lap. The photograph is composed so as to include the pub sign: above Elaine's head is the word 'Lion' and above Valerie's the word 'Lamb'.

'Thanks so much, ladies, that's great. Gotta get on, loads to do, ciao-ciao.'

Click.

Colonel Markham, standing to attention outside his white-painted garden gate. Behind him dahlias, camellias and gladioli march away in military rows. In the bottom right-hand corner, a small child toddles into view, finger in nose.

Click.

Through the railings, a glimpse of an Edwardian primary school building; in the background children playing on the grass; in the foreground Mrs Fratterbury, cigarette dangling from lips.

Click.

Lorraine Watford sitting in her back garden at a table set for tea. Cups and saucers commemorating royal weddings (Charles and Diana, Charles and Camilla) surround a teapot in the shape of the Queen's head. Lorraine holds aloft a plastic Union Jack in one hand and a chocolate eclair in another. She wears a T-shirt emblazoned with the slogan 'I love NY'.

Click.

Sinead Dumper looking startled. She kneels on a waterproof gardening cushion by a flower bed at the edge of her garden. She wears a pink twin-set, pearls and flesh-coloured tights. In her hand is a pristine trowel which hovers above perfectly-tended, weed-free soil. In a window behind her, Coco's small grey face stares out.

Click.

Jerry Brewer behind the bar in his empty pub, brooding. Motes of dust stand out as gold flecks against the dark wood, spinning through the gloom.

Click.

Alice, caught unawares. She is crouching on the pavement outside her house, stroking Tom; a sound has made her raise her head but the look of warm affection still lingers in her eyes. Tom's mouth is open, mid-miaow, and his ginger tail points ramrod straight towards the sky.

Chapter 13

Sinead poured herself a glass of white wine and opened her dinner party planner file. She had planned to drop Derek faster than you could say 'sucker' after he'd got her to the front of the queue at the interviews, but something in the back of her mind had whispered that he might not have outlived his usefulness. It didn't harm to keep him sweet and, after all, if she hadn't invited him round for dinner, she would have spent the evening watching her box set of *Downton Abbey*, again, while intermittently shooing Coco off the settee. Now. The menu. She had bought the ingredients for Menu Number 23: a starter of twice-baked smoked salmon soufflés, followed by rack of lamb with fondant potatoes and chocolate pots for dessert. She pulled out the laminated sheets and got to work.

As usual, she'd followed her plan to the letter and when the doorbell rang at 8pm sharp, everything was ready. She had laid the table with the second-best service, showered, changed, lit the candles, arranged the gerberas in three separate vases (grouped in height order) and made the butter pats with her favourite handbag-shaped butter mould. Derek stood on the front doorstep: pink, scrubbed face sprouting out of his thick, pink neck which in turn thrust its way through the collar of a black shirt so pristine it still had the creases in it from the packaging. The shirt was tucked into a smart pair of jeans and his feet were shod in brand-new desert boots – bought earlier that day in an effort to look cool, yet casual. The great, hulking bulk of his top half sat on top of slim hips and legs, making him, in his black shirt and blue jeans, look like a Liquorice Allsort from the rejects bin.

'Come in,' Sinead ordered, briskly. 'Shoes there,' she said, indicating a neatly-ordered rack. 'Cream carpets,' she added, by way of explanation.

He knelt down and removed the desert boots to reveal white terry-towelling sports socks. Having placed the boots on the rack, a safe distance from a pair of Sinead's white suede high heels, he followed her into the living room and thrust a bunch of gerberas and a bottle of wine at her.

'F'you,' he growled.

'Gerberas! My favourite.'

Derek clocked the three vasefuls already scattered around the room and grunted.

'Now,' said Sinead. 'Drinks. Wine? Beer?'

He stood awkwardly in the middle of the living-room carpet and looked at his socks.

He wanted a lager but wasn't sure what the etiquette was. 'Beer, please. Small one.' It seemed a good compromise.

As the soufflés took their second turn in the oven, Sinead settled herself on the edge of an armchair and prepared to entertain her guest.

'So…' she purred, preparing to once again draw him out with intensive questioning on the ins and outs (mainly the outs) of the door supervision business. Coco, sensing a potential new friend in the house, came bounding out of his bed in the utility room, straight through the kitchen and onto Derek's denim lap.

'Coco! Bad boy!'

'S'alright,' Derek assured her, pleasure lighting up his face and uncrinkling the piggy eyes. 'Love dogs.'

He patted Coco, accepting a barrage of wet salutations without flinching.

'Really?' prompted Sinead.

'Yurr.'

'Got one?'

'Nope.'

'Why?'

'Mother.'

'Allergic?'

'Cats.'

'Shame.'

He pointed at Coco. 'Pedigree?'

'Yes.'

'Cross?'

'Yes.'

'Name?'

'Coco.'

'Nice.'

He was certainly a gifted conversationalist, she had to admit. She approved of his no-nonsense style.

She found that she'd relaxed so much she was sitting back in her chair with her legs crossed at the knee. She never did that in public. Not since she'd studied footage of Lady Diana and seen that she always sat with her legs to one side, crossed demurely at the ankle.

The timer went off and she leapt up to tend to the soufflés, calling over her shoulder, 'Through to the dining room!'

She returned with two small plates bearing the soufflés and salad garnish drizzled with balsamic vinegar. Derek brought a forkful of soufflé to his lips, the delicate silver fork looking like children's cutlery in his enormous fist.

'Delicious,' he informed Sinead, who was working her way through hers with workmanlike precision.

'Yes,' she said.

'Good cook,' he ventured.

'Yes.'

'Lessons?'

'Yes. London.'

'Shows.'

'Thanks.'

She smiled at him, a real smile that went right up to her eyes, and saw his face flush.

'Like to better myself. Keep learning. Be the best at everything I do. No excuse for failure. Got to plan and put the effort in. Didn't have much growing up but by working hard got all this.' Her hand swept round, taking in the ruched curtains, velvet tasselled tie-backs and framed photograph of herself, alone, in her wedding dress.

She sat back, surprised at herself. Probably the most revealing thing she'd said in years. Where had that come from?

Derek took a gulp of his wine. 'I think you're amazin',' he confided.

She was taken aback by his openness, and her initial pleasure was swamped by sensible thoughts marching across her cerebral cortex and slapping her emotions into shape. Her eyes were on the prize, and the prize was Noblet de Beeble. Yes, Derek was a great raconteur and had a certain raw sex appeal but he was not the main event. If Lord de Beeble was the Big Top, Derek was the bearded lady – worth a look, but ultimately a sideshow.

She stood up and whipped away his empty plate.

'Got to check on the main,' she snapped, ignoring his crestfallen look as she whisked out of the room.

When she returned with the main courses, she found Coco had snuck in. He was sitting at Derek's feet, looking disconsolately at him, first from under one eyebrow, then the other. She was in time to see Derek give him a pat and mutter, 'Messed up. Annoyed her.'

Coco licked his hand before retreating under the table as Sinead approached.

'Rack of lamb and fondant pommes de terres,' she announced. He thanked her as she put the plate in front of him and from then on, the meal went forward in silence. Derek would attempt a remark on the food or the wine, but other than a brief yes or no Sinead wouldn't be drawn out. When the chocolate pot was deposited on his place mat he set down his teaspoon with a crash on the china plate.

'Have I said somethin'? Offended you?'

At the look of anguish on his face, Sinead relented.

'No – no. It's not you. It's…' she cast around, looking for a plausible excuse – reasoning that 'you're not Noblet de Beeble or some other rich man with a title' wouldn't be diplomatic. Particularly if she wanted to keep him sweet for some, as yet unknown, purpose in the future. The photograph of herself in her wedding dress caught her eye. 'It's my wedding anniversary. Would have been. Brought it all back. You know. A man, saying nice things.'

Derek looked stricken. 'Sorry. Didn't know.'

'No! You wouldn't.'

'Sorry.'

'Forget it. It's all over now. He's gone and I'm alone.'

Coco gave a little cough and emerged from under the table, as if to remind her that remark wasn't strictly factual. She gave him a shove and he shuffled out of the room, tail drooping.

'Not allowed in here,' she explained to Derek.

Something about the slump of Coco's shoulders and his long-suffering expression was familiar to Derek.

'Reminds me of His Lordship,' he remarked.

'His Lordship?' Sinead's ears pricked up.

'Yurr. Not happy. Doesn't like havin' to do all this interview stuff.'

'No?'

Seeing that Sinead was thawing out, Derek warmed to his theme.

'No. Overheard him and his brother at the big house the other day talking about the next lot.'

'Really? You're still working there?'

'Yurr. Still need to keep an eye on the journos and that. Paps,' he added, darkly.

'So… the second-round interviews,' Sinead prompted. 'Noblet's not happy about them?'

'No. Thing is…'

As Derek relayed the conversation he'd overheard between Noblet and Henry, including detailed plans for the format of the second interviews, Sinead drank it all in, not a word escaping her. And when he had told all he had to tell she hustled him out into the night with a peck on the cheek as a reward. She had been right; he hadn't outgrown his usefulness. Knowing what the interviews would involve before everyone else would allow her to plan. And once Sinead Desiree Dumper began to plan, nothing could stand in her way.

Sweeping a surprised Coco out of his basket and into her arms, she waltzed around the room, muttering, 'An honour to meet you, Sinead, Countess of Pantling, Lady de Beeble, ma'am. A privilege to make your acquaintance…'

Chapter 14

Three days later, phones were ringing off the hook and text messages were flinging themselves through the ether the length and breadth of the country as successful interviewees let friends and family know they were through to the second round. Some took it in their stride. Sinead received the news as a formality. Others were shocked and delighted or shocked and nervous; or, in Alice's case, shocked and nauseous. The first interview had been an off-the-cuff kind of thing; Mia's way of dragging her out of the dumps. She'd been tipsy and reckless and looking back on it, she was taken aback by her own audacity. So when the call came through to say that she'd been successful and was invited back for a second interview on Saturday 20th June, just under two weeks away, her stomach started churning. It was a second interview which, it stood to reason, would be more gruelling than the first. It was unlikely she'd be drunk this time and the recklessness seemed to have worn off now that she was back into the humdrum of the working week, with tabloid exposés and miracle-working Argentines melting into the past.

After work, she called Mia.

'I'm not sure I can go through with the second interview.'

'That's what you said about the first one.'

'Yes, but that was different. I was drunk.'

'So, get drunk again.'

'We have to be there at 10 a.m. It doesn't give me much time.'

'Start the previous evening. Piece of cake.'

'Seriously, Mia, I'm terrified.'

'You won't be on your own. Lots of people will be terrified.'

Not Mia though, of course. She wouldn't even turn a hair. Alice hadn't even bothered to ask if Mia was through: it would have been like asking Elvis Presley if he'd made it through the first round of an Elvis Presley lookalike competition.

'I could pull out. Or is that rude?'

'I wouldn't worry about that. If you don't want to go, don't go.'

Twisting around in her seat and dislodging Tom, who shot her a dirty look, Alice mused, 'Is it a bit ungrateful when all those other people queued for hours and didn't get through? Basically taking someone else's place and then wasting it?'

Before Mia could answer, Alice heard voices in the background and asked, 'Where are you, by the way?'

'Marrakesh.'

'Oh! Right. Sounds noisy.'

'Yes, I'm in a police station.'

'Oh dear! What are you doing there?'

'Long story – work, mainly.'

The voices in the background were getting louder and more irate and Alice thought she could detect sounds of a fight breaking out.

'Do you need to…' she began, as Mia said,

'Listen, do what you feel comfortable with and don't worry about what anyone else thinks. I'll speak to you soon – back in a week or so.'

The phone went dead.

Alice gave Tom a stroke and he pushed his furry head up against her hand.

There she was again, Mia – off doing something adventurous-sounding while Alice was sitting on the sofa with Tom after a day at work, wondering what to make for dinner and if there was anything good on telly. She didn't even have the option of Scrabble, as Tom tended to cheat and chew her tiles when she wasn't looking. Nothing ever happened to her.

Except something had happened. She'd been successful at an interview and had been invited to de Beeble Hall for a day of unspecified 'interview activities' along with, the woman on the phone had said, around fifty other people. Of course, there was the rather important point that she didn't want to marry Lord de Beeble – but then that hardly mattered. The likelihood of being chosen by Noblet to be his wife and then having to turn him down was so remote as not to be worth thinking about.

In that case, what was to stop her going along on the twentieth? She'd never been inside de Beeble Hall. Mia would be there for moral support. It would be something to tell the grandchildren. (*What grandchildren?* asked a voice in her head. She told it to shut up.) Why the hell not? This was the new Alice, she did what she wanted when she wanted, she made decisions on the spur of the moment. She would go.

***

Henry was back in London for the week to check everything was ticking over at the office and catch up on some work. Walking into the flat at 9 p.m. he found the huge kitchen table covered with proofs and Annabel and Joel installed on either side of Saskia, poring over them and sipping diet Cokes.

'Hi, babe.' Saskia pointed to her cheek as she riffled through photographs and he planted a dutiful kiss on the indicated spot. 'You know I hate bringing work home with me, buggers up our feng shui. Can't help it today though, we've got the deadline for the English Eccentrics issue and we're way behind schedule. They're still pulling the copy together, I spent half the day chasing up PRs for missing samples and we've not finalised the spreads. Come and tell us what you think of these.'

Henry thought wistfully of the beer and bath he'd been promising himself on the way home.

'Hi, Joel, Annabel.' He picked up one of the A3 sheets from the table. 'What am I meant to be looking at?'

'We've gotta can some of these images – we have room for twelve but we've got at least twenty that we all think are the total vacuum. It's a fucking tough call, man.'

Joel and Annabel murmured something incoherent in agreement while looking as if, at this stage, they couldn't care less if all twenty of the pictures got canned as long as they didn't have to look at them anymore.

'And you think I can help?' Henry went over to the fridge, offered everyone drinks, then took out a beer and prised off the cap. Pulling up a chair opposite Saskia, he said, 'OK. Which ones are definitely in?'

Saskia picked up four or five and pushed them over to him. 'These ones have to go in or we wouldn't be able to look our own souls in the face – right, guys?'

They nodded.

'Fine. So we've got,' he counted them, 'five definites. That leaves, what – fifteen, sixteen possibles?'

'I wish we could put them all in. Joel worked so hard on them,' she pinched that unfortunate man's cheek, 'but it would throw out the whole balance of the magazine.'

Henry reached out and swept all the sheets into a pile in front of him.

'Right. We're going to do this methodically. I'll hold up a picture and everyone votes – either yes, no or maybe. There are fifteen pictures and you're allowed five yeses, five noes and five maybes each. Then we'll do it again with the maybes pile.'

He grabbed some plain sheets of paper for them all to rip up and make into their 'yes', 'no' and 'maybe' tokens.

'First one.'

He held up a picture of a woman standing in a playground smoking a cigarette. Joel gave him a 'Yes' token, Annabel a 'Maybe' and Saskia, after five minutes of agonising, during which she vocalised her every deliberation, a 'Yes'.

'Great. That goes in the Yes pile then. Moving on.'

They went through six pictures the same way. Henry picked up the seventh, a picture of a young woman crouching down to stroke a cat. Glancing down at it, he saw kind eyes staring into his with such genuine warmth that he felt something catch in his throat. Realising that he'd been staring at it for much longer than necessary, he made himself look up and say to Saskia, 'I recognise her – isn't she…'

'From the interviews. Yes. Friend of that tall bitch who booked The Proxy.'

Something about the contrast between Saskia's sour face and the look of straightforward affection in the woman's eyes in the photograph made him feel as if everything had shifted a little out of position.

'Her name was…' he trailed off, waiting for Saskia to finish his sentence.

'Oh God, I don't know – Ellie or Ally or something.'

'He looked down at the photo again: real. He looked up at his girlfriend. Real? Well, yes. In her own way. But was her own way something he admired anymore?

'Anyway,' Saskia continued, oblivious to Henry's sudden road to Damascus moment, 'I'm voting no for that one. Not sure why I left it in.'

Apparently, they didn't need Joel and Annabel to vote on that picture – Saskia whipped it out of Henry's hand and dumped it on the 'no' pile.

'Next! This is a great idea, babe,' she added, reaching over to stroke his arm, 'we're really getting through them. Reckon we'll be finished by ten.'

The touch of her hand on his arm made him feel horribly disloyal. There she was, still the same old Saskia – she'd done nothing wrong, she hadn't changed. She would be stunned if he told her he was having doubts, out of the blue. He wouldn't even be able to explain his feelings clearly, seeing as they weren't clear to him. He'd sleep on it. He was tired. Things might look different in the morning.

The next day, driving into work, Henry thought about Saskia. Taking a step away from their relationship and viewing her through the eyes of a stranger was revelatory. As he drove down Hatton Garden and on to Holborn Circus, his brain shuffled between avoiding head-on collisions with cars flinging themselves across the junction and listing out Saskia's core character traits. Insensitive. Self-absorbed. Shit – nearly drove into the back of a Vauxhall that had pulled up with no warning. God, he was painting such an unattractive picture. She couldn't be that terrible or he never would have been attracted to her in the first place. He thought back to when they'd first met and tried to remember how he'd felt. It was like trying to remind yourself why you'd first made friends with that guy you'd known since school, who all your other, more recent, friends couldn't stand.

He'd just turned thirty when he met Saskia. Single for a couple of years, he was starting to get a niggling feeling that something was missing from his life. He'd been working hard since leaving university, gaining experience at work, establishing his own business and making a success of it. He'd enjoyed working hard and going out and having fun with friends, but now that was all starting to pall. He didn't want to be clubbing every weekend, getting home in the early hours before meeting up with the same people for a hungover brunch the next day. Then, one evening, a friend had invited him to a dinner party. He hadn't suspected it was anything other than your run-of-the-mill weeknight dinner party; but as soon as he'd got there, he could see he'd been set up. There were four couples around the table – and Saskia.

Initial impressions had been good – bright, full of energy, attractive; he forgave the match-making friend before he'd finished his starter. Her passion matched his own. They'd both been working hard at what they believed in. They were driven and enjoying life. Three months down the line and they were already living together. It had made sense – despite her inheritance Saskia hadn't bought a place of her own, she'd been too busy setting up the magazine. The lease was coming up on her flat and his was more than big enough for both of them, so she'd hired a removals truck and had her seventy-two boxes of possessions transported from Kensington to his warehouse conversion in Clerkenwell. Everything seemed right. She introduced him to some of the more avant-garde cultural events London had to offer and he introduced her to Hitchcock, jazz and cricket – with varying success.

On Shaftesbury Avenue the traffic was stop-start and at one point he had to manoeuvre past a broken-down van, coming perilously close to cars in the opposite lane. That obstacle cleared, his thoughts veered back to Saskia. He had been drawn to her drive, but now he wondered whether she was capable of being passionate about anything other than herself. Work wasn't everything; he was proud of his business, but he wanted something else out of life. Helping his brother plan his interviews, Henry had found himself reflecting on his lifestyle and values – and what, ideally, his wife would be like.

At Piccadilly Circus, he stopped at the lights and watched a young, Scandinavian-looking woman in a headscarf cross the road in front of him, one arm cradling the baby in a sling on her front. Children – there was an interesting topic. One of Noblet's criteria for a wife was a desire to start a family. Did Saskia want children? Would she make a good mother? He couldn't imagine it, somehow. He felt like his eyes were blinking open after a long sleep and the light was blinding. However unsure he was about quite what it was he wanted out of life, Saskia didn't seem to fit into any of his vague, unspecified yearnings. Henry wasn't a cruel man and he wasn't indecisive. He may have been drifting along with Saskia unbeknownst to himself for some time, but now he'd seen the light he knew what to do. Glancing in the rear-view mirror he indicated right and turned off Piccadilly towards home.

Saskia was working from home that morning. She'd told him she'd probably be at the flat until about midday, using the peace and quiet to get some final checks done. He knew his timing was dreadful, the last thing she needed was anything distracting her from the magazine deadline, but it couldn't be helped. If he tried to keep how he was feeling to himself she would be able to tell something was wrong. He locked the car and took a deep breath before taking the lift from the underground garage to their flat on the top floor.

Inside, all was quiet. He'd expected to find her at the kitchen table with her laptop, but there was no sign of her. She wasn't in the living area either. Maybe she'd decided to go into work after all. Or maybe she'd overslept.

He pushed the bedroom door open a few inches, not expecting her to be there – and there she was. He went in. She was lying in bed with her face away from him, eyes shut. Something in her attitude made him suspect she wasn't asleep.

'Saskia?'

She fluttered her eyelids and turned towards him, affecting to be waking up. She'd never been a good actress.

'Oh hi, babe. What are you doing here? Did I oversleep?'

'You must have done – it's nine thirty.'

'Nine thirty! Shit! I've gotta get into the office, fuck.'

Something didn't ring true. Henry watched her as she pushed the covers away and scrambled out of bed.

'You never sleep this late. I thought I heard you getting up as I was leaving.'

'No, babe, I must have slept through. Anyway listen, I've gotta get ready now, we'll talk later, yeah? You can tell me what you came home for.'

She was bustling around the room, grabbing bits and pieces of clothing.

'Don't mind me. I'll give you a lift in when you're ready.'

'Oh! Don't worry, babe. I'll get a cab.'

He noticed she'd got a top and some underwear out of the drawers, but seemed reluctant to open the large fitted wardrobe where her skirts and trousers were hanging.

A moment later he thought he understood why. A noise like a muffled sneeze came from inside the wardrobe.

Saskia, it seemed, hadn't heard it as she continued to rifle through a pile of jewellery on the dresser.

'What was that?'

'What, babe?'

'That noise. It sounded like a sneeze.'

Saskia tried to laugh in an offhand way. 'Must have been next door, babe, I didn't hear anything.'

Henry had started to move.

'I'll check.'

'Unless,' Saskia screeched, spinning round and holding out a preventative hand. 'Unless it's my wardrobe declutterer. Oh my God, babe, yes that's what it'll be.'

'Your what?' The words snapped across the room.

'You know, babe. My woman who comes every few months to declutter my wardrobe, get rid of last season's pieces, mend any rips and tears, that kind of thing. She's an angel. Pares things right down so everything's zen again.'

She was relaxing a little now, even coming over to pick a stray piece of thread off the arm of his suit.

'And you're saying,' Henry was speaking very slowly to allow all the words to sink in, 'that she does this – decluttering – in the dark. In the wardrobe. With the doors shut.'

'Uh-huh.' Saskia nodded, eyes wide. 'She's a shaman, man, she has her special ways of being and doing. She finds it calmer in the dark.'

Looking like he would take issue with this statement and then deciding against it, Henry went on, 'And how would she have got in the wardrobe without waking you up? You're not suggesting she's been in there all night, burrowing through your skirts and cardigans?'

Saskia's laugh was forced and shrill. 'No, of course not, babe! No, she's got keys so she can come in while I'm at work. She must have come in, seen that I was asleep and slipped in there without disturbing me.'

Henry could see that Saskia was almost convincing herself now.

'Ah,' he said. 'Well. In that case, I'm going to have to speak to her. I don't want her having keys to the flat.' And before she knew what he was doing he was standing at the wardrobe with the doors open.

Inside, between a kimono and a feather boa, was Joel; naked. After a pause of a year or so, Henry picked up the end of the boa and tapped it against Joel's nose.

'Allergic?'

Joel nodded, then sneezed again.

'Shame.'

Turning to Saskia, he drawled, 'Perhaps you're going to tell me that Joel doubles as your wardrobe declutterer? And that he prefers to work naked because it's good for his aura?'

For a moment Saskia looked like she might be sick, then she dropped onto the bed and rolled her eyes.

'Oh God, babe, tell me you're not going to be bourgeois about this?'

'If it's bourgeois to object to my girlfriend entertaining naked men in our bedroom when I'm out at work then yes, I'm going to be bourgeois about this.'

She plucked stroppily at the bedspread.

'I'm not like you, babe. You know that. I'm a free spirit. A wild thing. Can't you accept me as I am?'

During this exchange, Joel had remained motionless in the wardrobe, one sleeve of the kimono protecting his modesty.

'I don't think Joel needs to be here while we air our dirty laundry. He's spent more than enough time with the clean stuff.' Motioning him out of the wardrobe, Henry stepped back to allow him to pass which he did with alacrity, darting out of the open bedroom door.

'Unless of course, I should be checking for other naked intruders. In the dresser perhaps? Or under the bed?' Getting into his stride, he pulled up the edge of bedspread and crouched down to look underneath.

Annabel was lying naked on the floor. She attempted an apologetic smile.

'Darling?' Henry said, as he let the material fall again. Saskia looked up at him, white-faced. 'Sack the cleaner, would you? I've found something alive under the bed.'

***

'Well,' said Noblet, with a shake of his head. 'I have to admit it, old man, I am surprised.'

The two brothers were sitting once more on the terrace at the back of the Hall, Noblet with a fresh G&T at his elbow, Henry with a glass of white wine. The sun had sunk almost to the horizon, throwing long shadows which revealed every lump and bump in the luminous green lawn. A wood pigeon cooed nearby and Martyr's black-and-white cat was stretched out along the warm, yellow stone of the balustrade.

'Yes,' he confirmed, 'surprised. I knew she was a stupid woman, but to actually pay cold hard cash for some gibbering idiot to come to her home and help herself to perfectly good clothes from the wardrobe! It beggars belief. I don't like to sound hard, Henners, but you're well rid of her.'

Henry opened his mouth to defend her and then remembered that was no longer his responsibility. He'd leave that to Joel. Or maybe Annabel.

'And as for the bedroom antics,' Noblet was continuing, 'that's just adding insult to injury. To think we entertained that little ménage-a-trois under our roof. Goodness knows what was going on right under our noses.'

He looked down as if to check that nothing of that nature was going on under his nose, spotted a stag beetle lurching across the stones by his feet, and crouched down to examine it.

'Funnily enough, the Joel/Annabel thing doesn't bother me,' Henry said. 'I doubt they had much of a choice. Saskia probably added "sex" onto their to-do lists after "making tea" and "proofreading". She always clung to this mental image of herself as a bohemian, and there were certain things she did to reinforce that image. Smoking weed, for example.' He sighed. 'She would have been a much happier person if she'd been able to stick to what her family expected her to do: work in the City for a few years, marry a banker, have a couple of children, move out to the countryside and meet up with friends every day to play tennis and complain about the nannies. After she had her breakdown, she couldn't do that – she needed to prove that she wasn't a failure, and getting married and settling down with kids would have equated to failure in her eyes.'

Henry's phone made a subdued beeping noise.

'Wish you'd leave that in the house, old man. Preferably in the wastepaper basket.'

Henry was reading a message.

'It's from Saskia.'

'Again?'

'Mmmm.'

'She sent one ten minutes ago. What on earth can have happened since then?'

'Nothing's happened, she just wants to speak to me.' He put the phone back on the table. 'But I don't think that's a good idea. I've said all I want to say.'

'That's the spirit! Don't let her wear you down. Before you know it, you'll be yes-Saskia-ing and no-Saskia-ing and bombing back down the motorway for a plate of conciliatory lentils.'

Henry shook his head. 'I know I've made the right decision. She'll be ok once she calms down.'

Shooting an inquisitive glance at the phone, Noblet prompted, 'Getting a bit hysterical, is she?'

'You could say that,' Henry grimaced. 'I won't tell you what she says verbatim, but the gist of it is she's going to call me every hour on the hour until I agree to let her see me.'

'Good God! Yet another reason to throw that piece of devilment in the fire.'

'If I didn't need it for work, I'd be tempted.'

'I feel guilty, old man. You having to help me with these blasted interviews when you've got all this nonsense going on.'

'It'll take my mind off it. Which reminds me, I must talk to Mother later. Make sure she's prepared. It's a week away now.'

'Don't remind me, old chap. So, Mother's happy to be involved now, is she?'

'Jumped at the chance,' said Henry, remembering the good forty minutes he'd put into convincing her. 'She wants to make sure you find the right person.'

Chapter 15

They were heading for London, it seemed. Sitting in the back of Piers' beaten-up BMW, Alice watched the motorway signs flash by. Her planned evening of re-watching *My Fair Lady* for the hundredth time had been interrupted by the unexpected arrival of her sister and her boyfriend.

'We're on a mission of mercy and we're taking no prisoners. Or – in fact – we are taking one prisoner, and that's you!' Piers had announced as soon as she'd let them in; hands on his hips, head thrown back and guffawing like a mediaeval king surrounded by his court.

Cecily took advantage of Piers being engrossed in mediaeval-king-style merriment to explain.

'We were talking about you the other day, Al, and I was saying what a nightmare you've been having with all that rubbish in the papers. We thought you might need cheering up.'

'Ergo,' continued Piers, 'we put on our capes and our underpants on the outside and here we are, SuperPiers and his trusty sidekick to the rescue! Tonight, Cinderella, you shall go to the ball.'

'That's sweet of you both,' said Alice, 'but I'm not up to a big evening out yet.'

'Nonsense!' roared Piers. 'Take her upstairs, Cess, and don't come down until you've rolled her in a bucketful of glitter.'

In the end, it had been easier to give in.

'Enjoying the magical mystery tour so far, Al?' called Piers over his shoulder. Alice pasted on a smile and said yes, she was having a great time. 'Enjoying the eighties tuneage?' Alice said yes, she was very much enjoying the eighties tuneage. 'Ready for the night of your life?' Alice said she couldn't honestly say she was ready for the night of her life, but she was very grateful to them for taking her out.

'No problemo, Alster! Kill two birds with one stone whenever the occasion arises, that's my motto. I wanted to check out this gig anyway and catch up with some of my hombres, and when Cess told me about all the shit you've had thrown at you I said hey, babe, we're going to take that sister of yours with us and we're going to show her a fucking good time! Yeah!' Piers' excitement had risen to such a pitch that he punched the air and swerved into the next lane, earning himself a sustained beeping from the alarmed Renault Clio to his left.

When her heart had stopped trying to hammer its way out through her chest, Alice ventured, 'So we're going to a gig?'

'Damn!' Piers was crestfallen. 'Oh, damn it to hell, Cess, I said I'd keep to myself and I've messed up! Damn it all to fucking hell!'

Cecily reached over and squeezed his arm. 'It's alright, it doesn't matter! She still doesn't know who we're going to see, do you, Al?'

Alice shook her head earnestly.

'No, no it's ruined now,' fumed Piers. 'The secret's out and it's all my fault. I might as well come right out and say we're going to see The Proxy and it was going to be a big surprise because you had them at your party and you were going to walk in not knowing what to expect and you'd be all like "wow, yeah, it's The Proxy!" and we'd be like "Yeah!" and you'd be like "Oh my God!". But now it's all turned to shit. Typical fucking Piers and his big fucking mouth. Barely any point in going now.' He put his foot down, glared at the road and refused to be comforted by anyone.

In a heaving bar a couple of doors down from the club where The Proxy would be playing, Alice obediently downed tequila shots, trying not to gag on the salt and lemon. Cecily had taken Piers to one side and talked him out of his mood, and he was now more upbeat than ever.

'Down it! Down it! Down it! Yeah! That's the spirit, sis! Arriba, arriba! Get those shots inside you!' He gave her shoulder a playful shove, sending her careering into a man and splashing drink all down his shirt. 'Nothing like tequila to get you in the mood for a Par-Tay! Wooh!'

Despite the forced jollity, Alice was having a hard time pretending to enjoy herself. The music was far too loud, she found herself thinking – feeling very middle-aged – and she didn't recognise any of the songs. There was nowhere to sit and people kept shoving her in the back on the way to the bar. She hadn't eaten anything and was feeling faint.

They headed over to the gig. The queue snaked from the door of the club right down the road and round the corner. Everyone looked ultra-cool and edgy and Alice found herself feeling a bit provincial in her jeans, black heels and sparkly party top. In Gently Rising her look would have been considered chic, but here she looked like she'd ram-raided Next on her way over. Resigning herself to a long wait in the queue, she was surprised and horrified to see Piers marching past everyone and planting himself in front of the bouncers. She tugged at Cecily's sleeve.

'What's he doing? The back of the queue's way over there.'

Cecily threw a fond glance at Piers. 'Don't worry – come on.'

They followed him to the front in time to see one of the bouncers check something on his clipboard, nod curtly and step aside to let them through. Inside, Piers explained.

'My firm's got the ad account for their record label. I pulled a few strings, got us VIP backstage passes. Only the best for you, Alster!'

And then they couldn't say any more because the crowd went wild as lead singer Luc appeared on stage, followed by the rest of The Proxy.

***

A luminous pink skeleton, which reminded Alice of Sinead Dumper in her PVC jumpsuit, hung from the ceiling. Huge, squishy leather sofas were draped with people drinking and smoking. Vast floor-to-ceiling windows revealed the glittering London skyline – she picked out St. Pauls, the Gherkin and even the London Eye in the distance. Alex and Rollo were having a friendly dispute about something which had gone wrong in the set, both picking out chords on their instruments to demonstrate their point. Luc sat on a barstool at the counter of the huge open plan kitchen, reading a slim volume of what looked like poetry and drinking orange juice from the carton.

A voice beside her said, 'Are you wishing you hadn't come?'

She turned round to find Stein Avery grinning at her. Feeling a little starstruck – after all, she'd just watched him being screamed at by hundreds of adoring fans – she shook her head and said, 'Oh, no! No, it's great.'

He shook his head at her. 'You don't have to say that. They're pretty boring, these aftershow parties. Luc always insists on inviting a load of strangers back to his place and then ignores them for the rest of the evening. Here, have some of this.' He proffered the cardboard box of pizza he'd been helping himself to. 'I bet you haven't eaten for hours.'

Alice took a slice. 'Thanks,' she mumbled through ham and mushrooms.

'So, you came with that guy Piers?'

She nodded, still chewing.

'Known him long?'

'A couple of months. He's going out with my sister, Cecily.' She pointed out Cecily perched on the arm of a sofa looking out of place and watching Piers, who lay on the floor challenging a succession of tattooed and dreadlocked opponents to arm-wrestle.

'She looks besotted,' remarked Stein. 'Like she'd do anything for him. Lucky guy,' he added, with a sigh. 'Bit sorry for myself. Split up with my girlfriend a couple of weeks ago. We were all set for a tour in America when the deal broke down – record companies can't take any risks these days and no one's guaranteed to make it in the States. Anyway, she thought we were set for the big time and when she heard about the cancellation she upped and left. I heard yesterday she's started hanging around with The Cross Fires – obviously thinks they've got a better chance of superstardom.'

'But you're already famous, aren't you?' questioned Alice. 'I mean, I hadn't heard of The Proxy but then I don't know anything about music. Mia says you're the hottest band around.'

'Mia Wild?'

'Yes – she organised for you to come and play at my birthday party a couple of weeks ago. In Mereshire,' she added when he continued to look blank.

'Oh, that weird gig in the village. Sorry, I didn't recognise you.'

Why would you? thought Alice.

'Yeah, that was a bit of a crazy one,' he went on. 'You know some madwoman splashed red paint all over me?' He grinned. 'I've heard of people throwing knickers, but paint's a new one.'

He was very nice, for a rock star, Alice thought.

'Can I get you a drink?' Stein asked.

Alice looked down at her mug of tepid white wine. 'Erm…'

'Not that rubbish. That's for the freeloaders and the groupies. Come on, I'll make you a Stein Special.'

A Stein Special, it turned out, involved digging around in a James Bond-style secret cocktail cabinet hidden behind bookshelves in Luc's study and mixing blue curacao, grappa, angostura bitters, Grand Marnier and a sugar cube.

'And there we have it, ladies and gentlemen, the Stein Special. What makes it special,' he informed her, 'is that it's never the same recipe twice. Down the hatch.'

Alice took a sip, prepared to grimace, and then took another, bigger sip. 'It's actually quite nice,' she said, surprised.

'What do you mean, "actually quite nice"?' he demanded as he led her outside onto the balcony overlooking the city. 'You sound surprised. Almost as if you think I don't know what I'm doing.'

'Almost.' Alice agreed, smiling at him as she took another sip. Gosh, he was nice. So nice, that with a few well-chosen questions on his part she found she was confiding in him – everything from her quiet life in Gently Rising, to Mia arriving, Lord de Beeble's newspaper advert, her party, the tabloid story, the interview at the village hall and finally, Cecily and Piers hauling her up to London to take her mind off things. It took quite some time and they were down to the dregs of their Stein Specials when she'd finished.

She noticed and said, 'God, sorry. I've really been banging on. When stuff's been playing on your mind you forget that it's boring for other people.'

'It's not boring at all. You've had a pretty shit time by the sounds of it.'

'So have you. Tell me about your girlfriend – how long had you been going out?'

Stein stood up, taking their empty glasses from the table. 'I'll give you the full lowdown – once I've topped us up. We're both going to need some super-strength Specials to make it through a blow-by-blow account of me and Millie.'

Chapter 16

In Mereshire, a trespasser had snuck into the grounds of de Beeble Hall. The interloper was covered from head to toe in camouflage gear, allowing her to slip unnoticed through the trees while also working some totally fashion-forward squaddie chic. Her trainers made no noise as she tiptoed to the very fringes of the wood that bordered the formal gardens behind the house. Despite the lateness of the hour, several windows were still lit up on three of the four floors. One of the full-length windows at the far right of the house was open onto the terrace, and she thought she could hear the tap of a computer keyboard.

She counted the windows across from the left on the second floor. There, that was the one. Wasn't it? A light shone through a sliver in the curtains, but even as she watched it was extinguished. He was preparing to sleep. Would he dream of her? God knew she'd dreamt of him enough times since he'd left, over a week ago now. That was when she could get to sleep, which wasn't often, no matter how many drops of valerian she took, not to mention the whale songs on her Sonos. They belonged together – it was written in the moon and the stars. Even the spirits had confirmed that they should be together, via the most expensive new spiritualist in London, Susannah Windle. Two thousand pounds had been a small price to pay to discover that one day they would be reunited and, what was more, the spirits positively encouraged her to hasten that day's arrival. He didn't pick up the phone when she rang and, according to the read receipts, didn't read her WhatsApps. If Mohammed wouldn't come to the mountain, the mountain would hire a Ferrari at great expense, speed down motorways and A roads, dump the Ferrari in the village, get covered in cobwebs and God knows what else, and gaze up at a window which may, or may not, be his.

But she had not come to stand and gaze. No way, man. She needed to convince him she loved him and would never again betray him. (If he considered a little thing like a friendly threesome a betrayal. Totally suburban, but she'd let it go.) She had come in search of an ally.

***

In London, things had gone a little hazy and soft around the edges. Piers had stood up at about 3 a.m. and declared himself ready to drive them all home, before blinking twice and keeling over like a felled redwood. Cecily had found a small unoccupied bedroom and managed to heave him into it with the help of Rollo and Alex. No one had seen Alice or Stein for some time.

Up on the roof, Stein was pointing out various landmarks. Alice was very aware of his arm round her waist.

'That's the office building in the City where I worked for a couple of years before jacking it in to go full-time with the band. There's Liverpool Street station. I used to get the Tube into there for work when I was still living out with the pazzers in Epping Forest. That's the big roundabout by Old Street station – beyond it, past that tower block, is the pub where we had our first proper gig.

'And this,' he said, turning to face Alice, 'is the rooftop where I kissed a lovely girl called Alice.' As he drew her towards him, she almost resisted but at the last moment gave in to a rush of excitement and anticipation as his lips touched hers. And if there weren't quite banks of fireworks going off, there were one or two sparklers and perhaps a small Catherine wheel.

***

At the sight of a figure in camouflage gear and a balaclava sidling up to him with one finger to its lips, all Derek's security training kicked in.

'Wha' the...?' he exclaimed, while scratching his head and letting his jaw hang open. A second or two later he'd grabbed the intruder round the neck and was attempting to operate his walkie-talkie with his free hand.

'Shhh!' hissed his prisoner. 'It's me, man! Take my balaclava off!'

He did so, ignoring her squeals that he was pulling her hair. She looked at him, eyebrows raised. He looked blank.

'It's me, Saskia Stonor! Henry de Beeble's girlfriend! You've seen me around the place loads of times.'

He shrugged. She couldn't help noticing that he bore a striking resemblance to a hippo.

'And...' she added reluctantly, 'you threw me out of the party at the village hall.'

He turned her round to face the light. 'Urr!' he agreed, 'the ejection.'

'Yeah, man, whatever. But you know who I am now, right?'

'Yurr.'

'You've seen me around the place.'

'Yurr.'

'OK, fantastic. Now listen, babe, I've got a favour to ask.'

Derek looked guarded. 'Yurr?'

'Yurr – I mean yeah.' For her plan to succeed she had to hope that Derek hadn't been privy to news of the break-up. 'It's mine and Henry's anniversary coming up next week, and I want to make a big deal of it. I'm stuck in London working and Henry's down here so I want to arrange lots of special gifts and surprises for him. So, I need someone here to help me deliver stuff, you know?'

Derek still looked unsure.

'Someone discreet, who can keep a secret.'

Derek continued looking unsure until a wad of fifty-pound notes was pressed into his hand. He wavered for a moment. Was it unprofessional to accept money from his boss's girlfriend? It couldn't harm, could it? The thought of all the gerberas he could buy Sinead with the cash clinched it. He pocketed the wad of notes.

'Well done, babe, there's plenty more where that came from.'

She led him off the terrace and into the shadows.

'This is what I need you to do…'

***

How to Bag Yourself a Rock Star – Ten Top Tips by Alice Brand:

1. Play it cool. When he asks you back to his place, respond coquettishly, 'I'd love to'. Do NOT say you'll need to check with your sister.
2. If you feel he's taking things too fast, say so. Do NOT make up excuses involving fungal infections.
3. Avoid drinking so much that you wake in the middle of the night to discover you've been sick over the edge of the bed.
4. Should the aforementioned vomiting take place, do NOT compound matters by trying to clear it up with the nearest thing to hand. In case the nearest thing to hand happens to be the Rock Star's favourite T-shirt.
5. Should point 3 and 4 unhappily both occur, do NOT attempt to creep out of the flat like a thief in the night. Have more faith in the Rock Star's good nature.

6. When the Rock Star persuades you to stay and offers to make you breakfast, DO mention that the smell of bacon may make you feel sick again.

7. If the Rock Star should ask for your number, jot down EITHER home, work or mobile.

8. Arrange for your sister's boyfriend to pick you up some distance from the Rock Star's flat, to avoid him yelling across a crowded street, 'Look who it is! Little Alice "bury me in a Y-shaped coffin" Brand!'

9. Do remember to pack earplugs in order to drown out the sound of your sister's boyfriend singing, all the way down the M4, 'Alster and Avery up a tree, k-i-s-s-i-n-g'.

10. Do remember that pretending to read your book in an attempt to avoid speaking to said sister's boyfriend is a sure-fire route to further vomiting.

**

It was the week that would be forever engraved in Henry's mind as the Seven Days of Weirdness.

'On the First Day of Weirdness, my true love gave to me/
A sheaf of illegible scrawl.'

He read the first three pages of the wad of paper which sat, ominously, outside his bedroom door that Sunday morning, and took an educated guess that the remaining twenty-five contained more of the same. Summarising it for Noblet's benefit over breakfast, he described it as a love letter seasoned with resentment.

'I never thought Saskia would react like this. It's madness.'

'She is mad,' Noblet pointed out. 'The woman has somehow infiltrated our staff in order to have her stream of consciousness delivered to your bedroom door.'

'That's the oddest part. How did it get there?'

Lady Caroline, who had joined them, asked, 'Have you asked Sally? Sally will know.'

Henry shook his head. 'She's stumped too.'

'Have her round everybody up, force it out of them.'

'Already done. No one's owning up.'

'Have them whipped.'

'Yes, Mother. Excellent suggestion.'

'Soon have them talking.'

'Talking, screaming, suing…'

'It does seem ridiculous, old chap,' said Noblet through a mouthful of scrambled egg, 'when we've got these security fellows pounding the terraces, that the wacko somehow still got in. Can't believe nobody saw a thing.'

'And yet that's what they claim.'

'Ask Saskia how she did it,' suggested Noblet.

'No,' Henry said, firmly. 'That would mean opening up the channels of communication again. Exactly what I don't want to do.'

'See what you mean, old man. Negotiating with terrorists.'

'A little extreme, but that's the gist.'

'Poor dear Saskia. I never would have thought it of her. So undignified,' sighed Lady Caroline.

'I would,' declared Noblet. 'Anyone who cavorts around the lawn in a leotard has no notion of dignity.'

'I think,' pursued Henry, 'unless anyone decides to make a clean breast of it, I'll have to let it go. She's made her point, hopefully that will be the end of it.'

'On the Second Day of Weirdness my true love gave to me/
A gold-plated vial and a sheaf of illegible scrawl.'

The beautifully-wrapped box was waiting for him when Henry opened his bedroom door on Monday morning. He found himself instinctively looking down as he exited the room

– and yet it still gave him a jolt to see the blue and silver wrapping and another wodge of paper covered in Saskia's huge, looping handwriting. He sighed and carried box and papers down to breakfast with him.

Noblet was there before him, one hand shovelling in sausage, the other holding open the pages of a paperback. As soon as he'd swallowed, he accosted Henry.

'It makes my blood boil! Three typos – and I'm being generous in calling them typos, you understand, I'm giving them the benefit of the doubt that they know how to spell – three typos and I'm only a hundred pages in. I mean to say, is it not worth their while to read the text with a modicum of care? Perhaps it was a rush job, I hear you ask? Perhaps, yes! After all, it's been a mere matter of a hundred and sixty years since the thing was written.'

'Collins?' ventured Henry.

'Collins! I think not. I dare them to publish a new edition of Collins with so much as a page number askew. I have written to every publisher of every Collins novel and listed the errors in order that never again may the readers of that genius suffer from an editorial oversight. No, this is Dickens. Oh, yes!' Splashing coffee all over the tablecloth as he gestured at the book. 'Merely the Master, Dickens!'

With his brother's blood pressure in mind, Henry changed the subject. Placing the box on the table beside his plate, he said, 'Not quite as noteworthy as an error in a Dickens novel, but I've had another delivery.'

It had the desired effect. Noblet put down his book.

'What is it?'

'I haven't opened it yet.'

'Well open it, man, open it. And stand back, one never knows what that degenerate might have sent you. Dynamite. Anthrax. Could be anything.'

Henry undid the ribbon. Pulling off the lid he found, nestling in swathes of silver tissue paper, a gold-plated bottle engraved with his initials. Noblet craned his neck to see.

'Well? What is it?'

Henry held up the bottle.

'What's inside?'

'I'm not sure I want to know.' Picking up the sheaf of papers, he read the first few lines and then dropped the bottle back onto the tissue.

'It's blood.'

'Whose?'

'Hers, apparently.'

Henry scanned some more of Saskia's letter.

'She says she's been to see a shaman-slash-oracle, in Kensington – of course, where else would you go to find a shaman-slash-oracle? – and he told her that if I could be persuaded to intermingle a little of my blood with her own, my negative energy would drain away and the true path of my destiny would reveal itself. I don't mind telling you, Bob, I feel pretty guilty about all this. I think she's having a breakdown.'

Noblet waggled a finger at him. 'That's what she wants, old man – for you to crumble. You've got to be cruel to be kind, Henners – keep a stiff upper lip and before you know it, she'll have forgotten all about you and be living in a commune with sixty organic lesbians. Or something like that – you take my meaning.'

Henry packed the box up again gingerly.

'I think I'll return the letters and this to her without a message. You're right, Bob, consistency is the key.'

175

On Tuesday, Wednesday, Thursday and Friday mornings more gifts appeared for Henry, no longer outside his bedroom door where a security guard had been put on watch, but instead in various places around the house and grounds. Each time Henry would pack the letter and gifts up and return them to Saskia, receiving in return a bombardment of aggrieved text messages and voicemails.

On Saturday morning, the day of the second-round interviews, no gift or letter appeared. Henry breathed a sigh of relief. Perhaps Saskia had got the message.

Chapter 17

The week before the interviews was a dreary one to Alice. The initial euphoria of her encounter with Stein had worn off and she was left deflated and sad. Stein wasn't someone she had strong feelings for; he was just a nice enough man who had shown her some timely attention. On Monday she got a text from him, a breezy bit of nonsense, and she replied in a similar vein. Work seemed to drag and in the long evenings, she would sit alone, trying to occupy herself with a book, TV, cooking: anything that could distract her for a short while from feeling flat. Added to this was the looming interview. She'd promised herself she would do it and to back out now would be cowardly, but it was the last thing she needed. Particularly after a strange conversation with Sinead in the community shop which increased her apprehensions.

Sinead had volunteered for more and more shifts in the shop recently. Almost every time Alice popped in, she seemed to be behind the counter, immaculately made up and flicking through a copy of *Hello!* or *Country Life*. Alice felt her heart sink whenever she caught sight of the sleek blonde head over the top of a magazine. Sinead had a habit of picking up Alice's purchases with the tips of her fingers, a sneer on her face, as she tapped the price into the low-tech till. Several times Alice had popped in to buy a ready-meal but at the last minute had come out with cashew milk and tempeh.

Today, however, she was determined to come out of the shop with what she'd gone in for. It was Friday evening, she was tired, and she was going to treat herself to a high-fat, low-fibre, fully-salted ready-meal for one. She was going to eat it in front of *Pretty Woman* with a box of Ferrero Rocher to follow.

She marched over to the ready-meal section and made her selection. Sinead's beady eyes followed her round the shop as she picked up the chocolates and a bottle of wine. When Alice arrived at the counter and presented her purchases, Sinead's eyebrows had disappeared under her glossy fringe.

'Treating ourselves?' she enquired.

'Yes,' Alice agreed, trying to keep the defensiveness out of her voice. 'It's Friday night, after all.'

'Exactly. Saturday tomorrow,' Sinead replied, looking as if this should mean something very particular.

'Ye-es.'

'The interviews. Hear you've been invited back.' Whether Alice's progression to the second round had been via a clerical error or temporary insanity on the part of Noblet de Beeble wasn't clear. That it must be one or the other, was.

'Yes, the interviews,' echoed Alice, wishing Sinead would tot up the offending items and let her escape.

'Need to be alert. On top form.' Sinead paused and let her eyes linger on the chocolate and wine. 'Looking our best. No extra pounds.'

Alice stared at her. Even for Sinead, this was unsurpassed rudeness.

Glancing up and seeming to reflect that she had gone too far, Sinead continued. 'Going to be a long day. Need to be in peak condition.'

'How do you know it's going to be a long day? All they said to me on the phone was to be there at ten and that lunch would be provided.'

'Little bird told me.'

'Oh.'

'Mmm. Could be there for hours. Strenuous.'

'Really? What kind of things are they going to ask us to do?'

Sinead began jabbing at buttons on the till and hurling Alice's shopping into her reusable bag.

'Couldn't say. No idea. Sixteen pounds forty.'

Alice handed over a twenty-pound note, took her change and left, clutching her bag of indulgences.

Her enjoyment of film, ready-meal, chocolates and wine was marred by Sinead's words echoing round her brain. Strenuous, she'd said. A long day. Be alert. Why was she putting herself through it?

In homes around the country that Friday evening, many women – and some men – were echoing Alice's words, or some approximation of them, not least, Noblet de Beeble.

**

On the way back from Morocco, Mia stopped off in the South of France to catch up with some old friends. At the moment when Alice was braving Sinead in the community shop, Mia was leaning back in her chair, glass of wine in hand, watching the sun sink behind distant hills. The long, rickety table had been laid in the orchard behind the rambling old farmhouse. As darkness fell, candles were lit to allow the twenty or so guests to continue their conversations as they lingered around the remnants of a hearty meal. Helping herself to a piece of cheese, Mia smiled across at her neighbour.

'This is what I miss.'

'I'm not surprised, my dear. Tasteless, mass-produced cheddar is no substitute for good French cheese.'

'Not the cheese, you nincompoop. The atmosphere. People who know how to live. You.'

The older woman took her hand. 'I'm here whenever you want me.' She stroked Mia's cheek with soft fingertips and smiled. Then, from a bag on the floor, she brought out an old photograph. 'There. Is that the one you wanted?'

Mia looked at it for a moment and nodded. 'Thank you. I hope I won't need it.'

***

Alice stood before the full-length mirror and tried to look at herself objectively. This dress made her look fat. That much was certain. However, this dress also looked something like her conception of what the upper classes wore. It was a demure shift dress, in thick silk patterned with bunches of pale blue flowers on a cream background. She'd bought it for a wedding but never worn it, having decided on getting it home that it was too unflattering. She'd ended up in her old fail-safe, faded, black A-line skirt with cream silk top and pearls (fake). Alice took the dress off. It was too hideous, even if it did make her look posher. She reached into the wardrobe for another rarely-worn outfit.

Two hours later, she raced out of the house in her old fail-safe, faded, black A-line skirt with cream silk top and pearls (fake). Mia was waiting in the lane in a vintage Jaguar.

'What a lovely car,' gasped Alice as she climbed into the passenger seat.

'I borrowed it.'

'Who from?'

'I didn't catch the name. How are you feeling?'

'Nervous.'

'I'll bet you anything you like Noblet de Beeble feels worse.'

***

Noblet wasn't feeling nervous. He was feeling distraught.

'Why am I doing this? Why? What kind of an infernal, wrong-headed, madman am I? They ought to take people like me and lock us away in padded cells for our own safety. God knows why they don't. It's irresponsible.'

Sally, to whom this tirade was directed as she attempted to smooth the lumpy knot in Noblet's tie, tutted.

'You know, this is all Henry's fault,' he continued. 'If it had been left to me, we would have had a few sackfuls of post to trawl through, yes, but letters I can deal with. But no! He has to be clever about it. "Invite the many-headed beast to our home," he says! "Tart yourself up," he says! "Parade yourself about like a prize pig," he says!'

'I'm sure he said nothing of the sort,' frowned Sally.

'He might as well have done, because look what it's come to. Me, quaking in my boots, about to receive into the sanctuary of my home hundreds of strange women as if I'm some kind of – of – sultan recruiting his harem. It's not dignified, Sally. Goddammit, it's not English!'

Finishing the tie with a final jerk, Sally gave a couple of brisk brushes and slaps to Noblet's shoulders and shirt front.

'Quite presentable. Well,' she added under her breath, 'better than usual anyway.' Clipping off the head of a white rose she stuck it into his buttonhole. 'There. Very smart. Now don't stay up here too long, they'll start arriving any minute. Shoulders back and face them like a man.' With one final, rather hard, slap on the solar plexus, she was gone.

Noblet looked at himself in the mirror. 'And the most ridiculous thing of all is, I don't even want to get married.' He ruminated for a moment. 'Perhaps none of them will do. Yes, that's a thought. Mother will dismiss all the applicants, agree that I did my best and we can all settle back to how things were before. I can carry on writing undisturbed. After all, I have just embarked on that rather gripping deconstruction of his attack on Walford…'

When Henry popped his head round the door fifteen minutes later, he found his brother sitting at his desk, scribbling furiously, ink all over one of his cuffs.

'Bob?'

'Yes?'

'You're on.'

'Oh, dear.'

'Courage, Bob!'

Noblet screwed the top on his pen and stood up. 'I'm ready, Henners. My upper lip is, I can confirm, stiff. Lead the way.'

Chapter 18

As he descended the great sweeping staircase, what seemed like several thousand faces turned, as one, towards him. Rows of chairs had been set out in the large entrance hall; chairs which now held eager and excited applicants.

'Good God!' croaked Noblet out of the corner of his mouth. 'How many are there?'

'Fifty-four. Forty-nine women and five men.'

'Is that all? Looks like ten times as many.'

'Don't panic. Stay calm and take your time.'

'Easy for you to say.'

'Just a couple of welcoming words. Keep it brief,' Henry murmured as they reached the bottom of the stairs.

There was silence as Noblet made his way to the top of the room.

'Ahem!' he began, looking flushed and uncomfortable. He wrung his hands together, registered that they were clammy and wiped his palms on the front of his trousers. 'Ahem. Yes.' In an effort to sound confident, he roared, 'Welcome!' One or two in the front row flinched. 'Welcome,' he repeated in a stage whisper.

Looking round the room in some desperation he saw, above the heads of the interviewees, his mother's sardonic face as she watched from a doorway. There was an awkward silence. One or two people coughed and someone dropped a handbag with a clatter. He'd had a week to think about what to say, why hadn't he planned something? He began to say 'ahem' again, realised he'd already said that twice and changed it halfway through.

'A… ha! Yes, a-ha! There you all are!'

He beamed at them. He'd carried that off rather neatly, he felt.

He'd try it again. 'A-ha-ha-ha!'

Out of the corner of his eye, he saw Henry drawing a finger across his throat.

'And that about wraps things up, I think. My brother, Henry!' He finished with a flourish, before beating a hasty retreat.

Henry stepped forward and smiled at the audience.

'Good morning and thank you all for coming. First up, we're going to divide you into groups of five or six for the first activity, which is a balloon debate. We'll reassemble here at eleven o'clock for the next exercise.' He signalled to his team of helpers who stepped forward and organised the interviewees, leading them off to different parts of the Hall.

When the room had cleared, Lady Caroline's voice rang out across the hall.

'Congratulations, Nobby. Henry's been looking for ways to whittle down the number of your potential wives. Portraying yourself as a tongue-tied halfwit ought to do it.'

'Thank you for your loyal support, as ever, Mother.'

'And of course, if we discover any really promising girls who would benefit from elocution lessons, we know we can rely on you, with your innovative system of "ahems" and "a-has".'

Before Noblet could retaliate, Henry stepped in. 'I need you to make your way round to the different groups and observe, Bob. Take notes. I'll be doing the same. Mother...'

'I,' she cut in, 'will be in my old sitting room upstairs if anyone wants me. I said I would help, Henry. I did not say I would traipse around with a clipboard noting down the inane bleatings of a flock of sex-starved women.'

'Sex-starved?' Noblet looked horrified. 'What a thing to say, Mother.'

Lady Caroline crossed the hall to the staircase. 'I know a sex-starved woman – and man – when I see one. And I've never seen so many in one place before.'

When she was out of earshot Noblet turned to Henry. 'I told you. Didn't I tell you, Henners? Going loopy.'

'You're forgetting. She's always been like that. Come on – I need to get back in there, why don't you start with the group in the summer house?'

***

The group of applicants in the summer house included Sinead, who had spent hours researching balloon debates and was praying to be Mother Teresa.

'...and so,' the young woman facilitating was saying as Noblet inched his way through the door, 'you will need to present a compelling argument why you shouldn't be thrown out of the hot air balloon.'

Turning and seeing a startled look on Noblet's face, the woman smiled. 'Your Lordship – I was explaining the rules of a balloon debate. It's a hypothetical situation where the group imagines they are in a hot air balloon which is rapidly losing height. Someone has to be thrown out in order to save the rest. Each person takes on the role of a different historical character and tries to persuade the others why they shouldn't be the one to go. So – for example, if one of the characters were Charles Darwin, he could argue that the world would remain in ignorance about evolutionary theory should he die.'

'Oh yes, yes,' mumbled Noblet. 'I do remember my brother mentioning something about that. Carry on. I'll sit back here with a cup of tea.'

The facilitator invited the group to pick names out of a hat. Sinead opened hers and almost had to stop herself from punching the air: 'Mother Teresa'. She sat back, feeling smug. There was no way she'd be thrown out of the balloon. Once everyone had picked a slip of paper and had a few moments to think about their arguments, the facilitator invited them to begin. A thirty-something, well-groomed woman in a chic suit went first. She had been given Shakespeare and spoke eloquently of the eradication of the most sublime beauties of the English tongue should she be the loser. The next applicant had drawn a short straw with Diego Maradona, but she did her best, waxing lyrical about sporting genius and the social impact of football. Next up was Sinead. Noblet had finished his cup of tea and was about to slip out and move on to another group when he found his gaze arrested by the gimlet eye of the Irish woman who knew so much about Collins. She smiled and proceeded to direct her speech exclusively at him.

'Mother Teresa. Can't throw her off. Almost as good as Jesus. Or God. Gave her money away. Don't remember Shakespeare doing that. Got to think logically too. Old woman, small, light – should throw off someone heavy like Maradona.' She concluded, crossed her legs with an air of triumph, remembered that she was in public and swiftly uncrossed them, staring deep into Noblet's eyes all the while.

Noblet swallowed and managed to tear his eyes away. After an uncomfortable pause, the debate continued and he made his escape.

In other parts of the house, debates of varying levels of eloquence were raging. Noblet wandered from one to another, occasionally making a note such as 'Ginny – too much make-up' or 'Sarah – annoying laugh'. After half an hour he was hungry and ambled into the kitchen to see what he could find. A team of catering staff were preparing lunch with Martyr at the helm. As soon as she saw Noblet she barked, 'Hands off! This is for lunch.'

Noblet looked hurt. 'But I'm half-starved, Martyr. I couldn't eat any breakfast; I was too nervous.'

She shooed him towards the pantry. 'There's a pie and some cold meats in the small fridge and bread in the bin. Just don't touch anything in here. I've enough to do as it is!' Bustling off to berate a sous-chef for some misshapen julienne vegetables, she left Noblet to fend for himself in the pantry. Taking a napkin from the drawer, he loaded it up with a large slice of chicken pie and a couple of ham sandwiches. As he turned to leave, he heard the sound of the key in the lock and found himself face to face with an intruder.

'Who the devil…?' And then he remembered. He had met this particular crazy-eyed lunatic before.

'Yes, Your Majesty, and so I thought it would be nice to have a chat in here. Cosy. Seeing as they forgot the invitation.'

'Forgot…? Invitation…?'

'They must have meant to invite me. I'm a relation of George the Third. Bloodlines – they wouldn't have let me slip through their net. Your people, you know. Who organised it. So I thought I'd pop in and we could do it on our own somewhere.'

The blood drained from Noblet's face.

'Mind if I sit down?' he asked, and without waiting for an answer, slid to the floor.

'Keep your strength up,' Lorraine admonished, nodding her head at the napkin of food still clutched in his hand.

Noblet looked unseeingly at the pie for a moment and then inserted it into his mouth and chewed. He had to do something. Call for help. Or faint. But right now, all he could manage was to eat his pie.

'Right, Your Honour,' Lorraine trilled as she settled herself on the floor opposite him, her yellow-legging-clad legs stretched out in front of her, 'what would you like to know?'

'Know?' Noblet echoed through a mouthful of pie.

Lorraine laughed and reached forward to pinch his cheek. 'Silly-billy! You need to know something about me before the wedding. Can't wait till afterwards.'

Gulping down the remnants of the pie, Noblet moved on to the ham sandwich.

'Like a nice sandwich, do you?' she asked. 'I like sandwiches.'

'Ever found yourself short of a few at a picnic?' Noblet enquired between bites. He was starting to get reckless. Here he was, locked in a pantry with a madwoman. She would probably leap up and smack him round the head with a leg of lamb at any moment; he had nothing to lose.

'Picnic in your lovely garden – we could do that one day. How about tomorrow? I'm free tomorrow.'

'Tomorrow! Yes, why not?' agreed Noblet. 'I'll bring the port and cocktail sausages; you bring a sherry trifle. We'll invite the Queen and the Dalai Lama.'

Reaching over and taking one of his sandwiches, Lorraine thrust it into her mouth and chewed at him before responding. 'The Dalarama? He's a foreigner. Don't want any outsiders at our picnic, Your Graceship. You leave the invites to me. We'll have the Queen, if she's free, and the Prince of Charles. And his wife though she's a no-knickered hussy if ever I saw one. What else?'

'What else?'

'What else do you want to know?'

Could he perhaps spring up and smash his way out through the window? He could scream for help but she wouldn't like that and who knew what kind of a bloodied mess they'd find when they got the door open. He had to play for time.

'Questions, questions… Right. What, erm, what star sign are you?'

'Jupiter.'

'Excellent – most compatible with Aquarius. That's mine, I believe.'

'Aquariums.'

'Aquarius.'

'No,' Lorraine insisted, 'the plural of aquarium is aquariums. I know because I had one myself in 1983 to keep my mussel collection in. You like them too, eh? You must be Pisces, that's the sign of the fish.'

'Exactly so.'

'Next?'

He noticed she'd absent-mindedly put the key down on the floor beside her.

'Who is your favourite author?'

'I love reading. Read all the time. Speed read. Yesterday I read seventeen books. I speed write too. I'll show you if you like. Need some paper…'

'Right!' Shooting up like a jack-in-the-box, Noblet grabbed the key and was over to the door in a flash and unlocking it. 'Let's go and find some paper!'

Darting out he ran straight into Henry.

'There you are!' Henry expostulated. 'I've had people searching all over for you.'

'Well,' Noblet retorted, making extraordinary grimaces as he motioned towards Lorraine who had emerged from the pantry, 'I've been otherwise occupied. In the pantry. With the door locked.'

'Mrs… Watford, isn't it?' said Henry, surprised.

She curtseyed. 'Yes'm.'

Henry said 'Kitchen' into his walkie-talkie and then smiled at Lorraine. 'I hope you found everything you needed?'

'Most accommodating, thank you.'

'Excellent. This is Derek,' as Derek barrelled into the kitchen, his face darkening when he recognised Lorraine, 'and he will escort you on a private tour of the grounds terminating at the gate. I hope you enjoy it.'

'So gentle. Such nice teeth,' Lorraine enthused before curtseying once more and allowing herself to be led away.

Noblet was enraged. 'Is this what we pay all these so-called security guards for? To hand dangerous criminals our pantry keys and tell them to get on with it? Abducting and imprisoning willy-nilly?'

Henry looked grim. 'Believe me, Bob, once today is over I'll be reviewing our security arrangements. After Saskia's deliveries, this is the icing on the cake. Sit down here and I'll get you a cup of tea. Once you've had that come and join us – we'll be in the blue drawing room,' he called as he headed out of the kitchen.

***

Henry should have stuck to the day job. He found the whole event more stressful than he'd expected, what with attention-seeking applicants, the security lapse and his mother's lack of cooperation. At least he hadn't had to deal with any more Saskia-related oddness. When he entered the blue drawing room, he was pleased to find his mother ensconced in a chair at the top of the room, as requested via Sally a few minutes previously. He stood beside her and called for attention. The room fell silent as the rows of applicants stopped chattering and turned to face him.

'I hope you all enjoyed the balloon debate and have had chance to take a quick break. I'd like to explain the next – and final – exercise of the day.'

A puzzled murmur rippled round the room. Only one more exercise?

'I have asked my mother, Lady Caroline, to join my brother and me in judging the next activity. We would like each of you to reflect on a skill you have, which perhaps sets you apart from others, and which would be useful as the wife of Lord de Beeble. We would then like you to either give a short presentation or demonstrate your skill, if practical.'

More murmuring – much of it panic-stricken.

'The time is now,' he checked his watch, 'eleven fifteen. The hour before lunch will be spent preparing your presentation and discussing with the team the necessary requirements for any practical elements. We will take an hour for lunch and you will then be called back one by one to this room where we will hear your presentations.' Henry signalled that they were free to go. Uproar. Babbling voices, white faces, people clamouring round the facilitators – the pure horror in the air was palpable. Lady Caroline watched in silence for a moment.

'No composure, these modern girls – or most modern men, for that matter.' She lit a cigarette and blew smoke towards the herd of people stampeding out of the doors behind the team leaders. 'Apart from that girl,' she qualified, eyes narrowing as she leant forward in her chair to examine the person in question more closely. 'Who is she?'

Henry looked over.

'Mia Wild. Interviewed extremely well in the first round. Noblet was very keen.'

'Ha!' snorted Lady Caroline. 'I'm sure he was.'

Mia, seemingly deaf to the uproar around her, was trying to coax Martyr's cat inside from where she sat on the sill outside the open window. The cat rubbed her head against Mia's hand and then, startled by a shrill voice nearby disappeared out of sight. Mia strolled out of the room.

'No doubt utterly wrong for Noblet,' Lady Caroline remarked, 'but very charming to look at.'

***

Alice sat quietly in the corner and tried to conjure up a special skill that would set her apart from the others. She mustn't panic. After all, everyone else was in the same boat. And she did public-speaking for a living. She would make-believe that Lady Caroline, Noblet and Henry were five-year-olds and it would be fine. Someone tapped on the window behind her; Mia. Slipping out of the room and into the garden she resisted the urge to throw herself into Mia's arms, such was the relief of seeing her.

'How are you getting on?' Mia asked.

'I'm trying not to panic. But I haven't thought of a skill yet.'

'Oh, you've got hundreds. Thousands.'

'Name one.'

'I'll name three. You can teach, cook and speak German. Probably all at the same time.'

'I can only speak German to GCSE level. And I'm not sure how teaching would make me a good wife to Noblet. Unless he wanted to learn German to GCSE level.'

'Cooking then.'

Alice thought about it.

'I do love cooking and it's something I'd feel confident doing, but they've already got a cook.'

'So? She must have days off. A good cook is like gold dust – you should go for it.'

'You're right – I will. Thanks, Mia, you're a lifesaver. I'd better think of a recipe and see if they can rustle up the ingredients. What's your skill going to be?'

'No idea. I can't think on an empty stomach.'

Chapter 19

Lunch was over. It was crunch time. Those applicants who weren't preparing a practical demonstration sat in nervous rows in the hall, waiting to be called. Sinead, with the benefit of her insider information, had spent days agonising over what, from all her multitude of skills, her special skill should be. In the end, she'd decided to show off her prowess in shorthand. What better skill for the wife of a budding author and academic? Many would be the cosy evenings they would spend together; he pacing the living-room floor – *drawing-room floor, Sinead*, she corrected herself – in his smoking jacket, puffing on a pipe and dictating while she sat by the fire in very large, very expensive pearls, committing his brilliance to paper. Her name was called.

The regulation five minutes passed without incident. Sinead demonstrated her ability in shorthand, Noblet looked vacant and Lady Caroline wondered aloud whether she should hire Sinead to type up her memoirs. She left the room and the next applicant appeared. Henry looked at the name badge: 'Destiny'.

'I'm sorry – Destiny – I can't find your name here…'

'No,' admitted the woman. 'You wouldn't.'

She looked like a throwback to the 1950s in her headscarf, huge dark glasses and bright lipstick. Henry's heart sank. Could his woeful security guards have let another intruder sneak into the Hall?

'I'm sorry, but if you've not been called for a second interview, we can't see you,' Henry said, pushing back his chair and preparing to usher her from the room.

'I've not been called for a second interview. I've been called by fate. Your fate, babe.'

Oh God. He'd thought that voice was familiar, even with the Marilyn Monroe breathiness she'd been affecting. When the headscarf and sunglasses came off it was no surprise to anyone but Noblet, who hadn't been paying attention, that Saskia was underneath.

'You wouldn't reply to my messages so I had to find a way to get to see you. You're letting these saddos have five minutes of your time, don't you think I deserve at least that much?'

Turning to his mother and Noblet, Henry said, with a meaningful look, 'Would you mind…?'

Lady Caroline rose. Passing Saskia, she touched her on the shoulder. 'Dignity, Saskia. Nothing is more precious than our dignity.'

'Oh, fuck off, Caroline.'

***

Henry closed the door behind him. 'That wasn't very nice.'

'I don't feel very nice. I feel fucking terrible.' Saskia looked him in the eyes and he saw the anger vanish, swallowed up by a mixture of pain and longing. 'I miss you so much, babe. I wake up every morning and my heart's ripped out all over again when I remember you're gone.' Stumbling out of her chair and onto the floor by his feet she grabbed hold of his legs, crying, 'Tell me what to do to get you back! I don't give a fuck about anything else, not the magazine, not anything, I just want you!'

Henry looked down at her, stunned. He'd never suspected Saskia of this depth of emotion.

Stroking her hair as she sobbed against his knees, he said, 'I'm sorry, Saskia. I don't love you in the way I should. I can't think of any easier way to say it. I hope in time we can be friends.'

She sat back and looked at him with wild eyes.

'Friends? I don't want to be friends. My fucking heart is breaking, don't you get it? I wish I was dead.'

'Don't say that. We weren't right for each other. You need someone more…' He racked his brain for the word she used to bandy around when his opinions disappointed her. '…more spiritual. Why don't you take a break, get some space. Maybe go to your retreat in Goa?'

'Because,' she explained carefully, as if to a small child, 'I don't want a fucking retreat. I want you. Nothing else.'

Henry sat back, drained. He didn't know what else to say. Through the full-length windows, he happened to catch sight of Mia walking along the terrace. When he looked back at Saskia, she was staring at him.

'It's her, isn't it?'

'Who?'

'Don't give me that! It's that bitch, she's the reason you dumped me! I could see it all coming at the interview that night. You and Noblet drooling over her.'

'Saskia, I have met Mia Wild twice including today. The reason I broke up with you is because I no longer love you. That and the fact you were sleeping with other people,' he added, drily.

She wasn't listening. Standing up and gathering her things together she said, 'I'll show you. There's something not right about that bitch, I know it. I'm going to find out what it is and then you'll see you were wrong. You'll need me again.'

He tried to protest but she was already gone, knocking over an empty chair in the hall with a clatter.

***

As Alice edged into the interview room bearing a tray that trembled in her clammy hands, a glance at the three faces before her revealed they all looked rather tense. One of the kitchen staff had been sent in with her to carry the plates and cutlery, and together they arranged everything on a small table in front of the panel. When it was ready, Alice stood back.

'So,' said Lady Caroline. 'Your skill is to bake?'

'Erm, yes. Baking and cooking in general.'

'I see. You are aware that His Lordship has a full complement of kitchen staff?'

Henry rolled his eyes. 'Martyr can hardly be described as a full complement of kitchen staff,' he muttered to his mother.

'Well, yes, I did think of that,' Alice said, 'but I thought it might be useful to have extra help sometimes…' She trailed off. Mia had made it sound convincing, but now she felt like she was applying for the role of scullery maid rather than Countess of Pantling.

'Cooking,' Noblet declared, 'is always a useful skill to have. Wish I could do it.' He gave Alice an encouraging nod.

'I agree,' said Henry.

Alice looked down at her tart, wishing her cheeks paler.

Lady Caroline looked ostentatiously at her watch.

'I assume we are going to try some of that…?'

'Tarte aux poires,' Alice finished for her. It was one of her favourites. Juicy pears surrounded by frangipane in a crisp, buttery pastry. She cut slices, added a dollop of clotted cream to each dish and handed them round. For a moment there was silence while they all took a bite.

Lady Caroline was first to speak, looking up at Alice as if she hadn't seen her properly before.

'This is delicious. Truly delicious.' She took another bite. 'I've not had a dessert this good since the Clos du Roi. That little place near Montparnasse,' she added to Henry.

'Gorgeous!' enthused Noblet. 'Heavenly!' He held out his plate. 'More, please.'

Alice couldn't stop smiling as she handed him another slice.

Henry put down his empty plate. 'You're a very talented cook.' He looked down at his notes. 'I see you're a primary school teacher. Have you ever cooked professionally?'

'No, never.'

Lady Caroline nodded at her. 'Perhaps you should consider it, my dear.'

Once Alice had left the room, Noblet hopped down from his chair and helped himself to another large slice.

'Noblet!'

'Yes, Mother?'

'You've barely left any for Henry and me.'

She held out her plate for more.

***

By four o'clock most of the interviewees had been seen and sent home. The remainder were served tea which they drank dotted around the terrace in nervous little groups. At the end of the tea break, Henry went to round up Noblet and discovered he had gone AWOL again. Search parties were dispatched to the library, Noblet's bedroom and other likely places, while he himself tried the pantry. Having found it empty, he was returning to the interview room when he heard a loud expostulation from a small room known as the Games Room, as it was where board games were stored along with sundry items such as cricket bats and rugby balls. It was also, Henry remembered as he opened the door and received a small white ball in the face, where they kept the ping-pong table.

'Oh for goodness sake, Henners! Gave me a shock, coming charging in like that. Put me off my stride. That was going to be the most marvellous shot. Shall we mark that point down to me?' He asked his companion with a winning look.

'If you like,' she replied.

'Mia here,' Noblet said, motioning towards her, 'has trounced me three times in a row. I haven't even scored a point. Other than that last one.'

'Sounds like you're out of your league,' Henry remarked.

'Well, I don't know about that. We're going to make it best of five.'

'I don't want to be a spoilsport, Bob, but you've still got people left to see. Mia, would you mind if we postponed the final two games?'

She smiled at him and laid down her bat. 'Of course not.'

She really was jaw-droppingly gorgeous, Henry thought. He could tell Noblet was smitten, but – without being disloyal to his brother – he couldn't quite understand what the attraction was for her. She could have any number of eligible men at her feet with a snap of her fingers. He was almost jealous of his brother, having a woman like Mia prepared to consider marrying him. If she was, of course. He remembered what Saskia had said about there being something 'not quite right' about her; perhaps she had some other agenda. Then he remembered all the other things Saskia had said and warned himself against listening to the paranoid ramblings of a woman on the edge of a breakdown.

Mia had picked up her bag and was preparing to leave.

'Erm – would you like to come and discuss your special skill with us now, Mia?' asked Noblet.

'How about,' Mia suggested, 'we say it's ping-pong and leave it at that?'

Noblet simpered at her. 'Absolutely – I can testify to your skill in that direction.'

Henry looked withering when, after a few moments, Noblet dragged his eyes away from her retreating figure.

'Ping-pong? That's the skill you're looking for in a wife?'

'Correct. Nothing better to while away an evening than a good, long, table tennis tournament. Very creditable skill. More to my taste than half the balderdash I've heard today. I mean, Henners, if it's a choice between flower arranging, line dancing and – and what was it that gentleman offered us – "lifestyle vlogging", was it? – I'd take ping-pong every time!'

Chapter 20

Sinead woke up with a jolt. She lifted her head and listened, trying to quieten her breathing. She'd been dreaming about brass bands and Crufts. As she came to, she realised Coco was yapping and in the background, there was a muffled banging noise. There it was again. Coco continued to bark but whenever he paused for breath, she heard it.

'Yip, yip, yip, yip, yip, yip!'

Thud.

'Yip, yip, yip, yip, yip, yip!'

Thud.

'Yip, yip, yip, yip, yip, yip!'

Thud.

She pushed off the covers and slid out of bed. Switching on the light, she went straight to the wardrobe for her anti-burglar kit. Sinead had planned for the eventuality of a burglary. As a single woman in a large, desirable residence she was well aware of her vulnerability and had no intention of joining the ranks of sad saps who ended up in the papers: 'Wealthy homeowner gagged and bound while intruders ransack house'.

'Yip, yip, yip, yip, yip, yip!'

Thud.

She pulled on the bulletproof vest.

'Yip, yip, yip, yip, yip, yip!'

Thud.

The retractable truncheon was flicked out to its full length.

'Yip, yip, yip, yip, yip, yip!'

Thud.

The pepper spray was inserted into the correct loop on the bulletproof vest.

'Yip, yip, yip, yip, yip, yip!'

Thud.

The lipstick was applied. You never knew who might be burgling you, after all.

As she descended the stairs the thudding got louder. It was coming from the other side of the front door. Coco was shut in the kitchen, still yapping away. Sinead left him there, she was under no illusions as to his worth as an attack dog. Noiselessly, she drew back the bolts. The thudding continued. She turned the handle in her left hand while she raised the truncheon above her head in her right. She flung open the door. Instead of bearing down hard on the suspected burglar's head, she found herself flat on her back on the floor with sixteen-stone of man on top of her. The man grunted. Her arm, which had stretched out again ready to strike, checked itself.

'Ugh,' repeated the sixteen-stone of flesh.

She craned her neck to the side to get a look at his face in the dim light.

'Derek?'

'Yurr,' he confirmed.

She managed to wriggle out from underneath him. He remained face down on the floor.

'What were you doing?'

'Banging.'

'Banging what?'

'My head. Your door.'

'Why?'

There was a strangled noise that sounded like a sob and then something incoherent.

'What?'

'Meeyueediooo.'

'What?'

He raised his head and took a deep breath, holding back the sobs.

'I'm an idiot!'

The words shot through the air towards her, propelled on a wave of lager and spirit fumes.

Sinead looked up at the clock on the wall. One o'clock in the morning. She looked back at the prostrate form on the floor and put down her truncheon.

'Come on. I'll make tea.'

Derek allowed himself to be persuaded up, divested of his boots and led into the living room where he was equipped with a cup of hot, sweet tea. Sinead sipped a camomile infusion as she settled herself opposite him and asked, 'What's happened?'

Derek stared at his tea, took a sip and stared at it again without speaking.

Sinead tutted. 'It's the middle of the night. Woke me up. At least tell me what it is.'

Lifting his great head, he looked at the empty space over her right shoulder, two tears rolling down his cheeks.

'Lost my job. Because m'an idiot. Loved my job'

Something softened inside Sinead and, putting her mug down, she moved over to the sofa next to him and stroked his arm.

'Come on. Never mind. What happened?'

After the interviews were over, Henry de Beeble had called a meeting of all the security staff to tear a strip off them. He'd asked how their procedures had failed to such an extent that two intruders had made their way into the house and confronted Lord de Beeble himself. Derek, as on-site team leader, didn't have an explanation to give for Lorraine

Watford's unauthorised entry, but he had asked to speak to Mr de Beeble in private about the second 'intruder'. Once they were alone, Derek had confessed all about Saskia, expecting Henry to understand and perhaps even be pleased. As he was telling his tale, however, and Henry's brow was darkening, Derek had started to suspect that all was not as it seemed. When it came to how Derek had helped Saskia infiltrate the interviews so she could 'surprise him', he noticed Henry's jaw clench. Henry had said that although he understood that Derek had been misled, his first loyalty should have been to the de Beeble family and his actions were a breach of trust. In the light of that, and the security lapse which allowed Mrs Watford to enter the Hall, Henry had no choice but to terminate Derek's contract, and that of his company. Derek's termination was with immediate effect and the firm would be kept on for another week while a replacement was engaged.

This didn't come out very coherently but Sinead got the point.

'Stupid bitch,' was her first reaction.

'Who?'

'Saskia, of course. His girlfriend. Should never have involved you. Lied.'

'I shouldn't have listened,' agreed Derek, his words muffled against her shoulder.

'No. But you believed her. Wanted to help.'

'Wasn't that,' sobbed Derek. 'She paid me and – and – I was goin' to buy you...' he reached a crescendo of sobbing, 'gerberas!'

She looked down at his shaking head, shocked.

'Did it all for you,' he snuffled.

When she didn't say anything, he looked up and found his face close to hers. Before either of them knew what had happened, they were kissing. His shaking sobs died down as his kisses grew in enthusiasm and he drew her down onto the sofa.

In the kitchen, Coco began to howl hopelessly.

***

After the stresses and strains in Mereshire, getting back to the day job felt like a welcome break to Henry. He found he could come home tired after work in the evening and the flat would be blissfully empty and peaceful. He could open the fridge and find that his cheeses and cold meats were where he'd left them, instead of in the bin: sacrificed to one of Saskia's anti-fat, anti-meat scourges. Friends, however, seemed to find his contentment hard to take at face value. Particularly female friends, he noticed, who, soon after he'd broken up with Saskia, started dropping into conversation friends of theirs who had recently come out of relationships. 'I'm not interested,' he would insist until they got the message and left him alone.

One person who wasn't as easy to dismiss, however, was his mother. Given how fond she'd been of Saskia, he was surprised at the speed with which she started trying to matchmake. Every delightful, charming girl whom she'd once had earmarked for Noblet was now thrown, metaphorically, in Henry's path. As Henry was in London and his mother in Mereshire, this endless name-dropping was, for now, a minor irritant, but Henry had begun to dread Lady Caroline's annual summer party, a month away in July. Telephone conversations around this period took on a similar pattern.

'I'm so looking forward to the summer party, Henry, aren't you?'

Henry thought about it. Lots of his mother's aristocratic friends and their children standing around on the lawn in unflattering formalwear nibbling on finger food between 8 p.m. and midnight precisely; the same ancient Pantling string quartet who were hired every year; Noblet, a picture of misery, tightly buttoned into his dinner jacket; and his mother getting tipsy on champagne and holding forth on everything from immigration to road markings.

'It wouldn't be summer without it,' he replied diplomatically.

'I'll be sending out the invitations in a day or so. I do hope Camilla and Douglas can make it this year with Fenella. Such a charming girl,' she paused, inviting comment which wasn't forthcoming. 'And of course, Stephanie and Arabella Dryden will be coming. And Bo Searle.' She paused again. 'Such delightful girls. Can't think why they haven't been snapped up yet. Can't imagine they'll be on the shelf for long.'

At this point, Henry tended to wrap up the conversation to avoid being drawn on the relative merits of the various Arabellas and Fenellas laid out for his perusal. It wouldn't be as easy at the party, of course. He would have to keep out of Lady Caroline's way as much as possible if he wasn't to spend the whole evening making small talk with every eligible girl Mereshire and the surrounding counties had to offer.

***

'It's probably a stupid idea,' said Alice, 'but now the seed's been sown I can't stop thinking about it.'

She and Mia were sitting at a table by the window in the Lion and Lamb, driven inside by a sudden summer shower. Behind them Colonel Markham was sipping a pint of bitter at the bar, pretending to gaze into the distance while eavesdropping on their conversation. Mia caught Jerry Brewer's eye. He jumped to attention and set up another round of drinks.

'What's the idea?' Mia asked.

As she prepared to vocalise it, Alice felt the heat rise in her cheeks. Why was she so embarrassed about admitting that she had a dream? She took a deep breath and blurted it out.

'You know I told you they liked the tart I made at the second interview? Even Lady Caroline, I never thought she'd say anything nice but she described it as "truly delicious". Lord de Beeble had a second helping and Henry de Beeble said I was talented. I know it sounds big-headed but it struck me people are always saying how much they like my food. When I do the cakes for the WI stall at the fête, they always go like…well, like hot cakes.'

She paused for breath as Jerry deposited another whisky and glass of white wine on the table for them, with an appreciative smile at Mia.

'Go on,' Mia urged once he'd gone.

'The long and short of it is, I wonder if I could do it for money. Not instead of teaching of course, that would be silly, I've got to pay the bills. And I do like teaching, it's just that I love cooking and maybe I should do something about it.'

'You're a great cook. I'm surprised you never thought of it as a career before.'

'Well, to be honest, I did. As a little girl I always used to say I was going to be a chef, but then everyone thought that was a silly idea…'

'Who's everyone?'

'Oh, you know, Mum, and everyone. They all thought I'd make a good teacher and I liked children so… Teaching is secure and – I – I suppose in a way it "fitted", you know? Cess is a doctor, I'm a teacher – good, professional careers. I'm not blaming my parents, in some kind of "they thwarted my dreams" way, it's not like that at all. They wanted us to be happy, and in their world being happy is having a job that gives you security and that other people respect.'

Mia nodded. 'Whereas maybe for you, what makes you happy is being creative and doing something you excel at.'

Alice looked shifty. 'Well, I wouldn't go that far. I mean "excel" is…'

'Alice.'

'Yes?'

'You've got to stop being apologetic for being good at things. You are a great cook.' She waved a hand. 'It's very British, you know, this compulsion for putting oneself down. You don't find it in France, Italy, other European countries. In France, your skills are something to be proud of. Why pretend otherwise? You'll have to get used to talking about your talent without getting awkward. Especially if you're going to be marketing yourself. But I'm jumping ahead – you were saying maybe you could do it for money?'

'Yes. The summer holidays are coming up in a month and I thought maybe I could do some catering. Nothing massive – put some leaflets through doors in the village, maybe advertise in the *Gazette*. I wouldn't be able to handle anything too big, but…' She jumped as someone coughed in her ear.

'I couldn't help but overhear, Alice my dear,' apologised Colonel Markham. 'May I…?' He indicated an empty chair at their table.

'Of course, Colonel.'

He settled himself down. 'Alice, I think it's a marvellous idea. Your cakes and pastries are the talk of the village, I have no doubt the orders would pour in. That is the reason for my intrusion on your conversation. Rather than having to turn down lucrative orders, why not call on my help? You may not be aware, my dear, but I spent three years in the catering corps.'

Alice looked surprised. 'Well, if it wouldn't be too much bother it would be reassuring to know I had someone to help me. I don't know how much I would be able to pay, to begin with…'

He raised a gnarled hand. 'Stop! I should not be expecting any financial remuneration. The knowledge that I was supporting an enterprising young friend would be payment enough. That and the work itself, you understand. Those days in the corps were some of the happiest of my life.'

Mia raised her glass in a toast. 'Excellent! Here's to the Brand-New Catering Co. and all who sail in her. Which reminds me, Alice, you'll need someone to help you with the marketing – I'll put you in touch with a friend of mine.'

As they all clinked glasses Alice felt more hopeful than she had done in a long time.

Chapter 21

Mia's marketing friend designed some beautiful posters and leaflets which Alice distributed around the village a couple of weeks before the end of term. Before her advert had even appeared in the local paper, she had three jobs lined up: two dinner parties and a christening. And then came a call from Elaine Jowlett. Would she be able, for an old friend, to organise a simple, rustic supper for six on Saturday next? Nothing flashy, an *amuse-bouche*, starter, fish course – naturally – main and couple of sweets? Could she? Wonderful. Elaine assumed preferential rates for an old friend such as herself.

Preparing for Elaine's dinner party had caused Alice a certain amount of stress. Following the initial call, she had costed it up and presented Elaine with an estimate which Elaine, within minutes, had halved. Subsequently, sitting down to go through the menu, Elaine had tut-tutted at the pea and mint veloutés, I-think-not-my-dear-ed at the scallops and oh-dear-me-no-ed at the rack of lamb. A clean sheet of paper was produced and a new menu devised, consisting of such rustic fare as beluga caviar, fillet steaks and truffles. All to come out of the agreed budget of course: 'Because in a way, dear, I'm helping you out. You are fortunate in being able to hone your trade on an old friend who won't fly off the handle at the odd mistake. Although you will try not to make any mistakes, won't you, dear?'

Alice had called Colonel Markham, who, after railing at the ineffable selfishness of 'some people' had proved invaluable in helping her shop economically; bartering at the fish market over the lobsters and buying lumpfish caviar rather than beluga, asserting: 'If they notice the difference, I'll eat my apron!'

On the big day Alice prepared as much as she could at home and then she and the Colonel loaded up the car mid-afternoon and drove the few hundred metres to the Jowletts'. Elaine opened the door to them in an eye-watering orange and brown floral print dress.

'Welcome, friends! Come in, come in. Go straight through. Ted will give you a helping hand. Ted!'

Ted came darting into the gloomy corridor and wordlessly gathered up a large plastic box before darting away again like a downtrodden bellboy. Alice and Colonel Markham set to work in the kitchen, interrupted every few minutes or so by Elaine popping in to stick a sturdy finger into a pan of sauce or snaffle a canapé with a playful 'Oopsy! One for little me!' leaving the Colonel growling obscenities under his breath. Soon, the more pressing business of last-minute preparations consumed her and she left them in peace.

***

Something smelt bad. Rotten, even. Saskia sniffed and pinpointed the source as being the small shed to her left. If her nose didn't deceive her, it was where they kept the bins. Not the best place to hide next to, but she couldn't risk moving. Someone might see her. Peering through the binoculars, she refocused on The Bitch. She was sitting on a work surface in the kitchen, laughing at something one of her companions was saying. Saskia made a small note in the notepad on her lap. 'Sat 1st August, 6.30 p.m. At her cottage in GR. Laughing. Drinking from a mug. Five or six others in the house – men and women. Not Him.' Not that she had expected Henry to be there. They wouldn't be so stupid as to meet in public. They'd be doing it in secret. That was why Saskia had to be patient, watching and waiting.

Management of *The Vacuum* had been handed over to her assistant editor while Saskia focused on her temporary new vocation: Unmasking That Bitch as Being a Fraud and Getting Henry Back. She'd already found out something rather interesting about The Bitch, but she wasn't about to reveal her hand at this stage. Who knew what else there might be to discover, and besides, she wanted to try and catch her with Henry, in flagrante. She shifted position. It was hard work, doing a stake-out. She'd done her best to prepare for a long night; she was even wearing flats which was practically unheard of (although they'd been huge in all the autumn/winter shows so she could at least justify it to herself that way).

The Bitch was now taking food out of the fridge. Someone else had got a chopping board and was slicing onions while a third person splashed red wine into glasses. Saskia was conscious of a slight grumbling in her stomach. She reached into her handbag and, feeling around, pulled out a pack of organic oatcakes. As she watched the convivial scene through her binoculars while munching on a dry oatcake beside the bins, Saskia felt a wave of self-pity. Self-pity came easily to her these days, but rather than let the waves engulf her she would soak them up with the kitchen-roll of self-righteousness. The end was all. Once she had her proof, she would look back on these days of squatting behind hedges in sensible shoes and laugh. She and Henry would laugh together.

***

'Right, my dear,' said the Colonel, hanging up his apron and giving Alice an encouraging pat on the arm. 'It's time for me to desert my post, I'm afraid.'

As well as helping to prepare dinner, the Colonel was to attend it as a guest, along with Valerie Tipperton, Jan Fratterbury, and the guest of honour – Elaine's elderly Aunt

Jennifer. Alice felt calm as she watched him march out of the kitchen. With the Colonel's help, everything was on track, just a few last-minute preparations to be done before serving. She pulled a mirror out of her bag to check her hair and tone down her flushed cheeks. Elaine had requested that she be the waitress as well as cook – and chief washer-upper of course, although the Colonel was due to come back and help her clear up later.

Elaine popped her head round the door. 'All under control in here, is it?' she enquired. 'Excellent, excellent. One thing, Alice dear – Aunt Jennifer has arrived and mentioned that she is allergic to lobster so we'll need to whip something else up for her starter.'

The colour drained from Alice's face. She looked over at the tray where neat discs of lobster ravioli waited to be dunked in boiling water before being smothered in sauce and drizzled with truffle oil. All carefully planned and prepared.

'Wh… whip something else up?' she stammered.

'Yes, dear. And she did mention how partial she is to whitebait so I thought you could do a few of those in some batter.'

'But… I don't have any whitebait.'

'Not a problem! Not a problem, dear,' Elaine assured her. 'I'll hold the fort here, hand round the nibbles, while you pop to the shops in the car. Yes? Good,' and, without waiting for Alice's response, she closed the door behind her.

Left alone, Alice panicked. Where could she get whitebait from in the next half hour? The nearest shop likely to sell it was the supermarket in Pantling, twenty minutes away. That meant a forty-minute round trip, then having to make batter and cook the whitebait as well as the lobster ravioli. It couldn't be done! Feeling about seven years old, Alice got out her phone and dialled her parents' home number. No response. Damn! She remembered they'd gone into London to see something at the English National Opera with friends. Cecily was in Suffolk on some romantic weekend with Piers... Mia! She'd said she was coming down to the cottage this weekend with friends. She would ask Mia for help.

***

Saskia pricked up her ears. The Bitch had slipped out into the quiet of the garden to take a phone call.

'What's wrong?' Mia asked the person on the other end of the phone. There was silence for a few moments while she listened.

'Whitebait?'

Whitebait. Whitebait. Saskia racked her brain. What could be the significance of that word? Some kind of a code word? A restaurant? A pet name?

Mia was speaking again. 'Shh, calm down, sweetheart. It'll be fine, don't worry.'

Sweetheart! That bitch. She was talking to him.

'I know,' Mia was saying. 'But it'll be fine, I promise you. Give me twenty minutes – I'll sneak in round the back.' She hung up and went back into the cottage.

That clinched it. They were arranging a secret meeting. Saskia sprinted to her car. A few seconds later Mia emerged and got into a Lamborghini parked out front. She roared away and Saskia followed in her unobtrusive hired Lexus.

They were heading for the green. Mia pulled up next to the pub and went inside. The pub? That couldn't be the venue for a secret meeting? Saskia was on tenterhooks. Ten nail-biting minutes passed before Mia re-emerged carrying a dish covered in silver foil. She put the dish on the passenger seat of the car, started up the engine and pulled away trailed by Saskia's Lexus.

The Lamborghini turned down one of the streets which led away from the green, turned right onto another lane and stopped. There was nowhere for Saskia to park without drawing attention to herself. By the time she'd parked the car round the corner and jogged back, Mia had disappeared.

The Lamborghini was parked between two houses: a thatched cottage and a larger double-fronted house. The thatched cottage was nearest; Saskia walked past as slowly as she dared and glanced in through the window. She could see a group of middle-aged people sitting around a dinner table. Not a likely place for Henry and The Bitch to be meeting. Continuing on, she peered into the windows of the next house. Draped over the back of a chair near the window was a man's jacket. She was convinced – yes, she was sure it was Henry's jacket. She'd seen him wearing it earlier that summer, many times.

With a quick glance up and down the street, she opened the garden gate and walked in.

***

'You've saved my life! The pub, why didn't I think of that! You're a genius,' gushed Alice as she unwrapped the plate of battered whitebait.

Mia smiled. 'How's it going otherwise?'

'Well, now I'm no longer having heart failure it's fine. They wolfed down the canapés and they're sitting down ready for the starter, so I'd better dish up.'

'I'll leave you to it.'

'Thanks again, Mia, you're a lifesaver.' Alice smiled at her as she set out the starter plates. Mia wasn't paying attention; she was looking at something through the window, a small frown on her beautiful face. The object of her scrutiny was a blonde-haired woman in the neighbouring garden who was shuffling along the side of the house and craning her head to peer in through the glass panel in a side door.

'Do you know who that is?' asked Mia, eyes trained on the woman.

Alice glanced through the window.

'I don't think so. Oh! Isn't it Henry de Beeble's girlfriend?'

'Ex-girlfriend, so I hear. Yes – Saskia Stonor.'

'How bizarre. What on earth is she doing?'

Saskia tiptoed past the side door and peered into a small window further along.

'Someone very like her followed me to the pub,' Mia remarked, 'and then again from the pub to here. I thought it was odd at the time.'

A bell tinkled somewhere in the house.

'Oh God! That's Elaine for the starters and I haven't plated up yet!'

'I'll get out of your way,' Mia said, 'and make sure Saskia gets everything she's after.'

***

Nothing. No one in any of the rooms she could see into, and all was quiet in the house. They must be upstairs. Her heart beat angrily in her chest as she thought about what they might be doing up there. She tried the handle of the door and took a deep breath as it opened. Inside she found herself in a large, luxurious kitchen. The oven was on and something smelled delicious. Henry must be cooking dinner for them; perhaps The Bitch had been buying dessert in the pub. But they'd decided to skip straight to the last course. The thought instilled her with sufficient courage to tiptoe across the room, into the hall and up the wooden stairs.

The landing was large and square, with a deep sash window opening onto a garden behind the house. All the doors were closed. She stood undecided for a moment – and then she heard it. A noise in the room to her right. Yes – there it was again. There was someone in the room. Someone making quiet scratching noises, like fingernails being dragged in ecstasy against bedsheets... She wrenched open the door. A pure white, pedigree cat trotted out and rubbed hopefully around her ankles. Behind it, the room was empty. When her heart had stopped pounding, she took a breath, kicked the cat and went into the room. A four-poster bed dominated; the sheets tumbled as if the occupants had got up in a hurry. A bra and skirt were draped over an armchair in the corner and the blinds were down. This was it then. This was where they had met. Why they'd left the room she wasn't sure, nor where they were now – perhaps they'd seen her in the street and had fled – but they had to come back. The clothes up here, the jacket in the drawing room, the meal in the oven: everything spelled their imminent return. And when they came back, they would find their nemesis waiting.

Saskia knocked the bra and skirt off the chair with a disdainful elbow and sat down to wait.

***

Alice had cleared the plates after the mains and was pleased to see them scraped clean. Before dessert, Elaine suggested everyone join her in a stroll round the garden. As their little party made its way down the garden path, sounds of splashing were heard in the vicinity.

'What's that noise?' demanded Aunt Jennifer.

'That will be the neighbours, Aunt, in their outdoor heated swimming pool. Super people, aren't they, Ted? Moved in last year and had the most wonderful pool built. It's on the other side of the little orchard.'

'Outdoor swimming? At this time of night?' Aunt Jennifer was horrified. 'They'll catch their deaths.'

The sight of a police car pulling up in the lane stopped the conversation dead. Two officers got out and approached the neighbouring house.

Aunt Jennifer was in high glee.

'Lovely people, are they, Elaine? Hardened criminals more like! Always were a shocking judge of character, weren't you, Elaine,' she added, shooting a derisory look at Ted.

***

Up in the bedroom, time weighed heavily on Saskia. She had calmed down a little and was starting to ask herself some uncomfortable questions. Such as, hadn't Mia been wearing a black dress? If so, whose cream skirt was she resting her Uggs on? And whose house was this?

She pulled up a corner of the blind, saw a police car outside and dropped it again. Before she had time to think, someone was calling up the stairs.

'Police, anybody there?'

Oh God. Oh God. Oh God. This could ruin her: her reputation, the magazine. Fucking fascist pigs, sticking their snouts in where they weren't needed! She hadn't even broken in; the door was open. She'd done nothing wrong – in all but the pedantic eyes of the law, anyway. Quick, must use razor-sharp journalist's brain, must think of a way to escape. Footsteps on the stairs. There was no escape. Only her wits stood between Saskia Stonor and ignominy. Stepping forward she opened the door wide and glared at the ascending police officer as her head bobbed up above the balustrade.

'What, in God's name, do you think you're doing?' she demanded, in her best home-counties tones.

The policewoman got to the top of the stairs and took her time surveying Saskia from head to toe. Then glancing down the stairs, she yelled, 'Up here.'

Saskia refused to be browbeaten.

'I asked you a question. I demand an answer.'

The officer pulled out a notebook.

'May I take your name, madam?'

'No!' Saskia flung back at her. 'You may not! You may get out of this house; you are trespassing on private property.'

The second officer now joined them, observing Saskia with a look not entirely respectful. He was young and spotty and Saskia's blood boiled.

'I shall be reporting your behaviour to your superiors as soon as you leave my house, and I can assure you that stupid grin will be wiped off your face!'

The first officer repeated her question.

'I'm not obliged to tell you what my name is. This is my house and I am ordering you to leave. Now!'

The officer consulted her notebook.

'We have received a report of an intruder, answering to your description, effecting an unlawful entry into this property. Am I to understand that you are claiming to be the householder?'

Saskia's glare didn't flicker as she snapped, 'You are.'

The police officer consulted her notebook again.

'I repeat, am I to understand that you are the owner of this property, Mrs Kalpna Bhatia?'

The hesitation was barely noticeable.

'Correct.'

The policewoman looked at Saskia. Saskia looked at the policewoman. The policewoman looked at her colleague, who returned the look.

While their attention was diverted, she made a run for it. Shoving one officer into the other, she hurtled down the stairs, through the kitchen, out the door and straight into the arms of the householders themselves. The policewoman was hot on her heels and as Saskia tried to sidestep the startled couple, the officer grabbed her and pushed her up against the wall of the house.

'Let me go! Let me go you fascist pigs! Do you know who I am?'

'Why yes,' quipped the young, pimply officer. 'You're Mrs Kalpna Bhatia.'

***

Over the dividing hedge into Elaine's garden a row of faces, whose expressions ranged from the flabbergasted to the horrified to the fascinated, were drinking in the scene. Alice, hearing the commotion, appeared at the kitchen door, wiping her hands on a tea towel as they were leading a still-screaming Saskia away. She saw Alice and fell silent for a moment. Then, dragging one of her arms free, she pointed straight at her.

'You! You did this, you shopped me! It won't make any difference, you can tell that bitch Mia Wild that I know everything! Tell her I know all about the whitebait!' she shrieked before being bundled into the police car and driven away.

Chapter 22

When Cecily and Piers popped in for tea with Alice on the way back from their weekend away, they found it hard to see the serious side.

'Elaine's aunt thought she'd been poisoned?' sniggered Cecily.

'Yes. She was quite upset,' chided Alice. 'See it from her point of view – a potential criminal was bundled into a panda car yelling that she knew all about the whitebait.'

'Whitebait!' snorted Piers to no one in particular before stuffing a huge scone in his mouth.

'And it was awful,' continued Alice, 'because of course then everyone wanted to know about the whitebait: where it had come from, if it could have been tampered with. I had to admit that Mia had brought it round from the pub.' Her face grew pale at the memory. 'I'll never forget the look on Elaine's face.'

'Poor Al!' Cecily reached over and squeezed her arm. 'The stupid woman shouldn't have made you get it at the last minute anyway. She deserves whatever she gets.'

'Anyway, it all calmed down eventually and the Colonel and I cleared up while Elaine put her aunt to bed in the spare room. I haven't seen Elaine or Ted since.'

There was a pause, and Alice and Cecily contemplated the pretty cottage garden in silence while Piers stalked a wasp with a rolled-up magazine. Having exterminated it, he put down the magazine and did a little weeding in Alice's borders. Alice noticed he was digging up an allium.

'Erm…' she began, pointing towards the plant.

'I know, I know!' He smiled and tapped the side of his nose. 'You have to get the whole root out to eradicate the weed completely. Never fear, little Alster, sit back and watch an expert at work. Now. The real issue we should be chewing over here is who is the blonde bimbo and what is her beef with battered fish.'

'The – er – blonde bimbo is Saskia Stonor. She's the girlfriend, or ex-girlfriend,' Alice tried to keep her tone nonchalant, 'of Henry de Beeble. Henry is Lord de Beeble's brother – the one who's been holding the interviews for a wife. I've no idea what she was doing in the neighbouring house or what she meant about the whitebait. Mia thought she'd followed her so I guess she might have been trying to find Mia and got the wrong house.'

'But why?' asked Cecily.

'Yes, why?' echoed Piers, soil-ingrained fingernails tapping against his cheek.

They all fell silent once more; the only noises in the garden humming insects, birdsong and the occasional rip of one of Alice's summer-flowering bulbs being wrenched from the soil and tossed aside.

'This is a bit of a long shot,' mused Alice after a while, 'and I'm thinking aloud here, but…'

'Spit it out, Alster.'

'Maybe Saskia's jealous of Mia and wanted to confront her? If she and Henry de Beeble have split up, maybe she thinks he's left her for another woman. Henry knows Mia via the interviews. Something might have happened to make Saskia think they're seeing each other.'

As she said it out loud her heart sank. What would be more natural? They were in the same league, Henry and Mia – the premier league, whereas Alice was way down in the Johnstone Paint Trophy or whatever it was called these days. It shouldn't hurt so much, she'd never seriously thought anything could happen between her and Henry de Beeble. But she'd cherished the idea of him, single, deep in the secret part of her brain set aside for fanciful daydreams. Stupid. Henry and Mia falling in love, that was the way the fairy tale ended. The prince didn't go down on one knee to the ugly sister, that would be repugnant to everything in nature.

Looking down, she noticed she was dipping a piece of fruitcake into her tea and the other two were staring at her.

'Anything wrong, Al?'

'Oh! No, nothing. Sorry, I was miles away. Wondering about Saskia and everything, you know. Fascinating stuff.'

Her phone rang – she answered it and after a short conversation put it down again, looking shell-shocked.

'What's the matter?' asked Cecily. 'Who was it?'

'It… It was Lady de Beeble.'

'What did she want?'

'She'd seen one of my posters about the catering. Or one of her staff had – I can't remember which now. I was so flustered when I realised who it was that I didn't take much in at the beginning.'

'She won't read posters herself, Alster. She'll have someone to do that for her.' Piers grinned.

Alice wasn't paying attention. 'She said she's having a party – her annual summer party – and she wants me to help with the catering.'

Cecily hugged her. 'Alice! That's amazing! It'll make your name.'

'She'd been so impressed by my cooking at the interviews that she thought she'd employ me to do one or two things her cook wouldn't have time for. Like the canapés.'

'Canapés – sounds fun. What are you going to do?'

The vacant look disappeared from Alice's face as she looked at her sister with wide eyes and said, 'Panic.'

***

'Scotch eggs?' asked Sinead.

Derek glanced down at the hamper. 'Yurr.'

'Smoked salmon sandwiches?'

Derek hunted around, picked up a cling-film wrapped package and peered at it.

'Yurr.'

'Bubbly?'

'Yurr.'

Sinead put a final tick against her list and laid it down on the worktop.

'Crockery's in there already. So are the serviettes – napkins, I mean.' Jerking her head in the direction of the hamper, she ordered, 'Fastened and outside, please.'

Derek pulled the leather straps through the buckles and tossed the hamper onto his shoulder as if it were empty.

'Careful!' chided Sinead. 'The bubbly!'

As he tiptoed out, she slipped into the hall and checked her make-up in the mirror. Immaculate, as usual. Although what her hair would look like by the time they got there was another question. Outside, Derek had strapped the hamper to the back of his motorbike and stood waiting for her, a pink and silver helmet in his hand.

'Oh!' she stopped, eyeing the helmet. It had her name picked out in crystals on the back. 'What's this?'

'Bought it. For you.' He beamed.

She took it from him and inspected it from all angles. He lit up as one of her rare smiles spread over her face. 'I like it.'

'Good. Knew you didn't like the bike. Wanted to make you feel more...' He ran out of words and finished with one of his all-purpose grunts.

The motorbike had been a topic of some debate between them in recent weeks. After their midnight tryst, Sinead had surprised herself by letting Derek take her out from time to time. She knew it was interfering with her hectic beauty and fitness regime but somehow, she kept finding herself saying yes. Until today, they'd gone everywhere in Sinead's car because she refused to get on Derek's motorbike. She had a niggling feeling that a lady wouldn't be seen in public on a motorbike. It involved postures which, from all she'd read, weren't considered ladylike. Derek had finally managed to convince her, by suggesting a picnic in an out-of-the-way spot.

The beautiful pink and silver helmet made a difference, of course. She felt sure that even Lady Caroline could be persuaded to ride pillion if she were wearing that kind of designer headgear. Derek was astride the bike, waiting for her to mount. She popped one pink leather-clad leg over the seat and slid into position, gripping the burly waist in front of her.

'Hold on tight,' growled Derek as he revved the engine three or four times before pulling away.

Something strange happened to Sinead Dumper within the space of that ride. Derek realised something was up as soon as she hopped off the bike, yanked off her helmet and planted a huge kiss on his visor (he whipped off his helmet in order to allow her to repeat the process on his mouth). Her eyes were wide, her hair dishevelled and her expression dreamy.

'It's wonderful,' she gushed. 'The most wonderful thing.'

She staggered a little way from the bike and back again.

'Never experienced anything like it. The speed. The freedom. I felt,' she looked at Derek as if seeing him with new eyes, 'I felt out of control.'

Grabbing his leather jacket with both hands she pulled him towards her and asked, huskily, 'How hungry are you?'

Dropping the hamper, he whooped, flung her over his shoulder and rushed headlong into the woods.

***

Later, lying on a blanket beside Derek, the remains of a picnic scattered around them, Sinead took a sip of her champagne and sighed happily.

'Should be doing an hour's circuit training now.'

Derek glowered at her. 'Don't need to exercise so much. Figure's perfect.'

'Takes work. Shouldn't have eaten those chocolates either.'

He growled and leaned across to kiss her. 'If it was up to me all you'd do is sit on a pink sofa eatin' chocolate and lookin' pretty.'

She giggled.

He did a double take. He'd never heard her giggle.

'Can't do that. Too much prep to do.'

Derek's face fell.

'For the interviews,' he assented.

'Mmmm. Got to get ahead of the competition.'

'Bound to win anyway,' he said, his face a picture of despair.

Why did he keep kidding himself, he wondered. She wasn't interested in him. Why would she be? An out-of-work door supervisor who lived with his mum. What kind of a mate was that for a woman who could marry into royalty? (Was a lord royalty? He wasn't sure.) Each time he saw her, he managed to convince himself that she liked him, but what good did it do? She was still preparing for the final interview. She hadn't had confirmation yet if she had got through, but to Sinead – and Derek – it was a foregone conclusion.

She interrupted his reverie by putting down her glass and becoming businesslike.

'Reminds me. Need your help.'

'Yurr?'

'Lord de Beeble's gardener was in the village shop yesterday.'

'Yurr?'

'Said he's run off his feet. Prepping for Lady de Beeble's garden party at the Hall.'

'Yurr?'

'Everyone will be there. Including His Lordship.' She paused and looked meaningfully at him. 'I need to be there. You have to smuggle me in.'

'But…' he grappled with the idea. 'Don't work there anymore.'

'No,' she agreed. 'But you know the grounds. The security arrangements. Easy.'

'Shouldn't really,' he said, a worried crease on his brow.

She leaned over and kissed him. 'But you will.'

He nodded and she flashed a brisk smile at him.

'Let's go. Got Pilates at six.'

Chapter 23

The long summer rolled onwards, heavy and close. In London, the air seemed to have tripled in weight and clung, clammily, to Henry's skin. He thought longingly of the high-ceilinged cool of the Hall and the breeze that ruffled the leaves of the trees on the hill behind the house on even the stillest August day. Work was quiet – the whole world seemed to be on holiday – and Henry decided the best he could do was to pack up and join them. He would head down to Mereshire a week ahead of his mother's summer party; it would give him a chance to talk through preparations for the final interviews with Bob.

The final interviews. The words were loaded with menace. What would ordinarily signify the approach of success for one lucky candidate and one well-satisfied employer, signalled, to his mind – and surely to Bob's – potential disaster. Henry had been focussing so much on the logistics until now, that the reality of life once the interviews were over hadn't sunk in. For, of course, the winner would expect Bob to marry her. Henry was far from confident that Bob would go through with it; which would mean further media frenzy and his mother's fury raining down on his brother. Even if the marriage did happen, was that any guarantee of greater happiness for anyone? His mother, perhaps, would be placated but long-term would the marriage last? Would the new bride be content once the excitement died down and she settled into life as the partner of a disorganised academic who forgot she existed on a regular basis?

Two women were being invited back for the last interview in three weeks' time. Mia Wild and Alice Brand. Would either of them make a good wife for Bob? He paused in his packing and thought about Mia. He didn't have to think for long. Intelligent, confident, stunning – a wonderful wife for someone, but not Bob. He couldn't see her being content rattling around in the hall with the country squire and his handful of domestics. And Alice? She seemed more domesticated, amenable: again, she would make someone a wonderful wife, no doubt, but Bob? Well, possibly. She was a more suitable companion for his brother than the glamorous Mia, that was for sure. He laid a couple of shirts in his suitcase, pausing with one hand resting on them. If that was so, then he should try and influence his brother in Alice's favour. Steer him away from the obvious charms of Mia to the quieter attractions of Alice. Henry took a stern, hard look at himself. Was he acting from altruistic motives? Yes. If the consequence was that Mia would be free to look elsewhere – well, so be it.

He tossed the suitcase into the boot of the car and slid into the driver's seat with an end-of-term feeling. He loved that moment when the last layers of London peeled away and he was out in the countryside, trees flashing by as he sped towards what would always feel like home. His phone rang as he put the key in the ignition. He looked at the screen: Saskia – and removed the key again. She had been strangely quiet since storming out of the interviews. He'd expected to be bombarded with vitriolic voicemails or at least the odd letter written in blood – but nothing. He'd half persuaded himself that she'd given up; but knowing Saskia's persistence the silence could suggest she was busy with something else. Such as trying to scare Mia away from the interview process.

He could ignore the call, but forewarned was forearmed.

'Hello, Saskia.'

She cut to the chase. 'Didn't expect to hear from me, did you, babe? Thought I was locked up in Wormwood Scrubs, I expect. Thought they'd thrown away the key.'

There were many places he could imagine her being – halfway up a mountain in Mongolia researching women's goat hair knitting cooperatives; flat on her back and naked under railway arches in Clerkenwell as part of an art installation; analysing her relationship with her vagina in a criminally-expensive wellness clinic – but Wormwood Scrubs didn't spring to mind. Before he could voice his surprise, she continued.

'Very clever of your friend Mia Wild to have me arrested. I know how she did it, babe, so you can tell her so. She lured me there and set me up like a sitting fucking duck.'

It seemed necessary to interrupt at this point.

'Hold on, Saskia. Mia isn't my friend, and I had no idea you'd been arrested.'

'Don't play the innocent, babe! You're all in it together – you, her, that little pathetic Alice creature from the village.'

Henry was baffled. 'Whatever you think, you're wrong. This is all gobbledygook to me.'

'Yeah, right,' she spat. He could almost hear the spittle hitting the phone. 'She's got you brainwashed. But that's OK. Because I'm onto her. I've got my evidence and I'm going to show you who that faker really is.'

'Be my guest.'

She sounded a little deflated. 'I will, man. I fucking will. I just need to get my final documentary evidence – not a problem for a seasoned journalist like myself – and then I'll be back. Like an avenging angel!' she finished, triumphantly, before hanging up.

Henry sighed and put the phone down on the seat beside him. He didn't know what it all meant, and he didn't care. He was going to put his foot down, get out of London and spend a peaceful evening with his brother, playing cards and drinking plenty of gin and tonics. The Aston Martin purred quietly and slid out of the garage into the hard glare of the East London street.

***

'Why do I have to welcome them? It's your party, why can't you do it?' complained Noblet, adding under his breath, 'Why couldn't you have it at your own damn house, for that matter.'

'Stop being childish, Nobby. You are the Earl of Pantling and you will receive your guests in the correct manner.'

'Your bloody guests,' muttered Noblet.

'Ah, Henry!' Lady Caroline greeted her younger son with arms outstretched, cutting through Noblet's mutterings. He had appeared at the doors leading out to the terrace, wearing a well-cut dinner jacket which further highlighted the shabbiness of Noblet's baggy-elbowed, sagging affair. 'You look very handsome.'

Noblet raised an eyebrow. 'Didn't tell me I look handsome.'

'You don't. Now, Henry, I want you to relax and have a wonderful time. Lots of old friends coming, people you won't have seen for a very long time.'

'Not since last year, anyway. And every single year before that,' snapped Noblet.

'Enjoy reacquainting yourself with all the young people.' She smiled at him.

'Always the way, isn't it? Henners gets to swan around knocking back the punch while I stand like a stuffed baboon on the terrace saying "Delighted" to any Tom, Dick or Harry who happens to shove past.'

'Oh, do stop blithering on, Nobby. It really is incredibly tedious.'

***

'So, we're clear?' Sinead demanded.

Derek nodded, a look of misery on his moist pink face.

'Good.' She reached out and touched his cheek in a rare gesture of tenderness. 'Relying on you.'

He couldn't stop himself from grabbing her and pressing his lips against hers. She yielded for a moment and then pulled away, patting her hair and pulling out a compact to reapply her lipstick.

She snapped the compact shut. 'See you later.'

He watched her retreating figure as it disappeared through the trees, Coco trotting alongside in his best collar and lead. She was a knockout, there was no denying it. He wouldn't be surprised if the deal was sealed before the evening was out once His Lordship saw her dressed like that. On the other hand, if anyone realised she'd gatecrashed… The new security team wouldn't take any hostages, they were going to be furious that someone had slipped through their net. Either way, he couldn't see this evening ending well. He slumped back against the bike and prepared to wait for the signal.

***

Noblet shuffled backwards into the shadow of the catering tent and yelped as he bumped into someone. He turned and found with relief that it was Henry.

'You here?'

Henry nodded. 'Strategic withdrawal. You?'

'Great minds, old chap, great minds. Couldn't take another second of polite chit-chat. And as for this…' he wrenched off his bow tie and stuffed it in his pocket before loosening his collar. 'Been wanting to do that since about seven fifteen.'

He looked his brother up and down.

'Who are you hiding from? Mother?'

'Mother I can cope with. Mother's apocalyptic armies of eligible, charming girls I'm finding tougher.'

'Catherine Clemmington-Jones?'

'Amongst others.'

'I single her out for particular mention because it was five minutes' vacuous conversation with that particular wet blanket that drove me round here.' He cocked his head at his brother. 'Show-jumping stories?'

Henry gave a wry smile. 'And the fascinating minutiae of her puppy's daily routine, including bowel movements and how to remove ticks from his genital area.'

'Oh dear. You got both barrels, didn't you, old man?'

They both held their breath as Lady Caroline's strident tones rang out on the other side of the tent and then relaxed as her voice drifted away.

Henry looked at his watch. 'Nine o'clock. I could have sworn it was later. It wouldn't be so bad if I didn't have the feeling that Mother has instructed these girls to keep up a pincer movement. Every time I extract myself from one there's another, waiting to pounce.'

'Poor old Henners. If we're lucky…' He broke off, looking with panicked eyes over his brother's shoulder. 'Clemmington-Jones! Heading this way! Quick, in there, I'll cover you,' he hissed, shoving Henry towards a slit in the side of the tent.

As Henry squeezed through the gap, Noblet stepped out of the shadows and intercepted the approaching danger.

'Cathy, old thing! Been looking everywhere for you. Dying to hear more about that fascinating point-to-point you touched on earlier…'

***

Inside the catering tent, Alice and Henry looked blankly at each other. Alice had frozen to the spot, a mini Kilner jar of chicken liver pâté in each hand, and a spatter of something yellow across the front of her white apron.

'Sorry about this,' Henry began. 'I was…' Catching sight of a tray of bacon rolls he realised how hungry he was. 'Would you mind?'

'No! No, help yourself.' Alice put down the jars and tried to smooth her apron, tugging the hem down over her shorts.

'I'm starving – not had chance to eat anything yet.' It was hot in the tent and he took off his jacket, tossing it onto a stack of empty crates before taking the paper plate she offered him and choosing a roll from the platter.

'Oh? Why's that?' asked Alice, as she turned away and straightened the rows of already neat jars on wooden serving boards.

'Too much small talk to get through,' he explained between mouthfuls as he perched on the edge of a stool. 'It's been one of those evenings.' He was going to stop there when he chanced to glance at Alice's open, interested expression as she looked over her shoulder at him. He shifted his weight further back on the stool.

'To be honest, my mother's trying to set me up with one of her friend's daughters.'

'Oh!' Alice looked down at the jars again. 'Which one?'

'Any of them. I don't think it matters as long as she's got a home-counties accent, comes from a landed estate and looks good on a pony. She's a terrible snob, I'm afraid, Mother.'

The jars were satisfactorily straightened, it seemed, and Alice moved on to another task: adding grapes from a large bowl to the cheese boards. 'I'm sure she wants the best for you.'

'Oh, she does, yes,' agreed Henry. 'But to be frank, if I have to listen politely while another Fenella or Arabella tells me an amusing anecdote involving some old Oxbridge pals and a punt, I might have to insert this fork,' he picked up a large, two-pronged number, 'up the aforementioned lady's Henley Regatta.'

Alice looked round, shocked, and then let out something between a snort and a laugh; which made her cheeks flush red. Henry smiled.

'You're lucky, hiding away here with the bacon rolls and cheese boards.' He helped himself to a piece of Brie.

'Oh God, I know,' agreed Alice, picking up her water bottle and taking a quick swig. 'I'm terrible at mingling. I never know what to say and I end up drivelling to fill the silence. I expect you noticed that at the interviews…'

She was nice, he decided. Unaffected and kind-hearted. Could be good for Bob. Perhaps he ought to make the most of this opportunity to get to know her better on his brother's behalf.

She noticed he'd finished the cheese and said, reluctantly, 'Would you like me to pop out and see if the coast is clear?'

He loosened his tie and looked around for more food to snaffle.

'Not yet. I'll stay here with you for a while. If I'm not in your way?'

Her cheeks were pink in the heat of the tent as she shook her head and said, 'No, not at all.'

***

'Right, Coco. Don't let me down, you little runt. One thing I ask of you. Do it properly,' Sinead snarled at the little grey dog as she crouched down next to him, unclipping his lead. Holding his collar with one hand she pressed 'send' on a text with the other. If all went to plan, at this moment Derek would be receiving the text and blowing hard on a dog-whistle. She waited a moment and then let go of Coco. He stood looking at her uncertainly for a moment and then lifted his shaggy head as if he were listening, before trotting away.

'Yes!' Sinead pumped a jubilant fist in the air before recollecting herself. No one had seen her. She was hiding behind one of the outhouses, out of sight of the party guests.

She straightened her dress and stepped out from behind the building in the direction of the partygoers dotted about the lawn.

'Jesus Christ, Bella. Who on earth is that?' A demure-looking twenty-something with a sleek chignon and tasteful grey silk tunic goggled at the apparition making its way through the crowds.

'What on earth, don't you mean?' sneered her companion.

Heads turned as the figure stalked across the grass.

Sinead realised that her entrance had attracted attention, which made it hard for her to slip unobtrusively into the crowd as planned. On the other hand, it was natural they were gobsmacked. She knew she looked good. And when she saw how drab the other women were, she wasn't surprised she was making an impression. She snatched a glass of champagne off a passing tray, snapping 'What are you looking at?' at the surprised waiter. Pausing for a moment to survey the scene, she took a deep breath and walked up to the nearest group whose expressions ranged from bemusement to contempt.

'Divine weather,' she announced. She was determined to get the word 'divine' in as often as possible. It was a very upper-class word – that and 'utterly'.

When no response was forthcoming, she followed up with, 'Utterly divine.'

A kindly white-haired gentleman smiled at her. 'Lady Caroline always arranges good weather for her summer party.'

'Yes,' said a waspish-looking woman. 'Last year's was glorious. Were you there?'

'Absolutely,' confirmed Sinead, sipping her champagne. 'Utterly glorious.'

'But Tilda,' exclaimed another woman, mock surprise on her face. 'Don't you remember last year was the exception? An absolute downpour? The whole thing had to move inside.'

They both turned eagerly back to Sinead.

'Absolutely. Utterly soaked.' She knocked back her champagne and tottered away in the direction of another knot of guests.

***

Noblet had shaken off Catherine Clemmington-Jones by informing her that she seemed to be triggering his horse allergy, only to be collared by his mother and roped into a discussion about his search for a wife.

'But how did you guarantee the quality, Nobby?' a friend of his mother's called General Boyer was asking him. 'The quality, you know. What I mean to say is, how could you guarantee you wouldn't spend the day interviewing women from, let us say, Luton? Or Wolverhampton? How did you know these young ladies would be good county stock?'

Noblet was saved from answering by the sight of one of the aforementioned interviewees heading straight for him. He elbowed his mother in the ribs. 'Who invited her?'

'Who? Good God.' Lady Caroline forgot to complain about the elbow in the ribs at the sight of Sinead in all her glory.

'Who is it?' she hissed.

'One of the interviewees, remember?' Noblet hissed back. 'Irish lady. Very interested in Collins.'

Lady Caroline shot a withering look at her son.

'She isn't interested in Collins, you stupid boy.'

***

Sinead saw and interpreted some of the pantomime going on between Lord de Beeble and his mother, but this was where the genius of her plan revealed itself. She knew that even if Lady Caroline realised that Sinead was a gatecrasher, her breeding would prevent her from saying anything in front of the other guests. She stepped forward, a smile on her face. Lady Caroline waited until they were a few feet apart and then called out in a ringing voice, 'You are trespassing on private property. Please leave.'

The colour plummeted from Sinead's face, dragged down by her sinking heart. That wasn't right! She'd researched the aristocracy and their manners. Lady Caroline should never have said that. She swallowed down her indignation at Her Ladyship's lack of breeding and proceeded to Plan B.

'Apologies, Your Ladyship.' She tried a quick curtsey: it couldn't hurt. 'Walking my dog. Lead broke.' To illustrate this, she pulled a glittery lead out of her clutch bag and displayed the broken clip.

Lady Caroline looked her up and down. 'Do you expect me to believe,' she drawled, 'that you have been walking your dog... in that?'

'Yes. Down in Eve's Wood. Must have wandered onto your land by mistake.'

Silent groups of guests inspected Sinead's ensemble over the rims of their glasses.

'This is something you would normally wear to walk your dog in, is it?'

Sinead glanced down at herself. 'Utterly.'

'My dear, you are wearing a ball gown and a six-foot train.'

Sinead nodded.

'And a tiara.'

Sinead looked at her as if struggling to understand what her point could be.

'Not to mention your satin gloves and diamonds. We'll call them diamonds, for want of a better word,' she added cattily. 'It's quite outrageous to…'

She stopped and listened. From somewhere close by came the high-pitched yapping of a dog.

Chapter 24

Alice thought this was the best dream she'd ever had. It was even better than the one in which she looked like a young Bridget Bardot and lived in a marshmallow with a tame tiger. In this one, she was alone in a darkened room (OK, tent) with Henry de Beeble, chatting about any old nonsense that came into their heads. They'd talked about everything – her life in the village, her cooking, his business, his split from Saskia. When she told him about the whitebait, the way he laughed – leaning forward, hands pressed against his knees, looking her full in the eyes like they were old friends – had been better than any of her daydreams. She didn't want it to end. But as he reached out to touch her on the arm mid-sentence, she caught sight of the time on his watch. Her hands flew to her mouth.

'It's ten o'clock! I was supposed to have put the bacon rolls out by now!'

'Don't worry, I'll give you a hand. Where do you want them? Out where the buffet was?'

They worked quickly, moving between the tents with trays until everything was set out.

'Thank you. You've saved my... bacon.' *Oh, for goodness sake, Alice!* she chided herself. *This is not the time for corny jokes.*

'You're welcome,' he smiled, holding her gaze for what they both knew was a fraction too long. Somehow, they'd ended up standing very close together; neither of them in any hurry to move apart. She could feel the heat coming from his body and it dawned on her that he was about to kiss her. Their eyes locked and there was nothing more natural at that moment than for them both to lean in and...

'Yip, yip, yip, yip, yip, yip!'

'Oh God!' Alice's eyes nearly popped out of her head as she whipped round in the direction of the barking.

The buffet tables were receiving the unwelcome attentions of a small grey dog, whose diamanté collar identified him as Coco. A tray of bacon rolls, balancing at the edge of a table, was the subject of a sustained attack by the greedy canine. He leapt at it again and again, managed to tap it with a paw, and as Alice and Henry reached him it tipped over, showering the dog with bread and bacon. Coco set to work demolishing the pile of eatables on the grass.

'Oh no!' wailed Alice. 'I should have been here!'

From behind her an icy voice said, 'Yes. You should.'

Lady Caroline strode towards Coco. 'Get away! Get away you horrid animal!' He yelped in pain as she gave him a sharp kick in the flank.

'Leave him alone, you horrible woman!' Alice leapt forward and swept the dog up and out of reach of Lady Caroline's court shoe. As she realised what she'd said, she turned ashen, but kept hold of the little dog who sat, submissive, in her arms. 'Well,' she added defensively, 'you shouldn't have kicked him,' before turning and walking away.

Once out of sight of Lady Caroline and the other guests, she put Coco down on the grass and crouched next to him to catch her breath, trembling. He turned a pair of lugubrious eyes on her and waited. She was glad she'd stopped Lady Caroline kicking the poor little dog a second time and if she didn't get paid for her catering that evening, well, it wasn't the end of the world. But when she remembered the look of surprise on Henry's face, she wondered what else she might have forfeited by playing knight in shining armour to someone else's pet. When her breathing had eased, she picked the dog up again and headed around the house to where her car was parked. She didn't know what she was going to do about collecting her pots and pans but she wasn't going to face Lady Caroline and the rest of them again now.

As she rounded the corner, she heard footsteps close behind her, and then a hand grabbed her arm and span her round. She had the briefest glimpse of tanned skin, dark hair and brown eyes before she was being kissed firmly on the lips. Coco, pressed between them, made surprised snuffling noises. Henry stepped back and looked at her without a word before turning and striding away. Behind him, high in the sky, fireworks soared and crackled; reds, golds, blues and greens lighting up the tops of the trees.

***

Once everyone's attention had been distracted by the yapping, Sinead hadn't hung around. Her plan had fallen to pieces. Lady Caroline hadn't behaved the way she was supposed to, they hadn't believed her cover story and Coco hadn't followed orders. Storming through the undergrowth to where Derek was waiting, she ripped off her tiara, grabbed the pink helmet, slammed it on her head and barked, 'Drive!'

Derek watched with anxious eyes as she straddled the bike with difficulty, train over one arm. 'What…'

'Drive!'

'Why…'

'Drive!'

'The dog?'

'Get on the bleedin' bike and drive!' she screamed.

He got on the bleedin' bike and drove.

***

Later that evening, there was a ring on the doorbell. Sinead put down her glass of wine and shuffled unsteadily out into the hall. Derek looked up from his black gloom.

'Shlligo?'

242

She shook her head.

She'd barely spoken to him since they'd got back; locking herself in the bathroom where he heard her sobbing as he lingered outside the door, then reappearing with the apparent intention of draining every bottle of alcohol in the house. All he could get out of her was that her plan hadn't worked and that she'd blown her chances with Lord de Beeble. Despite a secret thrill of delight at this disclosure, Derek was thoroughly downcast. She was devastated and he didn't know what to do to help. When he ventured to ask her what had happened to Coco, she'd glared at him and announced that Coco was a 'usheless, mangy, brainless fluff of ball.'

Sinead opened the front door and found Alice on the doorstep. Noting the look of shock on Alice's face, she glanced in the mirror by the door and saw that her mascara was streaked down her puffy face, her blonde hair was a mess and her peach quilted dressing gown had a red wine stain down the front.

'Are you OK, Sinead?'

'What's shit to you?' demanded Sinead. She paused, reflected, then clarified, 'What's it to you?'

'Well… You look upset.'

'*You* look upset,' she retorted.

In fact, nothing could be further from the truth. Alice looked radiant, glowing, like a newly-opened summer flower which had escaped the ravages of Piers; and she appeared to be hovering a few millimetres above the ground.

Clocking some of this, Sinead revised her assertion.

'You're a shit,' she said, and nodded.

'Right… Anyway, I came to bring Coco back.' She handed over the grey bundle who whined excitedly and licked Sinead's salty face.

'Fine. Good riddance.'

The door slammed in Alice's face.

Inside, Sinead swayed for a moment or two, glaring at the dog in her arms. Then she crumpled to the floor, squeezing the dog and kissing his curly head.

'Poor ickle Coco,' she crooned. 'Poor, sad, lonely, ickle Coco.'

When she felt Derek's arm around her, she didn't resist, but leaned back against his chest and let the tears trickle down her face.

***

The feeling of unreal ecstasy hadn't diminished the next day as Alice joined the rest of her family for Sunday lunch. As it was a special celebration – her parents' wedding anniversary – they had booked a table at the Lion and Lamb to save Mrs Brand cooking.

'We could have gone somewhere nice. That new Spanish place in Pantling,' remarked Cecily.

Her father waved a deprecatory hand. 'This is quite posh enough for us. I've got a soft spot for the old Lion, you know. Plenty of happy times had by all here.' He smiled at his wife, who squeezed his arm.

'Well said, that man! A bit of hot grub, barrel of good ale and a hearty welcome from mein host, that's all we simple folk want from our hostelries, isn't that so, Papa?' roared Piers, dealing his honorary papa a mighty slap on the back.

'Steady on, Piers, he's not as young as he used to be.'

'Very true, Cecily. I'm feeling it in my joints these days,' Mr Brand said, laughing. 'Once knelt there's no getting up again. I almost had to call for your poor mother to come and get me to my feet yesterday after an hour weeding the vegetable patch.'

With a steady flow of gentle conversation streaming over her, Alice was able to sit almost in silence, paying scant attention to what was passing. She put in a word here and there, but mostly the bright summer garden was dimmed by the vibrant vision of a firework-strewn night. The starters were served and everyone tucked in. Alice picked at her battered mushrooms until she realised Piers was watching her.

'I've got me a little notion, ladies and gentlemen. I've been watching our favourite little lady and if my peepers deceive me not there are symptoms of lurve in that young lady.'

Alice frowned and shook her head but he continued.

'Doesn't speak, doesn't eat, moons about. Admit it, Alster! You're in love!'

Of all the people, she inwardly ranted, *of all the people to notice –* Piers! Normally as unobservant as a banana, why did he have to start paying attention to other people's feelings today?

'Come on,' he urged, 'tell all. Who's the lucky man?'

She had begun an earnest denial when her phone rang; a number she didn't recognise. She answered it.

Before the voice had got as far as the 'H' of Hello she knew it was Henry. She went beetroot.

Piers was in high glee. 'That's him! I'll bet my bottom dollar that's the feller!'

Oh God, she wished he'd shut up. Henry would be able to hear every word.

She got up from the table.

'Hello? Are you there?' he prompted when she didn't speak.

'Hi – yes, yes, I'm here. Sorry, I'm in a beer garden, I'm moving somewhere quieter. Right, that's better.'

'Good. It's Henry. de Beeble,' he added, superfluously.

'Yes, I know.'

There was a short silence.

'Your equipment is still up at the hall.' She felt a chill of disappointment. Was that why he'd called? 'I wondered if I might bring it round to you?'

The sun came out from behind a cloud and the previously hateful Piers, capering around making lewd gestures in the background, transformed into a charming, whimsical imp.

'That's kind of you. If it's not a bother?'

It appeared that it wasn't a bother and once times and addresses had been discussed, she hung up and returned to the table under the trees. Even Piers' steady stream of musical references to 'Mr Loverman (Shabba)' throughout the meal failed to dent her happiness.

***

Henry was due at eight o'clock, and by ten minutes to Alice was a bundle of nerves. The house was tidy, Tom was brushed, she had applied a little make-up, as José had taught her, and was wearing a new yellow sundress. The radio was murmuring in the background and she sat at the kitchen table with the crossword in front of her, to help her appear unflurried by the prospect of Henry's arrival. She wasn't sure why she was attempting the charade seeing as, sure as eggs were eggs, any semblance of calm would vanish upon his arrival.

She heard a car pull up outside. Her heart beat madly. There was a knock at the door.

She opened it – and found herself enveloped in Piers' embrace. His clammy cheek was pressed against hers as he breathed whisky fumes into her face.

'Desperate straits old girl, and only you can save me. First up, that feller out there wants paying.' He let go of her neck and lurched past her into the hall. 'You take care of that while I ex-she-cute a tactical chunder. Lead me to your vomitorium.'

'Oh God.' She grabbed his arm and shoved him into the downstairs loo, then snatched her handbag from the hall table and dashed outside. Once the aggrieved taxi driver had been paid off, including a generous tip, Alice came back in, shutting the front door behind her.

'Piers?' She listened at the door of the downstairs loo and then wished she hadn't. 'Piers, are you OK?'

The doorbell rang. She hurried to open it.

Henry stood on the doorstep, handsome as a god in the sunshine. He held a large box of pots and pans.

'Hi,' His smile made her stomach flip over.

'Hi… Thanks so much for bringing the stuff round.' She went to take it off him but he pulled it in closer to his body.

'It's heavy. I can bring it in, if you like?'

Yes, she bloody well would like under normal circumstances. If there wasn't a Piers-shaped bomb in her bathroom, primed to go off at any moment. Right on cue, the door to the downstairs loo flew open and Piers stood in the opening, naked except for a pair of Superman underpants.

'Right then, Alster!' he yelled, hands on hips. 'Are you ready for me?'

She saw surprise and then displeasure pass across Henry's face.

'This, this is…' she stammered, waving a hand in Piers' direction. But before she could complete the introduction, Henry had pushed the box into her hands.

'I'm sorry, you've got a guest. I won't interrupt. Thanks again for last night.'

She stood speechless as he turned and strode down the path, the silence broken by a loud belch behind her. Henry was already in his car by the time she called after him.

'It's not… you've got it wrong…'

The engine revved and he was gone.

A pair of sturdy arms slid round her waist and Piers rested his chin on her shoulder.

'Good. Glad he's gone. Now we can talk.'

Alice unclasped his hands and pushed him off her.

'For God's sake, Piers! What the hell are you doing here – and why are you in your underpants?'

She followed the direction of his hand as he pointed through the bathroom door to a pile of clothes on the floor.

'Barfing casualties.' He tried to take her resisting hand again but she snatched it away, marched him into the kitchen and pushed him into a chair. Setting a glass of water in front of him, she instructed him to drink it. When he'd drained it, and she'd had the chance to let some of the anger flood out of her system, she sat down across the table from him.

'Please tell me why you're here. If you can't tell me in ten words or less, I'll call Cecily and ask her.'

Piers put the glass down on the table and contemplated his ten fingers, marking each word off as he said it.

'Drank too much whisky, started a fight, Cess kicked me…' He curled the tenth finger shut and mouthed 'out'.

After more water and coffee, the full story came out. Cecily and Piers had stayed at the pub after the rest of the family had left and Piers had made his way through a bottle of whisky. He'd fallen out with a man at the bar, who had refused to agree that Abba was the greatest ever pop band, and Piers had punched him in the face. Cecily had had to separate them with the help of some regulars. She'd made it clear that he wasn't welcome at home and had stormed off.

'So you've got to save me, Ally-Pally. Don't let the world's greatest romance end this way.' His head was slumped on his crossed arms on the table and his eyelids drooped. Next thing, he was snoring.

Alice called her sister, who agreed to come and pick him up.

'Sorry, Al. It's not fair that he involved you in this. Hope it's not been too annoying.'

Alice put down the phone and sat looking at it for a moment. Should she text Henry and explain? She saw again that look of displeasure in his eyes at the sight of Piers half-naked in her hallway. Why would he believe her? A wave of frustration shook her and she banged a fist on the table, making Piers spring upright, eyes wide open; before resting his head back onto his forearms with a contented snore.

Chapter 25

In the tiny, dilapidated-looking hairdressers off the green, three ladies sat in a row. They were, left to right, Elaine Jowlett (cut and blow-dry), Jan Fratterbury (perm) and Lorraine Watford (peroxide). Each held a magazine on her lap, left to right: *Country Life*, *Hello!* and an ancient copy of *What Computer* that had somehow found its way into the stack of reading material left out for customers.

'No mention of Lady Caroline's summer party in *Country Life* I notice,' said Elaine with a satisfied sniff.

'Well, there wouldn't be, Elaine. It was only a week ago. They print these things months in advance, dear,' said Jan Fratterbury as she flicked through her dog-eared copy of *Hello!* 'More a *Harpers* kind of thing anyway, lovie. That might have some nice piccies.'

'Well, I for one won't be rushing out to buy it. Not interested in the slightest.'

'No? Oh, I'm not ashamed to admit I like to look at the dresses. All the belles of the ball.'

'You should always shut your computer down in the evening rather than keeping it on standby,' Lorraine informed them.

Jan nodded. 'Thank you, dear, I will.' Turning back to Elaine, she lowered her voice. 'You heard about what happened at the party, of course? The little fracas?'

Elaine flicked a page of her magazine and ran her finger along a line of print. 'No, dear. I don't indulge in tittle-tattle.'

'Of course, that's right, lovie. Very commendable. Neither a whisperer nor a tattler be, as the bard said. I shan't sully your pure ears, then.'

Elaine kept silent for a moment and then burst out, 'Oh, out with it, Jan! I know you're dying to tell me and far be it from me to deny you your pleasure.'

Jan had reached the part when Lady Caroline was viciously attacking Coco with a hammer, when the aforementioned canine's owner appeared in the doorway. Elaine and Jan looked up with guilty faces.

'Sinead, lovie,' gushed Jan, 'we were just talking about you…'

Sinead swatted this away like a troublesome fly. 'Never mind that. Remember that Saskia woman? Henry de Beeble's girlfriend?'

'One could hardly forget her,' retorted Elaine. 'Striding around the village in that ridiculous outfit taking photographs and then a few weeks later being arrested for breaking into the Bhatias' house! Her language on that occasion was far from ladylike, I may add. Ted was shocked to the core.'

'Here's something else to shock him,' snapped Sinead as she shoved a passing hairdresser out of the way and tossed a magazine at Elaine.

It was the latest issue of *The Vacuum*, which Sinead had ordered in to the local newsagent.

'Page thirty,' she added as Elaine picked it up.

Elaine turned to a photographic feature entitled 'English Eccentricity'. The first picture was of Elaine and Valerie under the Lion and Lamb sign. The image had been photoshopped, adding a mane and tail to Elaine and a woolly fleece to Valerie. Elaine's jaw dropped and Jan, peering over her shoulder, started to snigger. Elaine flipped the page and the sniggering turned into a gasp as Jan's eyes fell on a photograph of herself smoking in the school playground, with flames licking around her ankles and smoke pouring from every orifice. Opposite her was a picture of Lorraine having afternoon tea in a padded cell with a straightjacket hanging up behind her.

Lorraine caught sight of it and nodded approvingly. 'That's my best side.'

The next page showed Ted scurrying down an empty road, a mediaeval fool's bladder on a stick flung over his shoulder and a jester's hat on his head. Opposite him knelt Sinead at her immaculate flower beds, part of her clothes cut away to reveal robotic workings inside. Jerry Brewer was next, behind the bar of his empty pub, wearing a harlequin outfit with a large tear painted onto his face. The final image was of Colonel Markham, his rows of flowers erased and replaced with legions of toy soldiers over which he presided with a rifle at his shoulder.

Silence reigned for a good thirty seconds. Sinead waited, tapping her foot. Finally, Elaine found her voice.

'This is an outrage!' she spluttered. 'An outrage! How dare that woman trample over our good natures? We allowed ourselves to be photographed in good faith. She has shown an utter disregard for our dignity which to my mind is tantamount to mental abuse!'

Jan's face was white and clammy. 'Never mind your bloody dignity, Elaine, I could lose my job!'

Despite her own involvement, Sinead was watching them with a certain malicious pleasure.

'Annoying, isn't it? When people twist things. Make you look like an idiot.'

Elaine leapt from her chair and paced up and down the small shop, her black plastic gown billowing from her shoulders like a superhero's cape.

'We can't accept this. We won't. There are laws which govern this noble country of ours, laws to prevent the gutter press from libelling law-abiding citizens.'

Jan was standing too, twisting her hands together; a pathetic figure with a head full of rollers. 'That's right! We'll sue!'

'Lawyers can be very expensive, Jan,' countered Elaine. 'We need to be clever about this. We need to find a way to force her to issue an apology…'

'And compensation!'

'Indeed – and compensation. Not that any kind of pecuniary redress could ever compensate for our emotional distress.'

'No, lovie. Of course not. But it would be better than nothing. Especially,' Jan let out a little sob, 'if I'm to lose my job!'

'Shouldn't have been smoking in the playground,' remarked Sinead.

The others glared at her. They'd forgotten about Lorraine, who had got hold of the magazine and was flicking through with interest.

'Aren't they lovely and bright? The pictures? Lovely Jerry in his costume. I've never seen him in his costume. I'll ask him to wear it tonight, in the pub.' She flicked to the picture of Sinead. 'Have you had an operation, Shania?'

Elaine snatched the magazine from her hand.

'Has the Colonel seen this? And Jerry?'

'Not yet.'

'They must! We will convene a meeting without delay.'

***

A few days later, a minibus bearing the motto 'Gently Rising Community Transport' on its side chugged down the M4 in the rain. Ted was at the wheel, with Elaine behind him, calling out

253

helpful instructions about deploying his windscreen wipers and avoiding puddles. Other seats were taken by Sinead, Jan, Jerry Brewer, Colonel Markham, Valerie Tipperton and Lorraine Watford. Lorraine hadn't been invited along; however, with her usual unerring ability for being where she wasn't wanted, she had stumbled across them all boarding the minibus early that grey morning. She'd even made them wait while she popped back home for a banner.

'The idea is to make a protest, Lorraine, lovie,' explained Jan from her position on the floor as they pulled away from the village green. She'd called in sick to school and was keeping out of sight until they were out of the village. 'We're going to picket the offices of the magazine until that woman apologises.'

Lorraine looked dubious. 'Like the miners? I didn't like the miners. They were nasty to Mrs Thatcher.'

'No, not like the miners.'

'It's a peaceful demonstration,' explained Colonel Markham. 'A legitimate means of making our feelings on this disgusting article known.'

'Yes,' continued Jan. 'So, your banner isn't quite in tune with the mood, dearie.'

Lorraine had it unfurled across her lap. Beside a large-scale print of Cliff Richard's face, the words 'I love Cliff' had been crossed out and replaced with 'Lovely BRIGHT Pictures.'

'Do you see what I mean, lovie?' pressed Jan. 'We don't think the pictures are lovely at all. We think she's been rather naughty, tinkering with them like that.'

'Yes,' sneered Sinead. 'Meant to be a protest. Not a vote of thanks.'

The light seemed to break through the clouds of Lorraine's mind. She reached into her bag, drew out a marker pen and above the words 'Lovely BRIGHT Pictures' added 'Down With'.

Jan patted her hand. 'Much better, lovie.'

At one o'clock, after a couple of hours waiting for the RAC to fix their overheated engine on the hard shoulder of the M4, they pulled up in a dingy side street in Acton, tense and argumentative. Jerry was bemoaning their lack of satnav, Elaine was pointing out we hadn't needed satnav to win the war and Colonel Markham was trying to make sense of a dog-eared A to Z. Sinead was painting her nails and Valerie was trying to dissuade Lorraine from making menacing gestures at passers-by through the window.

At two o'clock they'd made it as far as Knightsbridge and parked up, to give Ted a break and refuel on Elaine's copious supplies of sandwiches, scotch eggs and cake. Jerry Brewer and Colonel Markham were washing it all down with a couple of beers at the back of the bus.

Three thirty saw them involved in a road-rage incident near Russell Square. Ted had accidentally cut up a man in a white van who had retaliated by overtaking and pulling up in front of them. Getting out of the van with a menacing look, he had demanded they get off the bus. A nervous Ted, Colonel Markham and Jerry Brewer had disembarked, followed by Lorraine, who broke the sticks of her Cliff Richard banner over the stranger's head and hopped back on the bus. The men scrambled back on behind her, Ted firing up the ignition and slamming his foot on the accelerator. The bus careered down the nearest street which turned out to be one-way. As a result of their attempts to extricate themselves, they found they were heading west rather than east.

At three forty-five they pulled over for Ted to recover from a delayed panic attack brought on by the road-rage incident.

Jerry and Colonel Markham stepped out for a breath of fresh air and were eventually tracked down in a nearby pub, in suspiciously high spirits.

At four fifteen, Valerie noticed that Lorraine was no longer on the bus.

At four forty-five Lorraine was discovered holding a one-woman protest with her I Love Cliff (Down With Lovely BRIGHT Pictures) banner in the pouring rain outside an art gallery.

At five o'clock Jerry Brewer pointed out that they would have to start heading back if he was to have any chance of opening up that evening.

***

It was a sad and jaded bunch which unpacked themselves stiffly from the minibus onto the village green that night: even the Colonel and Jerry's high spirits had faded. Everyone was annoyed with everyone else, and particularly annoyed with Lorraine. They were about to disperse with a few terse words of farewell when Elaine stopped them.

'Friends! Comrades! Don't let's let this one small molehill of an obstacle become an Everest! Yes, we have failed to make our peaceful protest outside the offices of that pernicious magazine today. But we will have other opportunities of making our feelings plain. I vow to you all, here on our hallowed green, that I shall find a way to punish that shameless London hack! We bucolic battlers shall overcome the urban usurper!' She knew usurper didn't quite work but it slipped off the tongue so well she hoped no one would notice.

Ted beamed and nodded, full of renewed hope, while the others mumbled non-committal something-or-others and scuttled off home through the drizzle.

Chapter 26

The champagne cork popped, startling a nearby moorhen, and Noblet poured the foaming liquid into glasses. He handed one to Alice, leaned back awkwardly on one elbow, and beamed at her.

'Well, this is very pleasant. I can see why you would count it an element in a perfect day.'

They clinked glasses and she turned to unpack the rest of the picnic on to the blanket.

The final assignment for the two remaining candidates had been to organise what they would consider to be a perfect day; all expenses to be defrayed by the de Beebles. Piers – dropping round to apologise, with a long-suffering Cecily – had suggested she should claim that her perfect day consisted of a trip to New York with unlimited spending money. She had ignored this mercenary counsel and decided to play it straight. Her perfect day probably wouldn't be the most exciting, but it would be representative of her. And after all, she didn't want to marry Noblet, so she didn't need to impress him. She didn't want to marry Noblet... so why was she still taking part in the interview process? The answer, if she delved into her deepest soul, began with an H, ended with a Y and intruded upon her every waking hour.

She hadn't heard from Henry since the day he'd stumbled across a pants-clad Piers at her cottage. Not a word. What could she expect? He'd kissed her under the influence of too much champagne, perhaps; had done the gentlemanly thing and brought her equipment back, but the sight of another man in her house had been enough to extinguish whatever faint interest she had inspired in him. Time and again her fingers hovered above his number in her phone contacts but at the last moment, embarrassment and self-doubt overcame the urge to explain.

When the call had come through, asking her to plan her perfect day and to coordinate arrangements with Henry's PA, she had accepted on instinct. It gave her a legitimate link to Henry, however tenuous. And the knowledge that her competition was Mia took the pressure off. It would be a competition in name only.

Alice's final interview kicked off at eleven o'clock with a walk along the river. She had spent the previous day making picnic food, and the hamper now groaned at the seams with pies, salad, cold meats, home-made chutney, a ripe Brie and various other delicacies. Far too much for two people, in fact. Which was lucky, because as she approached the meeting point that morning, she discerned not one but two men waiting for her.

'Morning!' Noblet approached briskly, one hand extended as if he were greeting his opponent in a duel. 'Good morning, good morning! Beautiful day.'

She shook his hand and agreed.

'Er – you know my brother, Henry?' He waved a hand in Henry's direction.

Alice felt her treacherous cheeks turning pink as he stepped forward. The way he couldn't quite meet her eye as they shook hands was discouraging.

'Brought him along as an independent adjudicator,' Noblet was continuing. 'Second pair of eyes on the day, you know.'

'Despite the fact,' Henry remarked, finally making eye contact, with a look that suggested they were sharing a private joke, 'I won't be there on subsequent days such as the day after the wedding and every single day after that.'

Noblet pshawed and waved this away. Alice was torn between a thrill of pleasure at the warmth of that look – and despair, as he casually wrote himself out of her theoretical future.

Alice's hamper came with four sets of crockery and cutlery, so once they had arrived at the picnic spot, they were all able to eat and drink without difficulty. Noblet devoured the food with gusto.

'This pie,' he said, holding up a slice of the Wiltshire ham and egg variety, 'is the most superlative pie I have ever had the good fortune to eat. Hands down.' He regarded the slice in awe before wolfing it down as if he might incur a time penalty if he ate any slower.

The eating continued, punctuated with similar exclamations from Noblet and awkward thanks from Alice. Henry, taking his role as independent adjudicator seriously, remained silent, sitting a little apart from them on the blanket. When most of the picnic was in Noblet's stomach, it seemed to strike him that he should be finding out more about his prospective wife than how much of her cooking he could eat in one sitting.

'So, er, Alice,' he said, shaking out his napkin and brushing some stray crumbs off his trousers. 'This is your idea of a perfect day?'

She confirmed that it was.

'Good-o. Nothing like a picnic on a summer's day.' He lapsed into silence. The day was humid and the call of the woodpigeons as soothing as a lullaby. His eyelids drooped.

Henry coughed.

'Yes!' yelled Noblet. 'Yes, as I was saying, nothing like a picnic.'

He helped them all to more champagne.

'Now. Tell us about yourself.'

She looked horrified.

'What – erm, what would you like to know?'

'Oh, anything, anything,' replied Noblet. 'What you like to read, favourite subject at school, brothers and sisters, that kind of thing.'

Behind him, Henry rolled his eyes.

'I've got a sister,' Alice blurted, latching on to his last question. 'She's a doctor. She's got a new boyfriend, Piers.' Summoning up all her courage she looked over at Henry. 'I think you might have seen him, Henry, at my house. He got drunk at the pub, had an argument with my sister and she chucked him out. So he turned up at mine, threw up all over himself and stripped down to his underpants.'

Henry sat up a little straighter. 'That must have been... awkward for you.'

'I was bloody livid, if you must know! Anyone might have thought... Anyway. He's very contrite and Tom got him back by throwing up in one of his deck shoes while Piers was passed out at my kitchen table.'

'Who's Tom?' Henry asked, with an expression that suggested he was losing track of the hordes of vomiting men in Alice's life.

It must have been the champagne that made her reply, 'Just a little ginger guy I picked up a few years back.' They both looked blankly at her. 'He's a cat! Tom's my cat,' she said, joining in their relieved laughter.

The afternoon passed pleasantly and without incident: a long walk through meadows, woods and down country lanes culminated with afternoon tea at a café in a nearby village. Noblet and she spoke about issues of mutual interest, such as the quality of the jam in the cream tea, until it was time for them to be deposited back at the Hall for the evening's activities.

Having been shown by Sally to a room where she could shower and change out of her muddy things and into the turquoise strapless dress Mia had given her the night of the makeover, she paused in front of the mirror. For a moment she allowed herself to fantasise that she would be going downstairs to meet Henry, and that they would be spending this evening not as part of a bizarre interview process, but as two people who found each other attractive and enjoyed each other's company. It was a dream which evaporated as she descended the grand staircase to find Noblet's jovial face upturned to meet her.

'Jolly good!' he greeted her. 'Excellent, excellent, time for the next bit of tomfoolery!'

Henry, appearing through one of the doors leading off the hall, stopped dead.

'You look lovely,' he said, and then a momentary expression of annoyance passed across his face, as if he had spoken without thinking.

He looked lovely too, she thought, his light summer shirt revealing a tantalising glimpse of tanned skin at his throat. She turned back to Noblet. He looked – well – he looked dishevelled, and as if he may have had one or two fortifying drinks.

'So then! What do you have up your sleeve now, may one ask? Not that you have any sleeves, of course.' He paused, and she could almost see him burrowing around in his memory banks for a suitable compliment. 'Very becoming gown, that.'

She smiled. 'Thank you. I don't think anyone's told me my dress was "becoming" before. I feel like I should curtsey and say "lawks".'

Noblet looked confused as Henry laughed and led the way into the drawing room.

Once inside, Noblet turned to her, eyebrows raised in surprise.

'This is your evening activity?'

She nodded. 'Well, the first one, anyway.'

On a small table between two high-backed chairs near the grand fireplace, was a chessboard.

'Chess, eh? Keen player, are you?'

'I love it,' she said. 'My father taught me to play when I was little and I suppose I was a bit of a geek at school, I was in the chess club.' Perhaps Cecily had been right, the way to a man's heart was not through his chessboard.

'Very good, very good,' nodded Noblet, seating himself in one of the chairs. 'I may be a bit rusty but I know the rudiments. I hope I'll be able to give you a game of sorts.'

Fifteen minutes later he sat back, forlorn. Picking up his glass he wandered over to the decanters and splashed a triple measure of brandy into it.

'I knew I was out of practice, but that was shocking. I was putty in your hands. Take my cap off to you.'

Alice fiddled with a rook. She hadn't meant to beat him so quickly; the plan had been to drag it out, make him think he had a chance. But once she got a chess piece in her hand, she couldn't stop herself. Noblet was muttering something about moving on to the next bit of nonsense when there was the sound of someone clearing his throat.

'May I?' Henry took the chair recently vacated by his brother. Alice caught the challenge in his eyes and her pulse quickened.

'Oh yes!' said Noblet, his brow clearing. 'I forgot! Henry can give you a game. What was it you were, Henry – school chess captain or something?'

'Under twenty-one county champion,' said Henry, and the match was on.

Sally, looking in half an hour later with a plate of nibbles, was surprised to see the would-be husband snoring in an armchair while his brother played chess with the interviewee. Neither of the players so much as glanced in her direction while she was setting down the platter and clearing away glasses. All Alice's faculties were trained on the board before her. The man opposite was no longer Henry, he was an opponent, and a damn good one at that. She hadn't played against someone this good for years and it felt great.

Noblet snorted and woke himself up. Looking around blearily, he said, 'Still at it, you chaps?'

Alice moved her queen. 'Just finishing.' Looking Henry in the eyes, she smiled and said, 'Checkmate.'

He leaned over and shook her hand. His palm felt cool and smooth.

'Well done. I'll be expecting a rematch one day.'

'You're on.'

Noblet stretched and stood up. 'So, what's next?'

A rusting white moped buzzed up the long driveway and stopped in front of the Hall. Sally handed over some cash, took the white plastic bags and hurried off into the kitchen. Once ensconced in comfy chairs with steaming plates of curry, rice, dahl and naan on their laps, Alice explained.

'This is the best Indian takeaway in the world, ever. The chef is a genius, cooks everything from scratch, none of that soaking meat in brine rubbish. They don't normally deliver further than the outskirts of Pantling but I've known him for years and he makes an exception.'

Noblet was loading his plate but Henry raised his eyebrows towards the television. Their chairs were grouped around it.

'Oh yes,' Alice added. 'My perfect evening is Indian takeaway from The Mango Tree in front of my favourite film, *Leon*.'

Noblet looked blank.

'It's about a serial killer and a little girl.'

Blankness turned into doubt.

'Oh, I'm not explaining it well, let's just put it on.'

They all sat back with their plates of food, the lights were dimmed and the film began.

Chapter 27

'No, no, no, no, no.' Sinead looked again. 'No. Can't be. No!'

She sat on the edge of the bath and glared unseeingly at the geometrically-aligned set of towels hanging over the heated towel rail. What was going on with her life? She was Sinead: her life happened the way she planned it. This was all wrong. This weekend she should be taking part in the final interviews to become Lady de Beeble. Instead of which, that pathetic cow Alice Brand was up at the Hall in her place while she, Sinead Desiree Dumper, had been booted out at the second-round stage. Not only that, but if this stupid bit of plastic was correct (and the fact that it was the fifth stupid bit of plastic she'd tried meant it probably was), she was pregnant. Up the duff. With Derek's child.

She looked at the pregnancy test one last time before hurling it into the bin with the others. Children were not part of the plan. They never had been. The plan was to marry as much money as possible, live in an enormous house, have servants to boss about and spend her days shopping, working out and picking at minuscule plates of food in expensive restaurants with stick-thin, tanned friends. Children had no place in that utopian vision. From her small experience of them, she had learnt that their pink, clammy skin concealed ruthlessly efficient factories for the production of puke, crap, snot, tears and noise. Who in her right mind would sign up to carry one of those around like some kind of bad taste accessory? She caught sight of her face in the mirror and pouted, lowering her eyelids a little so she could look through her lashes. In her mind's eye, she saw Derek's podgy face, his crinkly eyes and bulbous nose. Try as she could she couldn't morph the two together. What would a child of theirs look like? Perhaps if it was a boy and he inherited her good looks and Derek's bulk…

But what was the point in thinking about it? The child would have to go.

***

Later that evening, Derek, who was treating her to dinner at a posh place in Pantling, noticed she wasn't drinking.

He jerked his head towards her empty wine glass.

'Not in the mood?'

She hesitated. Why wasn't she drinking? If she wasn't keeping the baby why did she care if she damaged it?

Before her brain could register what was coming out of her mouth, she said, 'Got to tell you something. Period's late. Took a test. Pregnant.'

Derek put down his forkful of well-done steak. He gazed at her, open-mouthed.

'Pre…' he croaked.

She nodded.

'Pre…'

Somehow a smile seemed to be tweaking up the corners of her mouth, and then she was gasping as half a tonne of overexcited male whisked her out of her chair and spun her round, yelling, 'Pregnant! Gonna have a baby!'

She managed to indicate to him that spinning her round his head wasn't a sensible way to celebrate and he replaced her in her chair, hands fluttering nervously above her stomach. Surprised fellow diners stopped staring and smiling and went back to their dinners.

She looked at him. 'Wasn't going to keep it, but…'

The colour drained from his face.

'But… Maybe it'd be nice.'

'Nice?' He took one of her hands. 'It would be the best thing that could ever happen in the whole world, ever.'

It was the longest sentence she'd heard him utter.

**

After the easy ride he'd had on Alice's perfect day, Noblet wasn't looking forward to Mia's. A picnic, followed by a country ramble, a game of chess and a film wasn't too taxing even for someone as unsociable as the Earl of Pantling. The film had made little sense and he'd fallen asleep halfway through, but his brother and Alice had seemed to enjoy it, and the curry had lived up to Alice's accolades. Mia, he felt, was another kettle of fish. If she knew what a cosy night in by the fireside was, it wasn't something she experienced regularly, he sensed. She was more likely to spend an evening sipping cocktails with billionaires on a private yacht in Monte Carlo; or hobnobbing with nomads under the stars in the Gobi Desert. (Were there nomads in the Gobi Desert? Probably, they got around.) He was looking forward to spending time with the exquisite Miss Wild, but would have been far happier if it had been on his terms. Now, if he had been allowed to plan his own perfect day... Vague visions of the Bodleian Library, cigars, Burgundy, roaring fires and roast dinners shattered into splinters at the sound of his mother's voice.

'What's that, Mother?'

'I said, you cloth-eared oaf, that at least the end is in sight. By this evening we will have identified the next Countess of Pantling. And not before time.'

No one was quite sure why Lady Caroline had joined them as they glided through the Mereshire countryside towards the assignation with Mia. Her chauffeur, arriving at the Hall to collect Henry and Noblet, had opened the door of the Bentley to reveal Her Ladyship ensconced inside. She had reprimanded them for keeping her waiting and snapped at Noblet for stepping on her foot, but had not as yet offered an explanation for her presence.

Noblet turned to her now. 'Mother. Much as I adore every second we spend together; may I ask to what we owe the pleasure of your company today?'

Lady Caroline looked out of the window. 'Curiosity.'

'I see.'

'No you don't, Nobby. I suppose it seems surprising to you that I should be curious to find out more about my future daughter-in-law?'

'You weren't curious about the other candidate.'

His mother's head snapped round. 'I know better than to think you would contemplate marrying a cook who insulted your mother in front of all her friends.'

'Oh, Mother...'

She held up a warning hand. 'There is one candidate for the position of my daughter-in-law, and we are en route to meet her.'

As the car purred to a halt, Noblet realised all his worst suspicions were true. They had pulled up in a stable yard and Mia was approaching the car, wearing jodhpurs which showed off her long, shapely legs; but which to Noblet spelt impending disaster.

'Oh – no. I'm sorry, but no,' he said, before he was halfway out of the car. 'No. Indeed not.'

'What my brother means,' said Henry, 'is what a pleasure it is to see you again and he hopes you're well.'

Noblet waved an impatient hand. 'Naturally, naturally, all that too – but no. I'm sorry Miss Wild – Mia – but horses, no. I can't.'

Lady Caroline shook hands with Mia. 'He's always been the most desperate little coward, but you mustn't let that put you off, my dear. He needs someone with energy and determination to give him a push in the right direction.'

'Like to push you in the right direction,' muttered Noblet under his breath, 'straight into that ditch.'

Shiny strands of Mia's chestnut hair danced in the breeze and her eyes sparkled. No one could fail to admire her, thought Henry; her beauty took your breath away. Lady Caroline was staring at her almost rudely. He touched her on the arm.

'Mother, you've met Mia before, of course.'

For a second, she didn't respond, then, dragging her eyes away with difficulty she put a trembling hand to her head.

'The heat is terrible. Let's go inside.' And without waiting for a response she set off towards the stable office.

Mia smiled at the brothers and agreed that the heat was terrible. 'But,' she added, 'the best way to cool down is a refreshing ride through the woods.' She looked mischievously at Noblet. 'It's the only way to start a perfect day.'

***

It took a good half an hour for the combined persuasive powers of Mia, Henry and Lady Caroline to coax Noblet out of the safety of the stables and onto a formidable-looking gelding.

'His name's Orion and he's very steady,' one of the grooms assured him. 'He's used for beginners because he's so gentle.'

'Nobby's not a beginner, he just does a good impression of one. His father put him up on his first pony when he was four years old,' said Lady Caroline.

'Yes, and I got off for good as soon as I was old enough to express an opinion. I don't see the point of it – no offence, Mia. I like my methods of transportation without muscles and minds of their own. Bicycles, cars – perfectly good means of getting from A to B. You won't find a car heaving you onto the street in a fit of pique.'

'I see,' nodded Mia. 'You prefer, say, a plane to a pony?'

'Absolutely,' he agreed.

'Excellent. You're going to love the next thing I've got lined up.'

As he watched her click her tongue and give a gentle squeeze with her heels to her horse's sides, then head off out of the yard, he wondered what kind of a warped world matched such an angelic exterior to such a diabolical core.

***

When Colonel Markham answered the phone, his first thought was that he was the recipient of a nuisance call. In response to his 'Hello, 744568?' he heard heavy breathing. He was about to replace the receiver, when a voice gasped,

'It's on, Colonel! Operation Fightback!'

'What? Who is this?'

'Elaine Jowlett. Spread the word. The quarry is sighted, we are in pursuit. Join us at Greenlands as soon as you can. Hurry!'

She was wheezing and short of breath.

'Mrs Jowlett, please. Calm down and tell me what's going on.'

There was more heavy breathing and then some muffled sounds. Ted's voice came on the line.

'I apologise, Colonel. My wife is out of breath. We had to run to keep up with the quarry.'

'What quarry? What on earth are you talking about, man? Spit it out!'

Ted pulled himself together and made his report with all the precision of a man who worked part-time in the accounts department of Mereshire police headquarters.

'At around eleven hundred hours today, we observed a female individual acting suspiciously in the vicinity of de Beeble Hall – or in the vicinity of the gatehouse, to be precise. The individual was parked in the layby, which you may be familiar with, some fifty metres along the lane. Myself and my wife – that it is to say Mrs Elaine Jowlett – were perambulating past said layby and my wife – Mrs Elaine Jowlett – remarked to me that the said individual appeared to be familiar to her.'

At that point, there was more rustling and Elaine came back on the line.

'It was her, Colonel! That Stonor woman, sitting as bold as you like in her car, right here in our Gently Rising. It was clear she was up to no good – no doubt planning another piece of vilification – she was slumped down in her seat, trying to keep out of sight. My first thought was to confront her, but then I reflected. No, I said – no, Ted. We must be canny. We raced home, got in the car and sped back: just in time as it turned out. Lady Caroline's Bentley had pulled out onto the road, and the Stonor woman was following it a good distance behind. Ted and I did the same.'

'She didn't see you?' asked the Colonel.

'No! Never so much as glanced in her rear-view mirror. Dangerous style of driving. Anyway, we drove out past Pantling and the Bentley turned into the riding school at Great Skelford. The Stonor woman carried on past and we followed her, all the way to Greenlands. She parked at the side of the road and darted off through the undergrowth and we did the same. We've got her in our sights as we speak. She's hiding behind a tree and we're keeping well out of sight in the undergrowth. Now, you must rally the others, Colonel, and come straight here. Bring the banners, but be as quick as you can.'

The Colonel sighed. The test match was on and an ice-cold gin and tonic awaited him by his easy chair near the open French windows. His duty was clear, however.

'Stay where you are, Mrs Jowlett,' he commanded, 'reinforcements are on their way.'

***

As much as a woman consumed with bitterness and envy can be, Saskia was pretty pleased with herself. One unexpected side-effect of Henry dumping her was that she had, she thought, become a much better journalist. She had learnt to think on her feet, to follow up every lead and, most importantly, to hack into voicemails and emails and glean vital pieces of information. Not that she did the hacking herself, of course – she'd found someone discreet who did it for her. This discreet contact had breached the firewalls at Henry's company in order to read Henry's emails and those of his PA; which was how Saskia had found out what the schedule was for Mia's final interview. Her background research on Mia herself had come together and she had quite an arsenal to present to Henry and Noblet about The Bitch; publicly and in as humiliating a manner as possible.

She had tipped off the paparazzi that there was going to be a sting in the tail of Lord de Beeble's final interviews, and told them the location, and at that moment tens of them were creeping through the undergrowth to position themselves in prime locations for the denouement. There were some odd-looking paps around these days. She'd noticed a hugely fat, middle-aged woman and a skeletal man hiding behind a bush a few metres away. They looked familiar and not at all like your standard London paparazzi. She wasn't interested in them, though. Her brain was intent on carrying out the unmasking of The Bitch, which, if it were to come off as she'd planned, required her best acting skills. She checked her watch. It was time to move.

Chapter 28

Noblet assumed that whatever was to follow couldn't be as unpleasant as an hour's bouncing around on an uncomfortable beast accompanied by two people who were thoroughly enjoying themselves, and to whom his discomfort seemed an added element of entertainment. Henry was a natural horseman and Mia could have been born on the back of a pony judging by the effortless way she handled her steed. Both of them kept pace with Noblet for the most part but were clearly holding themselves back, longing to be off, galloping across the hills. Noblet had all but ordered them to go on without him, saying he would catch up with them at the end. If there ever was an end to this penury.

When he and his horse stumbled out of the woods, both of them sore and grumpy, the sight of Mia and Henry waiting by a tiny aeroplane did not lighten Noblet's mood. He dismounted.

'What new hell is this?' he enquired, conversationally.

'Have you ever done a skydive before?' asked Mia.

'What kind of a question is that?' he snapped. 'You may as well ask me if I've ever purposefully stabbed myself in the eye with a butter knife. Or led a conga line into a lion enclosure in a suit made of steak. Of course I've never done a skydive before.'

'Bob,' warned Henry, 'remember this isn't *your* perfect day. You've agreed to go along with Mia's plans.'

'Oh, this isn't *my* perfect day, you say? Well, thank heavens you told me, because for a moment I thought I'd died and gone to heaven. Oh yes,' he added, 'I mistook this for my own perfect day, but luckily the fact that we're being given parachutes clarified things. On my perfect day, I'd simply hurl myself out of a plane and hope for the best, because that's the kind of adrenaline-loving daredevil I am, as you know.'

'Calm down, Bob…'

'I am calm!' his brother yelled. 'Perfectly calm! Now come on, what are we waiting for? Let's experience perfection!' he said before marching over to the plane and clambering in.

Once he had been coaxed out again and kitted out in a snug jumpsuit, padded hat and goggles, Mia took him through the drill. They would be doing a tandem skydive: he would be clipped to her front and she would operate the parachute. Henry would also be doing a jump and would be strapped to another instructor. She took him through the safety routine and explained that the pilot would take them up to 10,000 feet, they would jump out, freefall for thirty seconds or so and then deploy the chute, landing a couple of minutes after that.

Noblet was white-faced. 'I suppose at least you've done this before?'

She nodded. 'Once or twice.'

'I'm surprised Mother isn't here to see this,' he said to Henry. 'It's got to be her best chance of seeing you become heir.'

'Oh, don't worry,' replied Henry, 'she's waiting at the landing site with a pair of binoculars.'

'And a rifle, no doubt,' muttered Noblet as he climbed into the plane.

***

At that moment, Lady Caroline, sipping Irish coffee from a thermos in the back of the Bentley, was listening to the afternoon play on Radio Four and absent-mindedly watching a woman cross the airfield in front of her. Something about her was familiar, although it was hard to say what, as her hair was tucked up under a wide-brimmed hat and her face obscured by a huge pair of sunglasses. The woman disappeared around the side of a hangar and Lady Caroline dismissed her from her mind.

***

Saskia approached a woman with a clipboard.

'Hi there, could I speak to whoever's in charge, please?'

The woman looked surprised. 'I'm running the admin side of things, can I help?'

'Oh yes, I hope so,' Saskia simpered, taking off her sunglasses and treating the woman to a winning smile. 'You see my boyfriend is doing a tandem skydive today and I... well, this is a bit embarrassing but...'

The woman listened, a sympathetic smile on her face, and when Saskia finished, she nodded.

'No problem. What's your boyfriend's name?'

'Henry de Beeble.'

***

The plane rattled and lurched, Noblet moaning at each bump.

'Henry. Henners. Have I ever told you how much I really, truly hate you?'

'Why me?'

'You knew about this. You could have stopped it. Aarrghh!' The plane dropped and then righted itself.

'Look on the bright side,' said Mia. 'You'll be getting out in a minute.'

***

Saskia walked out to the landing area, accompanied by the lady with the clipboard. She held a roll of material under her arm.

The cluster of jumpsuit-wearing staff, waiting to help the landing skydivers, looked knowingly at each other.

'Alright, love. Proposal, is it?'

Saskia nodded. 'That's right.'

'It's the group that's just jumped,' the lady with the clipboard informed them.

'Right then, better hurry up and do your stuff, love, you can see them circling up there now.'

Saskia unfurled her huge piece of material and spread it out on the grass. It read 'Henry, will you marry me?' in large black letters.

Having secured the corners with stones, she stood back and looked up at the sky. Two parachutes, one blue, one green, circled high above them.

***

'I'm dying! I can't breathe! Help!' yelled Noblet.

'Relax,' advised Mia. 'It's the only way you're going to enjoy it.'

'Enjoy it? I'm not trying to enjoy it, you lunatic! I'm trying to survive it!'

Henry, having seen Mia and Noblet at the door of the plane one moment, and gone the next, had felt a sudden surge of adrenaline as the reality of what he was about to do hit him. His instructor shuffled them across the floor of the plane to the door, Henry crossed his arms across his chest and tilted his head back as instructed and then they were gone; air rushing past his face as if he'd dived into a strange waterless ocean. He felt a tap on his shoulder and an almighty jerk as the parachute deployed. Then silence. After the rushing of the air, it was unearthly, and he hung, motionless, not even aware of the parachute above him or the man behind him; alone and silent, suspended in the sky. Beneath him, Mereshire stretched far into the distance in all directions: fields, rivers, villages, towns. As they descended, he felt a reluctance to return to earth.

Looking down as they neared the landing site, that reluctance grew.

'What the…'

He heard the instructor chuckle behind him.

'Weren't expecting that then?'

'You could say that,' replied Henry, grimly.

As he watched, a figure stepped right onto the banner and seemed to be peeling something back. The words of the proposal were ripped away and underneath was another message, revealed just as Noblet and Mia were landing beside it.

'MIA WILD IS A FAKE. ASK HER REAL NAME.'

***

A minute later, Henry had landed in the middle of mayhem. Noblet was sitting on the grass, head in his hands. Saskia was confronting an amused-looking Mia, telling her her time was up and she was going to be unmasked for the fraud she was. Lady Caroline had got out of the car and was approaching the group, picking her way across the field in her high heels, clutching her handbag. Photographers had emerged from the undergrowth and surrounded the group, snapping away. Staff from the skydiving club were trying to calm Saskia down, roll up the banner and move everyone away from the landing area. They succeeded in shifting the group a few metres away, and Henry, pulling off his goggles, strode across to them.

'What's going on?'

Saskia spun round to face him.

'It's time for you to know the truth, babe. That's what's going on. This woman has duped you all but she couldn't dupe me.'

Lady Caroline was in earshot by this time and called out, 'Saskia, I think you may need professional help, dear.'

'Oh, Caroline, can't you see it's your sons that need help? They're the victims of fraud, perpetrated by this woman, Mia Wild. Or should I say…' Saskia turned and pointed at her with all the drama of Hercule Poirot unmasking a murderer '…Mia Falcone!'

Mia looked unperturbed. 'No, you shouldn't. That's not my name.'

Saskia smiled. 'I knew you'd try to deny it. That's why I brought these…' She reached into her bag for some papers.

'Falcone isn't my name,' Mia continued, 'it's my husband's name.'

Lady Caroline and Henry stared at her. Even Noblet raised his head for a moment, shook it, and let it drop back into his hands.

'I kept my name when we married. I've never been Mia Falcone.'

The photographers snapped away, capturing the looks of shock as Lady Caroline's chauffeur and a couple of the skydive crew tried and failed to move them back.

Henry recovered the power of speech. 'Why…?'

'You want to know why, babe?' Saskia cut in before Mia could answer. 'Because she's a freelance investigative journalist. I thought I recognised her the first time I saw her – I'd seen her around. She pretended to be interested in marrying Noblet to get intimate details of your family life and splash them across the gutter press.'

Mia opened her mouth to respond but whatever she said was drowned out by the strident tones of an enormous woman in tweeds who was parading across the field towards them. She led a motley procession of people waving banners with slogans ranging from 'Restore our Dignity!' to 'Down with lovely BRIGHT pictures'.

'This woman is a liar and a trickster! Don't listen to her, whatever she's saying! She doesn't deserve the title of journalist!'

For a moment all eyes turned to Mia, wondering what new accusations were about to rain down on her. As the procession approached, however, it became clear that Saskia was the focus of their attention.

Elaine continued. 'We are here to protest at the villainous actions of this woman, for whom we agreed to be photographed in good faith and who has abused our trust!'

'Trust!' echoed Ted, waving his banner.

'She came here, to our peaceful village, with her London ways and her London photographer...'

'London photographer!' growled Lorraine, shaking one washing-up-glove-clad hand at Saskia.

'...took our pictures and then defaced them in the most perverted manner before splashing them across her magazine for all to see.'

The paparazzi clustered round, shooting Saskia encircled by angry protesters. Derek, with one solicitous eye on Sinead, was videoing the proceedings.

'We demand justice!' declared Elaine. 'We won't leave without a full apology!'

'And compensation!' added a voice from the back which sounded suspiciously like Jan Fratterbury's.

'Apo-lo-gise! Apo-lo-gise!' Elaine chanted, the others joining in. 'Apo-lo-gise! Apo-lo-gise!'

Saskia looked bewildered, waving a hand as if batting away this annoyance. Henry, after trying to speak a couple of times but getting drowned out by the chanting, bellowed, 'Will you all please shut up!'

Taking advantage of the surprised pause, he continued, 'I have no idea what's going on and it seems explanations are in order, but can I suggest we do it somewhere more private.' He motioned towards the photographers. 'Saskia, Mrs Jowlett – all of you, please join us at the Hall where we can continue this discussion more,' he searched for an appropriate word, 'comfortably.'

Lady Caroline turned and stalked back to the car, helped over the muddy ground by her chauffeur. Noblet roused himself and followed her. Henry shot an enquiring look at Mia.

'I'll see you there,' she said. 'I need to pick something up on the way.'

He shrugged and walked away, wondering if she would turn up at all.

Seeing her audience drift away, Saskia hurried to her car, trailed by the protesters. Lorraine continued to chant, starting off with the original 'Apo-lo-gise!' but soon adding a little poetic licence with 'Com-pro-mise', then 'Past-eur-ise' and finally 'Damn-your-eyes'.

***

Barely was her bowl of muesli finished that morning when Alice found herself standing at the kitchen counter weighing out the ingredients for a Victoria sponge. There were some days when the only thing for it, was to bake. While some people preferred yoga or tai chi, for Alice a meditative state was achieved through sifting flour and beating eggs.

Her mind was a mess and she needed clarity. She would tackle the work side of the jumble first she decided, mentally pushing Henry de Beeble into a box and closing the lid. Her catering business had started to pick up again after the post-de-Beeble-party hiatus. A couple of her initial customers had commissioned her again and friends of theirs who'd tried her food had also booked her. When she looked at her calendar the bookings stretched beyond the summer into the autumn, when she'd be back at work. 'You mustn't let your hobby impact on your teaching, love,' she could hear her mum saying. 'Best to keep it as a summer-only thing.'

But she didn't *want* to keep it as a summer-only thing, she thought with a surge of petulance that made her bang the flour down so hard she was enveloped in a white mist. Going into school, seeing her friends there, teaching the children – she enjoyed it, it was rewarding on good days and at worst, on the bad days, it was a bit dull. Cooking, on the other hand; having people enjoy her food and ask her to cook for them again… It was like comparing a warm bath to the Caribbean Sea. One was pleasant, the other was sparkling and stunning and life-affirming and, oh God, she wanted to cook for a living.

She wanted to cook for a living. There it was. She stood immobile at the counter, one floury hand on the KitchenAid mixer, the other pressed to her cheek. Could she do it? Her heart beat faster at the thought. It wasn't feasible yet, she didn't earn enough; but if she built up her business, worked evenings, weekends, school holidays, then maybe she could hand her notice in, say… this time next year? It was terrifying – and overwhelming – and while her brain weighed up the pros and cons, her heart had already decided. She'd been good little Alice Brand for long enough, doing the sensible thing. Now it was time for the tulip to bloom.

She switched on the food mixer and watched the mixture come together, pale yellow and fluffy. Taking her cake tins out of the cupboard she divided the mix between it. This was her professional life, she thought, taking the first one and sliding it into the oven. The second tin she gazed into for a moment, as if she would find some answers there. Time to tackle this one – her personal life. That went into the oven too and she turned on the timer.

The day with Noblet and Henry had been a bit like the contents of her mixing bowl: many disparate ingredients whipped together over time. Instead of eggs and sugar, there was embarrassment, confusion, hope, excitement and happiness. She'd never felt the way she did with Henry with any other man. The fireworks she'd read about were real, and they went off at all kinds of unexpected moments, not just when he'd kissed her that time at the party. When she'd made a silly joke that went over Noblet's head but Henry got it straight away. When they'd turned to catch each other's eye at the same moment during the film. When they'd caught each other getting swept away with the excitement of the chess game. When Noblet had disappeared into the bushes on the trail of a rabbit and Henry had reached out to help her over a stile, and she knew – knew – that neither wanted to release the other's hand.

She loved Henry. It was preposterous but what the hell. Who was to say how long it took to fall in love?

She took some strawberries out of the fridge and washed them in a colander. As she chopped the red flesh into quarters, she felt a weight lift from her shoulders. She had no idea what to do about the fact she loved Henry, but the relief of admitting it made her feel as light as those gently rising sponges in the oven. And, she reflected, as she moved on to whipping the cream, there was one thing that had become clear. She should withdraw from the interview process. No matter how nominal she felt her candidacy for the job of wife of Lord de Beeble was, to stand down would be a step in the right direction. She would be taking back control of her own future.

What was the proper etiquette for letting an earl know that you were very grateful to him for considering you as a potential spouse, but you'd like to stop the whole goddamn circus and get off, please? She was sure Sinead would know, there was probably a chapter dedicated to it in Debretts.

With the cake finished on the worktop before her, she knew what she would do.

***

'Sally, we're expecting guests,' announced Lady Caroline when they arrived back at the hall. 'Tea for fifteen or so out on the terrace as soon as you can, please.'

'Yes, Your Ladyship,' said Sally through gritted teeth as she hurried off to break the news to Martyr.

Henry returned from briefing the security team on the potential arrival of paparazzi and took a seat next to his brother.

'Alright, Bob?'

Noblet turned a pair of weary eyes on him.

'Alright? I've been bounced through woods, fallen out of a plane, been revealed as the hapless victim of a con artist and got caught up in a village uprising. What do you think, old man?'

Henry got up again and went inside. Coming back with a gin and tonic he handed it to his brother.

'Everything will seem better after this.'

Noblet grabbed it and took a great gulp. The doorbell clanged. 'Just in time,' he said, taking another swig.

Everyone was settled around tables on the terrace and furnished with tea and biscuits, when Sally reappeared.

'One more guest,' she announced, stepping aside to reveal Alice, beetroot red and grasping a cake tin and card to her chest.

'I'm sorry,' she gasped. 'I didn't realise there were so many people here. I'll leave this for His Lordship and go.'

She put the tin and card down on a table and turned to leave. Henry sprang out of his chair.

'Please,' he urged. 'Join us. Don't go. We've got a few things to clear up but then Bob will be delighted to speak to you.'

She looked as if she wanted to sink into the ground but allowed herself to be led to an empty chair. Henry hovered nearby until she had accepted the teacup proffered by Mia, then went back to his seat.

'If Mrs Jowlett will allow me, I would like to clear up the mystery surrounding Mia Wild – or Falcone – first, if I may.' He had been surprised to see Mia amongst the first to arrive at the Hall, looking as unruffled as ever.

'Too right,' snarled Saskia.

'I'm more than happy to explain what I'm doing here and who I am,' Mia said, calmly. 'But I'd prefer to do it in private.'

Saskia leapt up and flung a pointed finger towards the other woman, head turned in appeal to Henry. 'Trying to wriggle out of it!'

Lady Caroline, sipping her tea, glanced at Mia. 'We're among friends here. I'm sure whatever you have to say will remain confidential.'

Mia looked her in the eye. 'Don't you know what I'm going to say, Lady Caroline?'

The hand which held the teacup shook.

'How on earth would I know?'

'I think you have your suspicions.'

When Lady Caroline tried to put her cup down in the saucer it rattled.

Noblet turned to her.

'Mother?'

'I really don't know…'

'She's not just your mother, Noblet. Nor yours, Henry. She's also mine.' Mia looked at Lady Caroline, whose eyes remained trained on her teacup.

'It's true that I'm a journalist,' Mia went on, 'and in a way, that's why I'm here – but not for the reasons Saskia has suggested.'

Saskia, along with the rest of the group, was staring at Mia, open-mouthed.

'I grew up in a commune in the South of France. I had a happy childhood but I wanted to find out more about my real parents. I knew that a woman had brought me to the commune and asked the people there to bring me up. They knew that woman's name was Caroline, that she was English and rich, but that was all. They had one photograph of her.'

Mia took a photograph out of her bag and placed it on the table in front of Lady Caroline.

In the foreground of the picture was a group of smiling people sitting around a table outdoors. Over one of their shoulders, unaware of the photographer, was a young Lady Caroline. She sat on a bench under a blossom-laden tree, talking to another woman.

Henry picked up the picture, looked at it and passed it to his brother who inspected it speechlessly.

Mia was speaking again. 'It took me years, but I discovered who the woman was – and a couple of weeks later I heard about Noblet advertising for a wife. I wanted a way to get to know the family without embarrassing Lady Caroline, or causing a scene. This seemed like a fun option.' She pulled a face at Saskia. 'Of course thanks to you, the embarrassment and the scene have happened anyway.'

Henry looked at his mother. 'Mother? Is this true?'

She looked around at the agog villagers, hesitated, then nodded.

'Yes, darling. It's absolutely true.'

Jan Fratterbury nudged Elaine and hissed, 'It's better than the telly!'

'It's absolutely true,' said Lady Caroline. 'I had spent the summer in Capri – your father had stayed here at the Hall, he never liked to be away from England in the summer.' She paused, drawing a pattern on the wrought-iron tabletop with her spoon. 'I had a lover – you needn't look so disapproving, Nobby, we all had them in those days.'

'Hmmph! That's all right then,' muttered Noblet.

'One day I realised I was going to have a child. I couldn't pass it off as your father's – even he would have worked out that the dates didn't add up. So, I wrote to him and told him I'd been ill, but not to worry, that I would convalesce in Italy over the winter and be home by the spring. Noblet was at pre-prep school by then and Henry hadn't been born.'

'I remember,' said Noblet, a faraway look on his face. 'The Christmas Mummy didn't come home.'

Lady Caroline nodded. 'I had the child – a little girl. A friend of a friend had told me about a commune in the South of France and I thought – well, I thought one more child running around won't make any difference to them. We travelled back overland and stopped at the commune. I asked them to take the child and arranged for monthly payments to be made for her keep.' She looked up at Mia for the first time. 'I kept up those payments throughout her life, until she turned eighteen, when she was to be given, via a French lawyer, a lump sum.'

There was silence. Everyone was on tenterhooks, waiting for the next revelation. Lorraine picked up a piece of shortbread and crunched noisily.

Henry looked at his mother, an inscrutable expression on his face. 'You had Mia before I was born? Did you go back to Italy after that?'

'Once or twice, yes.'

She flinched under the intensity of his questioning gaze. 'What, dear?'

He sighed. 'You know what. Am I... Am I Bob's half-brother or full brother?'

The way her eyes flickered before she answered said it all.

Noblet looked at his brother, comprehension dawning on his face.

'You mean... You're not...'

Henry gave a ghastly smile. 'It seems I'm half-Italian. Like our sister.' He and Noblet both turned to gaze at Mia as the words sunk in.

Elaine cleared her throat.

'Lady Caroline, Your Lordship, Mr de Beeble. I think I speak for all of us when I say we have intruded on your privacy too long. We will take our leave, if we can extract a promise from that woman,' she jerked her chin at Saskia, 'to print a full written apology.'

Henry, with some difficulty, dragged his thoughts back to the present.

'Could you explain the situation?'

Elaine told him about the photographs in *The Vacuum*: Saskia sitting in sulky silence as she spoke.

'And if Saskia prints a full apology, perhaps over a double-page spread in the magazine, as well as compensating you all for your distress, would that help?'

Elaine replied that it would, the others murmuring their agreement.

'I think perhaps compensation of,' Henry mused for a moment, 'five thousand pounds each would be fair, don't you?'

Saskia looked outraged while the others nodded with enthusiasm. She started to protest but Henry interrupted.

'If I were you, Saskia, I would settle out of court. A court case could look very bad for you and the magazine. The de

Beeble family would be prepared to finance any action our fellow villagers decided to bring against you.'

She glared at him for a moment and then capitulated. 'Oh, whatever, man. Fine. Have your stinking money. I've got my integrity.'

A buzz of excited chatter was interrupted by Elaine rising with a majestic flourish of her shawl and bowing to the de Beebles.

'Our sincere thanks to you all. We will leave you in peace.' She swept off the terrace followed by Ted and the others, with Lorraine walking backwards and curtseying every other step.

Derek and Sinead brought up the rear; Sinead seeming to linger as the others disappeared into the house. She paused on the threshold and placed a hand on her hip.

'By the way. Don't want to marry His Lordship anymore. Going to marry him' – jerking her head towards Derek. 'Going to have a baby. We're... happy.' A wide, genuine smile crossed her face, the first Alice had ever seen on that countenance. 'So take your Countess of Pantling and stick it up your arse! Who'd want to end up like her,' she continued, pointing at an outraged Lady Caroline. 'Me and Derek are setting up a security business. Got it all sorted. Stuff the lot of you!' Derek put an arm round her shoulders and gave her a proud squeeze. He started to lead her into the house but assuming a businesslike air, she darted down the stairs and pressed a pile of business cards into Noblet's hand. 'Don't hesitate to give us a call if you need security, Your Lordship. Tell your friends.' Without another word, they both disappeared into the house.

Noblet and Henry looked shell-shocked. Lady Caroline was throwing surreptitious glances at Mia. Alice was trying not to catch anyone's eye and watching the departing villagers as if she should join them. Saskia was frowning and drumming her fingers on the table. To Mia she said, 'So, you haven't been having an affair with Henry.'

Mia laughed and Henry looked up, amazed. 'No, of course not! I've known all along he and Noblet were my half-brothers. And as you know, I'm married.'

Saskia nodded. 'To an Argentinian called Hector Falcone. I've got a copy of your marriage certificate.'

'Bravo. You'll make an investigative journalist after all.'

Lady Caroline was now openly staring at Mia. 'You were right, you know. Something about the look of you this morning brought it all back: it was as if your father were standing there before me. He was such a handsome man. I always knew you would be beautiful.'

'Is he still alive?' asked Henry.

It was Mia who answered. 'No. He died twenty years ago.'

'And was he…?' He raised his eyebrows at Lady Caroline. 'Was he also my father?'

She dropped her eyes and motioned yes with her head.

'Well I'll be…' said Noblet, running his fingers through his already dishevelled hair. 'Well I'll be… What this situation calls for is booze, and lots of it.' He stomped across the terrace into the house. A second later he popped his head out again. 'You don't have any revelations about my patrimony, do you, Mother? Another exotic lover of yours? A souvenir of your travels around south-east Asia perhaps?'

'Don't be silly, Nobby.'

'Thought not,' he said as he went back inside.

When he returned he was clutching a bottle of champagne. Sally and Martyr followed with a tray of glasses.

'Brought Sally and Martyr out to meet the newest member of the family!' he announced. 'Sally, Martyr, meet Mia Wild-de-Beeble, our sister.'

Popping the cork, he poured out the champagne, handing a glass to Saskia who put it straight down on the table without looking at it.

'Listen, babe,' she said to Henry, 'I don't give a shit about any of this. You've got a sister, that's great. Weird, but great. I just want you back. I did all this to show you how much I love you. Please,' she reached out and took his hand, 'tell me we can give it another shot.'

Henry drew his hand away.

'I'm sorry, Saskia,' he said in a low voice, very aware of having spectators. 'I feel the same as I did when we broke up. I hope you find someone else and are happy, but I'm not the man for you. I'm not going to change my mind.'

Her eyes searched his face for any sign of vacillation, then she picked up her handbag from the floor and rushed, sobbing, through the house. They heard the front door slam.

'Another toast,' said Noblet. 'Good riddance to bad rubbish!'

'Not very good taste, dear,' reproved his mother.

Noblet ignored her. 'To Mia! I, for one, am delighted to find out that you are my sister and I don't have to marry you. If I had to spend the rest of my life with you, I'd have a nervous breakdown.'

'Of course,' gasped Sally. 'That means there's only one young lady left.'

'Yes,' agreed Noblet. As one, they all turned to look at Alice. Her cheeks, which had resumed normal service, flushed red again.

'Oh no! I'm sorry,' she stammered. 'That's what I came here to say. I wrote it all in the card. And I brought a cake to apologise for messing you around. I don't want to marry you.'

'Indeed!' exclaimed Lady Caroline, drawing herself up to her full height. 'The de Beeble name isn't good enough for you, perhaps?'

'It's not that...' muttered Alice.

'That's lucky.' Without anyone noticing, Henry had moved across the terrace to stand beside Alice. He turned her towards him so her back was to the rest of the group. 'I'm very glad you don't want to be Her Ladyship. I'm hoping one day you might agree to be plain old Mrs de Beeble. After we've done all the normal stuff people do, you know – getting to know each other on dates that don't involve my brother and fifty other women, that kind of thing.'

Her heart was pounding and she couldn't stop smiling as she replied, 'That sounds good. It'll be nice to go on a date where I don't have to bring my CV.'

Once he'd stopped kissing her and she'd stopped kissing him back she muttered, very aware of their audience, 'I don't understand, though. I thought you weren't interested. You seemed so cold.'

'I thought I was being selfish,' he explained. 'Bob was the one looking for a wife. What right did I have to stand in his way? Then I realised I was being an idiot. Bob doesn't love you and I was pretty sure you didn't love him.' He turned to his brother. 'That's right isn't it, Bob. You don't want to marry Alice?'

'Oh God, no,' Noblet confirmed, horror spreading over his face. 'No offence.' (Alice shook her head to indicate none had been taken.) 'I don't want to marry anyone. Not even the lady who knew so much about Collins.'

Noblet looked around him. At his newly-discovered half-sister. At the empty space where the lady who knew so much about Collins had been. At his brother and Alice standing close together, Henry's arm around her shoulders.

'Well, Mother. I hope you can admit I did everything humanly possible to find a wife. Now, will you give it all up and help me run the estate again?'

'Nobby,' she growled, 'you are a silly, silly boy.'

'Is that a yes?'

She glared at him for a moment, then threw up her hands. 'Fine! You've proved it. You are unmarriageable.'

Noblet raised his glass, pink with pleasure. 'That's the nicest thing you've ever said to me.'

Dear Reader,

Thank you for reading LORD SEEKS WIFE. The idea was based on wondering what would happen if you crossed the 'open audition' format of reality TV shows with a quintessential English village, peopled with eccentric characters and different social classes. Plus I've always been fascinated by the weird and wonderful announcements to be found in local newspaper classified ads - in LORD SEEKS WIFE that became the Situations Vacant section where Lord de Beeble advertises for a wife.

If you'd like to get involved in a wider conversation about my books, please review LORD SEEKS WIFE on Amazon, GoodReads, Bookbub, on any other online bookseller, on your own blog and social media accounts, or talk about it with friends, family or reading groups! Sharing your thoughts helps other readers, and I always enjoy hearing about what people experience from my writing.

Thanks again for your interest in this novel. For news about all my books, please visit me at my website – www.heatherbarnettauthor.com or join me on Twitter @WritesHeather.

All the best,

Heather

Acknowledgements

I would love to list out all my friends and family in this section, and all the people who've been such vocal supporters of my work. I've been told we don't have room, so I'm leaving a space here. You know who you are - say the word and I'll write your name in by hand:

....

This book is very close to my heart so it was a joy to find that my publisher, Serpentine Books, was equally enthusiastic about it. I'm incredibly grateful for their hard work and vision bringing it into the world.

I'm grateful to my editor Amanda from LetsGetBooked, and proof reader Abbie from Abbie-Editorial.

Thank you to three more very important 'A's who read, said kind and constructive things about, and generally supported the writing of, this book: Adele Barnett-Ward, Alix Hunt and Anya Tobin.

My thanks for too many things to fit on this page go to: the Barnetts – Joan & Bill, Nicholas, Hsiu-Fang, Rachel, Hugh; and the Barnett-Wards: Ed, Nathaniel, Griffin, Rory and Rosalind.

Thank you to Rosie Ruddock for the loan of an important family name.

Thank you to David Hart for keeping me relatively sane throughout.

Finally, my general gratitude goes to all the eccentric characters in life who make the world a more entertaining place to be.

Also by Heather Barnett…

ACTS OF KINDNESS

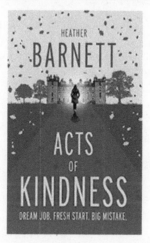

Dream Job. Fresh Start. Big Mistake.
When Bella Black arrives in a sleepy Wiltshire village, it
seems like the perfect place for a new start: a lovely home,
exciting job and an attractive colleague or two to take her
mind off her recent divorce.

When people start disappearing, she realises she holds the
key to a mystery bigger than she could have ever imagined.

Who is really pulling the strings at the secretive OAK
Institute?
Can anyone be trusted?
Will Bella make the right choices before it's too late?

*'fast-paced and fun…a terrific distraction from real
life'* —WI Life